ORIENTAL COVER-UP

A Novel

By

ELIAS SASSOON

ISBN: 978-1456558819

Oriental Cover-Up

Copyright © 2011 by Elias Sassoon

First Printing: January 2011

DEDICATION

To my Syrian grandmother, a woman filled with stories of a mystical past that encouraged imagination to bloom in the rarest of deserts.

TABLE OF CONTENTS

ORIENTAL COVER-UP

Preface To All Editions To Ever Be Printed

What you hold in your hands dear readers is a book written by an author, a writer, a newspaper reporter. I am that person, who is better known in literally circles as the ghost writer of the stars.

This book begins and ends on this one extraordinary night, a night like no others. The night was the one I got the biggest exclusive of my career. It is a story which centers around one man, Joseph Kabir. He is the same man who has committed the greatest crime of this century. But you are puzzled! You have never heard of a Joseph Kabir. There's a reason for that. The story was never released, that is, until today with the publication of this book. Kabir, who was he? How do I describe him? Impossible. I cannot begin to understand how the mind of that lunatic works. A complete puzzle, that's him, a man who exists as a riddle to be understood only by those who deal in riddles.

The night of his crime when Kabir was captured, I was there. For some reason I do not understand, I was singled out for the exclusive. I know it doesn't make sense, but nothing surrounding the person of Kabir makes sense. Nothing that he ever told me makes sense. His existence in general is senseless. What else can I say about Kabir? Read for yourself. What is about to unfold was told to me mostly from Kabir's very own mouth. I make no attempt to analyze it or make put it in a format to make sense of it. I just give it to you the way it was given to me. Good luck.

Montreal, Canada
January 17, 1978

CHAPTER I

Let the scene be set or let the scene be exposed, or let the exposed be expunged from the record or let the record be placed in a record book removed from the sight of all humanity but always on view to the solitary man.

We need the mood. It was nightfall, a hot night, so hot that earth worms crawled out of their holes below seeking relief. The story itself, what we are calling our story, it begins at a late hour, 11:00 P.M. to be exact. It would have gone down in history as another ordinary night if I hadn't decided to make the day live in the memory of all. Yes, it began on that night or maybe ended on that night. You decide.

The setting of the night: a gray stone building having green jade gargoyle-sculpted creatures hanging from its roof. The carved dedication on its front space explained it had been completed in 1810. This medium-sized stone structure was situated in the middle of a medium sized town filled with medium-sized churches, medium-sized supermarkets, medium-sized cars and, most importantly, medium-sized people.

Entering this building, called a precinct, that's what I did on this night, upon entering, you are thrust into small, red-walled, red-carpeted, furniture-less enclosure the size of a very small closet. The only thing breaking the monotony was a small red door, not much bigger than a large rat hole and the wall sign with its arrow pointing towards it with the words, "That a way," printed across it. Once you crawl through the red door, you must ascend a spiral staircase with a red carpet lining its steps. A top the staircase was a long hallway with a creaking wooden floor and its small offices with their red and white painted doors. Hanging from the ceiling were light bulbs dangling from long blue wires and all flickering on and off. The place smelled like it had been freshly painted.

I was in the building; I was in the room marked Detention Room A down the long hallway. I was handcuffed and thrown a top a bench. From this vantage point, I had an excellent view of the long corridor. I saw all who entered and left. I saw weaving in the hallway, everyone was weaving. I saw milling, everyone was milling. I heard buzzing in the hallway, everyone was buzzing. I waited for the beginning. The noise increased with the passing seconds. What would happen to me? Did it matter? What were they waiting for?

Very soon, the scene changed. Now before me was ticking, typewriter ticking. There also appeared lights flashing, powder flashing and the smell of sulfur. There were cameras snapping and questions popping out of the mouths of reporters of all description. They were here for me, to get a glimpse of me, to hear me speak. Outside the precinct too, they were there sounding like trumpets blaring an announcement of the arrival of life. The trumpets beat the building in a disjointed tempo. The building shook, the building tilted, the building danced an enchanting dance. My head throbbed from the trumpet notes. Soon I discovered through careful listening that it wasn't notes the trumpets were beating; they were beating out words to beat out sentences, "I'm from the Post," they boomed. "I'm from the Star. I'm from the Gazette." There was rushing and trampling and more words. "Will you come out of your offices? Can we come in? We wish to interview that mad assassin Kabir. All we are asking of you is to let us ask him one question. The public has a responsibility to know. Can you tell us anything? Where are you holding Kabir? When is he going to be arraigned? Is Kabir still up here? Kabir, Kabir do you hear me? Are you around here? Answer the call Kabir, answer!"

Clarinets screeched out a reply to the blaring trumpets. "No comment at this time. We are unable to answer your questions. No comment. We can't answer that. We couldn't do that. We won't endanger the prosecution. No, no, no, no. No comment. Kabir is in a safe place, that's all we can say. We haven't had the opportunity to question him yet. That's right. Yes we are terrible undermanned at this time. No, we haven't got a motive for the crime yet. No, no, no, no. As soon as we learn anything definitive, you'll all be filled in. Okay. Now, all of you clear out of here!"

The trumpets stopped their blaring and the clarinets stopped their humming. Nothing was to be heard or seen in the medium-sized stone building. The members of the press and other circus performers dispersed into the night air leaving a deathly silence behind. But the silence wasn't to last long. More noise was about to erupt from outside. The sounds of feet stamping on the pavement followed by shouts and cries. There was the din of hundreds of young voices raised in a harsh yell, "String him up! Butcher him! Stone him! Kill Kabir! Kill the Savage!

Frightened, yes, I was frightened. What if they broke down the stone building and carried me off? What would they do to me? Listening, waiting, dreading the worst, thinking the worst. Have any of them infiltrated already? Are they coming? They are capable of anything. They are cruel and vicious, the mob, the filthy dirty mob is capable of the most heinous of crimes. I couldn't keep my fears to myself any longer. I screamed at the top of my voice for them to go away. Nobody appeared. I was still alone with my fears and with my screams. Not one of the office doors opened. I covered my ears but I still heard the mob. My ears stung from the pitch of the chanting. But was there shouting or was I imagining it? Why didn't anyone come out of their office down the long hallway if there was trouble brewing? Yes and how could anyone have heard of me as what I had done occurred only a few hours before, not enough time for the news to travel to the general masses of men, women and children. It had to be my imagination. I faced up to the voices outside, I listened as they roared and very shortly thereafter fell silent.

Out of nowhere, or maybe out of the hidden microphone located in some remote place in the place I was being held, came the booming voice saying, "Listen up men, my men. We should get him out of the Detention Room A! It's not safe there! More protection is needed! Has space been found for Kabir yet? We are facing an emergency. When Kabir committed the gravest crime the town has ever seen, half the force was out on vacation. We can't handle him! What are we going to do? What? Report immediately!"

All the offices emptied out like bullets. "What are we going to do, what? This is serious, oh my. What? What are?" In and out of their offices they went, bobbing and waving, "Let's not panic," finally the call went out. "Let's leave him in the Detention Room A. He'll be safe there. We'll post two guards outside the room. Nothing to worry about. Stay calm. The crisis is over, the crisis is over."

In the hallway they - they being the authorities, the police, the fuzz, the flat foots, the figures in power, etc., etc., etc. - stood for some time longer. I heard them milling and singing such sweet tunes as, "Charlie do you have a cigarette? Why is it that I always seem to leave my cigarettes at home?" and, "Ron is that wife of yours making you go to the police auxiliary dance Saturday?" And, "Geez, I gots a rotten toothache. I gots to go to the dentists in the morning, I don't likes the dentists. You know I haven't gone to the dentists fa years." Chatter, I heard a lot of chatter, indistinguishable in content before one voice rang out above the others, "We must return to our work; responsibilities are waiting for us." Immediately like a cattle stampede, all rushed for their offices and were gone behind closed office doors. Once again, there was quiet.

*　　*　　*

During this interesting night, I had shed my garment of earthliness. I was no longer a mere mortal. I was the sun, yes the sun up above. I had always been this but never would admit it and when I did it landed me in Detention Room A. This night was the center, the pivotal point around which Earth, Jupiter, Venus, Mars, and Saturn revolved. They twirled and spun for me, the pied piper of wisdom. I had ordained frenzy for this night and frenzy there was. I was a celebrity, a man who had captured the hearts of millions by destroying hundreds, but there I was alone in Detention Room A with a mere two guards hovering by me - odd lookers both, thin like pencils in baggy blue uniforms and both wearing glasses in which one lens was tinted green and the other transparent - sitting there on a long olive wood bench so polished and slippery that it was a struggle for me to keep from sliding off. It was so shiny I could to see my own perfectly oval face, my beautifully groomed hair, my beautiful almond shaped eyes, my beautiful ears, so on and so forth in its reflection. Chained also, they had me chained; my hands were shackled behind my back. What did they think I would do, murder somebody? A joke friends, merely a joke. But did I deserve this, to be left in a small room like this. On one side of the bench where I sat were two wire-webbed windows which gave a good view of a used car lot. That's it. The rest just walls and that picture on the wall behind me, a huge portrait painting of a blind, black man with terrible misshaped eyes. The man had a tin cup in his hand and a jet black seeing-eye dog at his side and was standing in the middle of a busy intersection begging, while men in gray suits and women in tight white skirts passed. Was this a picture or not? So realistic, so penetrating, so illustrative of the individual's plight in modern day cultures of mass hysteria!

I waited alone for quite some time in Detention Room A and then it started; a parade of characters coming in and out. The first, a male flasher wearing red socks, a plaid trench coat, pink fluffy slippers, and a black beret cap. He approached my bench and stood next to me. "I enjoy showing myself off," he explained, striking up conversation. "The curvature of my form is a masterpiece to the eye. My skin covers my form with perfect symmetry. I am beautiful. I am breathtaking."

The guy slid closer to me, while I slithered farther away.

"I flash at anyone," he continued. "All enjoy me. I'm not particular who I show myself to. All are the same to me; they all have what I want. I'm so beautiful, so lovely, and so God-like."

I knew what would happen next and it did; the flasher did a little flash for me, and then waltzed over to the two guards and put on a show for them. It wasn't too long after that when a young man in a gray flannel suit and white hat arrived to escort my flasher out of Detention Room A. As the flasher left, despite his escort's acts at physical preventive, he managed to perform a few mystifying feats of aerial acrobatics to a captive audience. Then he was gone.

Companionship wasn't lacking very long after the flasher had departed the scene. Shortly thereafter, up to me came a quick stepping, beautifully proportioned, big-thigh lady with an unholy reputation. She stood before me, scanning me for a minute or two with her powerful blue eyes as if I was a sculpture and she a potential buyer.

"Are you him?" she asked. "Are you the character everyone's been yapping about? You can't be? Are you?"

"Who?"

"Kabir?"

"Yes, that's me. Are they really talking about me?"

"Not only are they talking about you, but they is moaning and groaning about you. None of them wants to be assigned to your case, none. They don't want to have anything to do with you. They don't even want to see your face. You're famous Kabir, real famous."

"Noooooo."

"Yeah, you buddy. A za-za-za-loey. I can't believe you're Kabir. Wow. You really pulled off something man. You don't seem the type; you look more the peanut butter sandwich and chocolate milk type. But I guess you can never tell about a person from his appearance."

"Ah, so true madam, so true."

My lady sat herself down as close to me as she could without sitting on my lap.

"They got you cuffed I see," said she as she swing her hand behind my back. "Ah thems are idiots, thems are fools. Kabir, good to meet yah. My name's Sable, Sable the bed buster or Sable the hair remover, or, Sable you make up a nickname. Yeah, like Detention Room A? Ain't it marvelous? Like home. Yeah know I slept here last week. Those creeps in the offices wouldn't even give me a proper cell. What type of inky-dink police house is this?"

"I think it's a lovely room, quite exquisitely decorated. What marvelous furnishings it has. I especially am enamored to its lovely webbed windows. Architecture is always a matter of taste as is art in general my dear."

"Man, you is a smart one, ha. You got a lot of education in yah."

"Yeah, unfortunately."

"Even with your highfaluting-learning I still like yah. Like yah for what yah did, like yah for what you stand for. You may not realize it but we're in the same line of business. Me and you are degraders. We remove to uncover. Yah do it your way and I do it mine. We know what's important." My lady thought it time to parade her business assets before my eyes. With precision, I analyzed her credentials. Out of the goodness of her heart, she allowed me to rub up against her in all the proper places. But my pleasure very shortly came to an end. A young man in white suit and blue hat came clanking in and escorted Sable into another realm. Her parting words to me were, "We'll be seeing each other again, honey; it's in the cards."

You, my readers are perplexed by my peculiar comradeship with the criminal element as you so basely put it. Don't be perplexed. There's nothing to be perplexed about. Criminals are the purest form of a man. They communicate from the heart. They're the vanguard of reform. Criminals therefore share common goals, and they being pure are able to communicate on a higher level then the common masses. It's the criminal who is great, it's the criminal who is always right, and the rest are the foulest dirt. But why am I making speeches. It's not fair you. Terribly sorry. Got carried away. Let me get back to the story. That's more important.

Okay, now the flasher was gone, now the lady with the unholy reputation was gone, now I was alone, alone feeling depressed. But fate was working for me or I had a friend in the precinct I didn't know for my solitary state wasn't to last long. Another visitor arrived upon the scene, a middle-aged man on crutches and wearing a black patch over one eye. He was escorted into the room by two gray bearded men wearing white suits. To the olive bench they moved him, planting him by my side. Once there mission was done they sped from the room. The one-eyed guy wouldn't sit still, making all sorts of snorting noises in my ear. From the corner of my eye, I noted he had this peculiar habit of wetting his upper and lower lips with the tip of his tongue. He inched closer and was soon staring into my ear lobe, but saying nothing. "You know you have a warm body," he said, breaking the silence. "It emits plenty of heat. This is a wonderful sign. You are a very good man."

I nodded my head in thanks.

The guy proceeded to tell me his life story. His name was Herod Kabala; his beliefs had died ten years back, his real life he said only began last night. When he found out I was Joseph Kabir, the Joseph Kabir they were all talking about, he took me in his arms and hugged, and hugged, and since I was cuffed, there was no way to break his grip. My head was tightened against his chest, his arm crushing my neck. "I want you in me," he yelled, as he pressed my body against him. I was turning blue. I had to do something. I used my head, literary as a battering ram against his chest, the chest that held me in captivity. He gave way to my pounding and slid all the way over to the other side of the bench only to return seconds later but this time more subdued.

"I'm sorry," said Herod, "really sorry. I just wanted us to join. I want our greatness to merge. I wanted us to become the ultimate in beauty." Herod took one of his crutches and pounded it into the floor and beamed, "I'm a great man like you Kabir. Tonight I was setting fire to the apartment building on Lawrence Street when they caught me. I've set more fires around this town over the last five years than anyone. Last night was the first time I've been caught. Wanted to be caught. Wanted my story to be told, wanted to be appreciated, and wanted every single one to understand."

I was awed by this Herod though not much what he said made sense and in fact frightened me to tell you the truth.

"You know what I wish, Kabir, I wish I would have had the opportunity to set everything on fire in this world, every building, every thing which had no heart. I wish I could have gotten my hands on an Atomic weapon and dropped it on the world. I would have delighted in seeing this planet Earth crumble into a thousand pieces. I would have loved to see each and every Earthling float solitarily into outer space. I shall never see my dream come true now. I'm gone."

I sat perfectly still afraid to make the slightest move.

"Of all nights to pick to let myself get caught, why this one?" continued Herod. "It's your night not mine. You'll get the headlines, all of them and deservedly so I might add. Ah, it doesn't matter, it doesn't. You'll be my representative. You'll deliver the message I would have delivered. We are basically one anyway."

I barely said two words back to Herod. What could I say? The only way I could reply to Herod was with a smile. Our tête-à-tête was interrupted when some one came racing out of the office carrying yellow papers. An ordinary sight, not a sight to get overly upset about. Herod though reacted strongly to the scene. He pointed to the office the man with the yellow papers had emerged from and asked, "Have you been in that room? Have you see it?"

"See what?"

"The blue divide, the blue divide is in there, the odious blue divide."

"The blue divide, what's that?"

"It's a snake that twirls effortlessly around and around. For centuries it's hid a variety of people between its coils."

"Hm, really, wow, interesting," said I when in reality I didn't understand a word the man yapped.

"The blue divide, the blue felt divide has an interesting history packed with macabre tales. The divide itself," rambled Herod, "is over two hundred years old. It presumably was constructed in eighteenth century France where it was used to house political prisoners who were to have their eyes, ears and tongues removed from their bodies. When liberalism came to France, the blue divide was sold to Turkey where the Sultans used it to house their concubines. Some of his black slaves were made into Eunuchs behind the divide. When Turkey abolished the title and office of Sultan the blue divide had to go and passed through various hands until finally finding a resting place in Russia where the Bolsheviks used it as their brain programming center. Surviving members of the royal family, their supporters and members of the hated upper classes were indoctrinated into the Communist way behind its walls. After the Bolsheviks were firmly in control in Russia, the blue divide was disposed of through some secret channel. For years it floated from country to country, from town to town, until finally finding its last resting place here in this medium sized stone building."

As Herod explained it to me the blue divide was now being used, or had been used in the precinct in recent years as a torture chamber. "They say ten men have been strangled in it. Amputated fingers hang from the walls of the thing, amputated fingers. The blue divide, the blue divide, the blue divide, the blue divide." Herod's eyes became dazed and he chanted the name. He began bobbing his head up and down like a duck drinking water in a pond, and then took one of his crutches and banged it against his head. His body, his legs, his arms, his head began shaking wildly as though he was suffering from an epileptic fit. I didn't know what to do. Unexpectedly he jumped up and bounded up and down on the balls of his feet. His face had a turned a pale white, as white as some angel up there in heaven. Herod gasped for every breath, his hand held to his chest. He was in pain, yet remained on his feet prancing about Detention Room A. It was all coming to some grand climax and the pain was the deliverer.

"Sit down please," I begged. "Herod stop before it's too late."

Herod didn't stop. He took his crutches and smashed them against the top of his head till blood flowed and he fell to the floor before me. I yelled for help but nothing. My two guards peeped in to see what the commotion was all about but then quickly hid their heads once more. I tried to run out into the hall. The guards bared my way. I screamed; I kicked them; I bit them, but all they would do was carry me bodily back to the bench, stepping over the fallen Herod in the process.

The same voice that had blared out of the hidden loud speaker now blared again. "Everyone out of their offices. All go directly to Detention Room A for there is a sight there I want you all to see." The edict was obeyed with steams of humanity pouring from their offices and congregating before Detention Room A. My guards mysteriously disappeared.

Herod lay cringing on the floor with a surprising smile upon his face. Looking straight at the crowd, I demanded that someone, anyone call for an ambulance. Nobody responded. The crowd could only whisper to themselves, "Is it possible to do anything? Why should we do anything? Do you want to be responsible? Oh no, no, no, not me. Never. No, not me. Why should we help him? He's our enemy and so completely dehumanized in our minds, a thing rather than a feeling human being. If not a man, what is he? He's an arsonist and will exist for all time as that only. Let him die. Vermin, he's vermin."

I rose and charged them. I couldn't do much with my hands cuffed but I kicked some, bit some, and spit some. In return, I received two fists to my face, one landing on my right eye and the other landing against the side of my nose. I was carried on someone's shoulders back to the bench and positioned in an upright position. From here, I could witness Herod cringing on the floor. He was choking. Would nobody help? Just then, a young man with red hair, freckles and a long curling, handle-bar mustache, came charging through the crowd. Looking down at Herod, he looked up at battered me, looked down at Herod, looked up at me, and then turned to the others. Jumping into action, he leaped into the crowd, and managed to land on top the head of a thin, long-haired man. Both fell to the floor with Freckles on top. The crowd retreated further into the hall while freckles thumped away at the long thin guy's body with his fist. The voice from the loudspeaker clicked on once more, "Get out," it ordered, "all retire to your offices. Don't watch. Retreat I say."

All scurried away in obedience and locked themselves back in their offices. Freckles, finished with the long-haired man, crawled over to the stricken Herod who muttered something or other him. Unable to hear at first, Freckles put his ear to Herod's mouth and listened. The expression on Freckles face changed from sympathy to horror. Then, taking Herod under his arms, he lifted him up and shook the last living breath from his body. I couldn't believe my eyes, couldn't accept Herod dying in the arms of Freckles. Nor, could I believe Freckles actions, nor could I believe it when the thin, long-haired man rose from the floor and mechanically took Herod's body from Freckles or when Freckles barked at him, "Make sure when you get rid of the body. Leave no traces of it anywhere. Burn it, slice it up, just destroy the carcass, and annihilate the horrid thing. Now hurry! Go!" No, I couldn't believe. I watched intently as long-hair disappeared down the hall dragging Herod's body. How could I believe it?

Now that we were alone, Freckles turned to me, "He was ready, but just needed a little help. I understood. He asked me, I gladly did what I could. He was ready. He'll never return, never. Ah, if only we could all reach that state."

"Who are you?" I asked.

"I am an individual who understands it all. I am in charge here but really not in charge. I can never be in charge. They will destroy me; there is a plot against me because I will not lead, not really. I choose not to lead men; my goal in life is to destroy leadership and destroy those who follow the leader. But today, now, this minute, they have given me the title. Is it all clear now."

"No really," I replied to Freckles. "What's your name?"

Strange, this man was strange, thought I. Freckles did not answer me. He'd made his little speeches and then left Detention

Room A quickly yet slowly and without saying another word. I was alone again in his strange room, in this strange building with these strange people in the middle of the night.

CHAPTER 2

Waiting, not understanding, feeling out of place, like I was put on some alien planet without the aliens. What were they going to do with me? Why were they just leaving me here sitting on this stupid bench. Why was no other human being addressing me, dealing with my inner turmoil and my inner beauty? Was this a waste or not?

But I was jumping the gun. I wasn't abandoned and I wasn't to be alone very much longer. From the office, directly opposite Detention Room A, two men and one woman who was carrying a small computer-type machine, exited. The one man was a pot-bellied, balding, middle-aged man chewing on a piece of gum. The other was Freckles, a guy I never expected to see again. Both had come for me. The woman, wearing a black dress and black eye mascara was young, thin, with large sagging breasts. All three escorted me out of Detention Room A. Sagging breasts followed us holding her machine; she said not one word throughout. To a staircase, we went and proceeded to walk down hundreds of steps to the very bowels of the building with both Pot-belly and Freckles arguing all the way down. Pot-belly was raving something about how all this was against regulations and how if it was discovered, they'd be removed from the force. There was also a report to the Commissioner. They must get the report to him by seven in the morning. Freckles just laughed. Pot-belly raved. I listened intently. Pot-belly raved some more. He called Freckles a shit-ass and the worst Captain the precinct ever had, a disgrace to the police force and a diabolical manipulator. "A madman, you are."

Freckles just laughed. "Regulations, do I care about regulations. I care nothing about what is external to myself. They are in the process of dismissing, no eliminating me. The plot is in motion. I know and I don't care. I have my soul to maintain. So I will be eliminated, but until then, you are my lieutenant, the next in command, a robot, like all are robots, a follower like all are followers. Understand that and follow. We must try to be with Kabir, get his side of the story before the FBI comes and his mouth and existence are permanently silenced. Have I made myself clear?"

Pot-belly said no more. Finally, we reached our destination, the basement. We glided down the well-lighted corridor with its black, painted walls until we stopped before a green door marked 'Officers Lounge.' Underneath was a hand-made sign that read: <u>Do not enter without knocking.</u> Pot-belly's grumbling began again and made him sound like a hungry bear but did not prevent Freckles from knocking at the green door. A little old man with a mop opened the door.

"What-a do-a you-a-want-a. No-a come-a in here-a," said the old man with the mop as he slammed the door in our faces.

Pot-belly came to the forefront now. "Let me handle this," said he. He knocked on the door himself now while Freckles, I, and Sagging Breasts moved out of the way. Again, the old man with the mop opened the door.

"Ow-a again you-a people-a bother-men-a. Why-a bother-a me. Closer-a the door-a."

"But-but-but," sputtered Pot-belly as the door slammed in our faces for a second time.

"Maybe we should forget about going in. We can find someplace else," reasoned Freckles.

Pot-belly wouldn't be chased away, not he, an officer of the law, a Lieutenant. It was the principle of the thing. Pot-belly opens the green door. This time the old man was inside with his back to us, mopping the floor. Taking a few steps forward, the old man grew aware of our presence and immediately turned to face us.

"What-a this?" he growled. "Why-a you-a sneak in-a here-a. I close-a the door-a for that-a mean-a you-a stay out-a. Now-a you-a in nothing-a to do-a. But-a I no want-a move. You-a on my-a wet-a floor-a. Stay-a there-a now-a."

"Listen you illiterate," snarled pot-belly. "We can't afford to play games. The criminal Kabir is with us and we must interrogate him immediately. We are going to use this room. Now old man let us through."

The old man picked up his mop and held it up like a club.

"No-a one talk-a to-a me-a that-a way. You-a not my-a boss-a. You-a better not-a walk-a on my-a floor-a or you-a going to get a wet-a mop-a on you-a head."

"Now listen here, this floor, this room is the property of the police department. I am a valued member of that department and so have an absolute right to it. You, on the other hand, are not part of the department and have no rights at all. Do you understand what I just said, you filthy peasant."

The cleaning man ignored Pot-belly's last words and went back to his work with the mop. Pot-belly by himself advanced another three steps, obviously believing he had won the battle of wills. The mop man stopped cleaning, glared at Pot-belly, who had a smug expression on his face, and turned a deep crimson while his eyes took on the intensity of a mad Doberman. "Look-a what you-a did-a to my floor-a. I told-a you-a not to walk-a on the wet floor-a. I warn-a you-a, but you-a do anyway. You-a filthy my-a floor-a. You-a ruin-a my work-a."

The old man took his mop and let it down repeatedly on the body of Pot-belly who went down quickly while Freckles and I ran for the nearest corner where we watched the festivities. Sagging Breasts, with her machine in hand, rushed back out the green door. Meanwhile the struggling Pot-belly was kept pinned as the mop landed blow after blow against his head, neck, shoulders, chest, arms, legs, feet. Tish, tash, tosh, were the sounds produced as mop met flesh. It was lucky for Pot-belly that the cavalry soon arrived; six men in boots came racing in through the green door and charged the old cleaning man who, nevertheless, remained undaunted. He waved his mighty weapon at them, swish-swash-shooo, swish-swash-shooo, felling every one of his attackers. As he swung his weapon, he roared, "Look–a what-a all you-a have-a done-a to-a my floor-a." But, alas, the old man was growing tired for as soon as he would knock down one of his attackers another would rise and then another and another, and another. His downfall, however, came from an unexpected source. Sagging Breasts - now having returned and putting down her machine - snuck up behind the old man, took off her high-heeled shoe, aimed it at the old man's head and fired. Bull's eye; the old man's tongue popped out of his mouth, his eyes bulged, and he slowly crumbled into the floor. Immediately all attackers pounced on their battered opponent as if they were hungry sharks, each grabbing some part of his anatomy. The old man still struggled but to no avail. They dragged him to his feet and then handcuffed him.

"Let's book him," came the common cry. "He'll get five years. Not enough. The bastard should get ten. Crazy bastard, crazy bastard, crazy bastard."

A line resembling a caravan now formed. Up front, was the old man with two husky guards, in the center was Freckles who was supporting the half-unconscious Pot belly; Sagging Breasts with her machine was behind them with the rest of the riffraff who had subdued the old man. At the command of one of the guards up front, the caravan marched in unison towards the door and in seconds were all gone, all except me that is. I was alone, completely isolated with my self, which gave me the opportunity to really observe the strange room I found myself in. Yes, strange is the right word. I walked around the room. It contained one bar, one refrigerator, one pool table, four crystal chandeliers, two magnificent reclining lounge chairs, and one tall metal sculptor of two nude men wrestling. Those were the conventional items in the room. Now for the unconventional objects dispersed haphazardly throughout. There were glass cases on high wooden stands; in these cases were old antique telephones, old police uniforms, old whistles and clubs, and my favorite display, old guns. Oh, those guns, brown guns, black guns, blue guns, long-barreled guns, short-barreled guns, machine guns, rifles, guns, guns, guns. I stood enthralled before the guns. What wonder drugs they are when used properly. To get a better look I stuck my face to the glass. Just then, a female shriek rang out from behind. Immediately I turned and saw a lady with a dust rag in hand and a white scarf rapped around her hair.

"Heeey, heeey, you, you there, hey," she whaled. "What are you doing by the gun showcase? Nobody is to look at that exhibit till next week. The showcase was covered over with a cloth, did you remove it?"

"No."

"Ah-okay. Anyway, you shouldn't have put your face to the glass. I bet you smudged the glass." Pushing me out of the way, she hurried to the showcase, examined it, eyed me angrily, and then for the next ten minutes lectured me on the importance of neatness. Thereafter, she just yapped about everything. She talked of the old cleaning man who had gone wild, and then relayed gossip about each cop in the precinct. She told me about her home life. She told me about her husband's problem. She told me about her kids. She told me about her brothers and sisters, aunts and uncles. She told me and she told me. Finally, she got around to asking who I was and what I was doing here in the middle of the night. When I explained I was Joseph Kabir waiting to be questioned about my actions of the last night, she became pale and shot out of the room at top speed. I walked around the room some more carefully viewing portraits of ancient old men with white beards hanging on the wall. While thus engaged, Freckles and Pot-belly came traipsing back in, though Sagging Breasts was nowhere to be seen. Pot-belly had a white bandage on his head and was limping perceptibly. We all then sat down, each one in a lounge chair by the couch. How cozy. If only Pot-belly could have calmed down. He began jabbering, cursing the day he was made to share an office with Freckles and so on and so forth. Bang, boom, bang.

I would find out that Pot-belly's real name was Lieutenant Talon, and Freckles appellation was one Captain Decarrie, but everyone still referred to him only as Detective Decarrie. He'd been made the Captain only a few weeks before and for reasons nobody ever really understood. He was generally hated in the station house and everyone considered him weird. How he even had maintained himself on the force was even of greater concern. A common theory was that he had some friend in high places. At first, he said nothing and we all just sat. Finally, he uttered, "Joseph Kabir your story shall be heard. People shall know it. The truth will be proclaimed like Herod wanted it to be proclaimed." Decarrie perplexed me; I never could understand a word out of his mouth. Talon interested me less. He was your common man attached to everything and everyone he could lay his authority-ridden hands upon and covering himself in the cloak of sanctimonious popular believes. Every so often Talon would grumble this and that, and make a lot of vulgar type faces at me and at Decarrie who he didn't seem to hold in any respect.

Decarrie unexpectedly exclaimed, "Why don't they stop?"

"What are you talking about, you idiot?" chided Talon.

"The crowd out there, the crowd that's yelling, 'Down with Kabir! Kill the disgusting vermin! Step on the filth! Butcher the varmint!'" Decarrie pointed to the back wall. "Don't you see them," he yelped, "they're waving torches to the sky."

"Yes, I see," I responded. "I knew they were out there, I knew."

"Both of you are crazy." barked Talon. "I hope the FBI gets here soon."

"They're out there, everywhere out there!"

"You're a lunatic, Decarrie. Thank goodness you'll be out of here soon."

Decarrie pulled keys from his pocket and threw them at the wall cursing as he did, "You'll never get Kabir, you bastards, you ugly bastards. You'll never get me, you'll never get Herod. You bastards, freaks, pornographers."

Decarrie was red in the face. Big blue veins were popping out of his neck. Smiling now, he said, "Joseph, you see they've disappeared for the time being. But they'll be back for us. They always come back."

I nodded in agreement while Talon continued to flap his tongue. He called Decarrie one unflattering name after another and I thought he was going to throw a punch, but fortunately didn't go that. Time passing, minutes, hours in the Officers Lounge. "Your story shall be told," Decarrie explained as we waited. "And it must be told before the federal storm troopers appear." Waiting for somebody or something, that's how it went, eat sat, and we sat, waited and waited, waited for something that would enable my spirit as Decarrie explained.

There was a knock on the door. Talon froze. I froze, while Decarrie yelled, "Come in, you're expected." The time had come.

CHAPTER 3

I entered the Officers Lounge, I remember that so well, so well. I, I being Arnold Bombser the chief crime reporter on the town's leading newspaper, The Star, in addition to also being one of the authors of this book which I have written about the perpetrator and which I have grave misgivings about.

Back then, the Officers Lounge, I remember. Strange. The secrecy. I had been waiting in the police precinct half the night with some twenty other reporters to get some information on Kabir and the crime he committed. My God was I ever surprised when Detective, or should I say Captain, Decarrie came up to me and offered an exclusive interview then and there with Kabir. I couldn't believe it. It didn't make sense. Kabir hadn't even been questioned by the police yet and here I was being offered an exclusive interview with this infamous scoundrel. Yes, why me? Why me? I guess I had been on a friendlier basis with Decarrie then any other reporter, as close as that jerk Decarrie would let me. Decarrie wanted Kabir's story to be widely known and he knew that my daily column, probably the most popular in the newspaper, would achieve that purpose. Decarrie must have also calculated that I was one of the fairest and most objective writers there was, who in the past had written absolutely splendid columns on numerous felons. From there it developed; from the exclusive story, to the exclusive book.

I originally wanted it not to be know that I am one of the men responsible for this book but since Kabir revealed the fact in his preface there's nothing I can do about it but accept credit for the book's composition. Why did I write the book in the first place if I didn't feel right about it? Well to be honest, financial considerations weighed heavily in my decision. But they were not my only reasons. I felt the public would be interested in learning some how the mind of a deranged, psychotic, mass murderer works, and deranged Joseph Kabir is. But you must have judged his mania for yourself in the first two sections which he authored.

One thing I must warn you about before you proceed; this book gives only Kabir's point of view. Now as Kabir is totally amoral, in other words a stinking no good liar, faith shouldn't be put in his words. I want you to observe the mind though, that sinister mind, that mind that seeks only to destroy us, to destroy society, to destroy the world, to destroy you and me. I know this only too well! I observed Kabir up close. The man has no grasp of reality. All he sees is himself. He doesn't see those around him, he doesn't want to see or work for the common good. He, that bastard, believes only in depravity, in grabbing whatever he can for himself. Bastard, bastard, bastard. But Kabir is no isolated case; there are hundreds, even thousands of Kabirs stalking the streets today. They all are an evil that must be stopped. Remember if we don't get the Kabirs, then the Kabirs will get us.

*   *   *

The first time, when it began, when I met Joseph Kabir, the first time in the precinct. Down into the bowels of the basement I went. Odd I thought, very odd. Upon entering the Officers Lounge, Decarrie directed me to sit on the couch in front of him, Talon, and Kabir, the bastard. Talon was sniping at Decarrie. Talon didn't want me there. Talon said it was against all procedure, that we should just be holding him until the FBI got there to begin the questioning. Talon was absolutely right, I didn't belong there, not one bit. But what was it to say. What went on behind the scenes wasn't my concern. My only concern was advancing my career and this interview would do just that.

But it wouldn't be easy. Ever since I remember, Decarrie and Talon were fighting; both shared the same office and were always slugging it out. Talon was the good cop, the one who cared, the one who did his job properly, but the one who never got ahead because he didn't have the connections. Decarrie, well Decarrie was another story. He was as lousy a cop as there ever was, doing his job halfheartedly if at all, but always getting promoted. I believe the truth is he didn't care to do his job or care about anything. He was a subversive plain and simple. I peg the guy as another Kabir, and maybe even more dangerous. He's the type that walks amongst us seemingly quite normal while all the while working to smash us all down. Yes, in the long run he's more dangerous than Kabir because a Kabir can be gassed while the supposedly moral Decarrie can't be touched.

I interrupted Talon's barking to Decarrie by explaining, "Look I have deadlines to meet so can't we simply proceed with this interview." Talon persisted, however, and was now begging Decarrie to get me out and put Kabir in total isolation until the proper authorities arrived. Decarrie wouldn't even give Talon the courtesy of an answer. Throughout this, Kabir was absolutely quiet. One would never imagine this young, angelic man to be a maniac which he most certainly was. I can't emphasize that enough.

Before we could begin, Decarrie inquired if any of us would like a drink. He and Talon declined. Decarrie offered a drink to Kabir to the great anguish of Talon and to the bewilderment of myself. Kabir gladly accepted. Decarrie removed Kabir's handcuffs and handed him a bottle of beer which he partook in. What a scene, I must say that, what an unbelievable scene. When both finished their liquid refreshment I declared "Kabir, let me begin by saying that you're crime baffles me, it really does. You are an educated young man; I looked at your record and found you had committed no prior offences. These facts make your crime even more unbelievable."

"Joseph didn't commit any crime, no crime at all," spit Decarrie.

"Shut up Decarrie. You shouldn't be saying such things to a reporter," whispered Talon to Decarrie but very loudly.

"Well to you, Decarrie maybe it's not a crime but to about ninety-nine percent of my readers it will sure be considered that."

"Screw your readers," stabbed Decarrie.

Decarrie had a big mouth, a very big mouth. I ignored his last comment directing another question at Kabir. "Is it true that you never were convicted of any major or minor offense and that you never even received as much as a parking ticket?"

"That's right. I was exemplary. I was the class athlete, the young genius, the Boy Scout leader, the lifeguard. In short, I was the moral idol for millions young and old, rich and poor, alike."

"Just answer the questions, Kabir," snapped Talon. "We don't want any sarcasm."

I didn't have time to waste if I was to get the story to the press by the afternoon edition so I put an end to all the rigor-more-all by saying, "Kabir, I don't believe in wasting time. Half the night is over already. There isn't much time. We must proceed. Now, I'd like you to explain the motive for your crime. If possible, I'd like you to provide me with a personal angle. Don't give me the regular pabulum, like that stuff that will appear in all the papers tomorrow. We need, I need something different. An underlying motive or motives that will satisfy the public's appetite to know and understand."

"Marvelous, just marvelous, super, just super," said Decarrie. "You see Joseph I selected the right person for the job. Isn't this Bombser something. The beauty of Kabir will become known."

Decarrie the idiot. Most of the time he sounded like a little old saint who no longer was such a saint.

"Okay now Kabir, your crime was against the university so I would like you to tell us all about when and how your association with the university began?" said I.

"Fine, fine, fine," chortled Kabir. "I began as a graduate student at the university last year. I had journeyed here from down south just to have the opportunity to study in the university's Middle Eastern Studies Department."

"Why did you want to study Middle Eastern Studies? Do you or your parents come from the Middle East?" asked I.

"Decarrie, must I answer that question, must I?" asked Kabir.

"You don't have to answer anything, not anything at all."

"I won't answer that question then. It's a barbarian question meant to destroy me."

Oh, that fuckin' Kabir. Every other word that came out of his mouth was barbarian. What an arrogant punk.

"Okay, fine. Let's take a step back, then. Tell me about the beginning of your association with the university. Try to be as detailed as possible."

"It was terrible, just terrible right from the beginning. I never fit in. I was always different, but I wanted to fit in, I wanted to be a scholar, I wanted to represent the university, I wanted to even be the university. But it just never happened."

"Why? What made you so different?" inquired I.

Kabir now gave us a lot of his specialty, bull shit.

"What made me so different, did you ask, well, it was the way I was raised. I came from a poor family, so poor that you could just cry to look at us. But I rose above it, I succeeded, I got to university. The university, well the university represented wealth and wealthy people. A poor boy like me just couldn't fit in, no sir."

"Tell me more about this poverty-stricken upbringing you had? It certainly will be of interest to my readers."

"Should I Decarrie, should I tell him?"

Decarrie leaned over in his chair and whispered in Kabir's ear, "Go ahead Joseph, tell him more, go ahead."

"Well okay then. My father was a hard-working man who whenever he could find work slaved in a factory, toiling fourteen hours a day at the drill press for twenty dollars a week. We barely had enough to eat. Thank goodness for the Welfare Department who supplied us with a large supply of stale white bread and jar upon jar of peanut butter. I had to start working when I was ten years old to raise money to help the family. I was a shoeshine boy, delivered newspapers, stole newspapers and sold them, did magic tricks on street corners, pretended I was blind and begged with a tin cup, helped put dogs to sleep in the pound, and worked in a plant shop mixing fertilizers."

"My God, and you're still so young," sounded I.

"Next I worked behind the fish counter in the local supermarket, slicing up smelly fishes, removing the bones, weighing, packaging, and selling them. That job didn't last long and I wound up selling ladies perfume in a department store. Then, I enlisted in the army reserve and stayed in for a few years until I was abruptly discharged. Between all these jobs, I managed to fight my way through high school and college. I was really lucky; the college I went to was free, so there were no financial problems there."

Talon began laughing and yapping, "You dishonorable bastard. Bombser, this guy's been telling you a pack of lies. I carefully read through his record before, and it plainly states much of Kabir's background. Kabir's father was connected with factories all right, but not the way Kabir said he was; his father owned a factory, a ladies underwear factory. His family had money, lots of it. Obviously then, a lot of what he just said is pure and simple crap although there were a few grains of truth there. Kabir was in the army reserve and he did attend a free public college. But I have my doubts about the rest."

I was mad and disgusted, ready to walk right out the door, ready to leave Kabir way behind. Something held me back though, something called responsibility. The newspaper was depending on me to bring in a great story, a newspaper which had fed and clothed my family for years. So I remained. I clearly and distinctly let Kabir know that if he pulled another stunt like that again, I would call it quits with the interview. Kabir promised to be a good boy, and in the course of his apology revealed that the other degenerate Decarrie had put him up to lying, advising that if all those huddled up idiots out there wanted to destroy themselves by perceiving only his outer-ness, his background, then he should have some fun with the fools and give them plenty to remember. A wonderful man, Decarrie. One of the pillars of society. What is society becoming? Why does it admit men like Decarrie into its body that will only bring about its destruction?

I yelled at Decarrie, then for putting Kabir up to his foul scheme. He gave me the same humble apology as Kabir did. Supposedly, everything Kabir told me from this point on was the truth but, in my humble opinion, this is to be doubted, scorned, and laughed at.

The room grew quiet. A pink veil had dropped down upon us signaling the close of one section and the beginning of a new one.

CHAPTER 4

Journalism, the interesting people you greet, the interesting you meet, and the interesting people you interview. Kabir was one of the interesting people I had to interview but it was never easy or very comforting. His answers were often incomprehensible, mystical, insane, and in general, rather stupid. I'd ask him a simple question and he'd tell me an hours worth of story and never were the answers factually. He liked to tell tall tales about the individuals he came in contact with, yet revealed little about himself. Worse, Kabir's mind is so disjointed that he would say one thing one minute, skip to another topic in the middle, switch back, talk about something else, reminisce and then do a little of everything, all to my chagrin. All I could do is write what he gave me and produce the best product I could which in my opinion is very good.

Decarrie only made my interview with Kabir harder. Every five minutes he would interrupt us asking if we wanted something to eat or drink. What unrelenting energy Decarrie has. But I plowed on. Between Kabir's bizarre mind and Decarrie's antics, I managed to get my questions in.

"You spent one year at the university, am I right?"

"Yes, one miserable year. What a God-damn university, I hate it. If only its walls would come tumbling down."

"But you didn't always feel that way, did you?"

"Of course not. When I first entered the university I thought it to be a most delightful place."

"What changed your opinion?"

"Not any one thing. Gradually, I turned against the university. It was a slow transformation which wasn't completed until last night, and you know what happened last night."

"Your transformation, yes, catchy, very catchy. Now that will make a good story. Readers jump at material that deals with personal transformations. Too bad, yours wasn't a religious transformation. The public likes those. I want to start from the beginning then, before the transformation when you entered the university. What were you like then?"

"I was a kid with a body and a mind."

KABIR THE MYSTIC.

"And I was a true barbarian."

"What do you mean barbarian? Define your term?"

"A barbarian is one who sees only a whole patch of grass and never sees each blade."

KABIR THE BAD PHILOSOPHER.

"No Joseph, you could never have been a barbarian," chimed in Decarrie.

"But I was. All I knew were books and what I could get from them. I was the amateur Middle East expert who wished to learn every fact ever produced and then spit them out in a very elitist intellectual fashion. My only interest in life was to read about people, philosophize about people, criticize peoples' governments, and to spout off about peoples' nations. Thank God I found the light in time, shed my skin and found the truth."

KABIR, THE RELIGIOUS-MYSTICAL FOOL.

Things didn't go so well between me and the university or between me and the department from the first day. Oh, what a first day it was. I had only arrived in town a few days before and I was still disoriented and homesick. I felt so alone and barren. I couldn't wait for the semester to begin so that I could begin participating and shed some of my isolation. On the first day was scheduled the department's annual orientation meeting where students, new and old, were brought together with their professors and given a solemn pep talk. But I'll get to the orientation meeting in a few minutes. First let me tell you what happened the morning before that meeting."

"Must you?" asked I, Bombser, the crack reporter for The Star. "Can't you begin with the damn meeting?"

"If you want the whole story of my transformation, then I will have to tell you about that morning before the meeting. It is then that it began for me, my rebirth, my coming of age, and my transmutation from gold to silver"

That morning I woke at the crack of dawn. I skipped breakfast and sped out of my crummy room in this old cockroach-infested boarding house close to the university where I was living. It was cheap and that's why I took it. And the grime of the place suited me, suited my disposition towards a world that is not perfect. Slowly I strolled over to the university savoring each beautiful moment of expectation. I can't explain how excited I was at the prospect of meeting renowned specialists of the Middle East. That's all I could think about.

A few blocks from the university, I saw a strange sight. There was a man, a tall man, a wide man, a man with grayish hair and a bushy beard, wearing an old black raincoat and a pair of dirty jeans which had white paint splattered all over them. He was standing in front of a huge office building banging on a metal sculptor of a man on horseback which stood in front of it. There are a lot of lunatics around, thought I. Another block I walked. Again, I saw the same guy who just a minute ago had been at the statue. This time he was standing on two wooden soap boxes in front of another office building and with a hammer and chisel in his hands, was attempting to remove the name of the business from the front of the building. I walked on.

Eventually I reached the university, a huge collection of eighteenth century buildings. What astoundingly magnificent architecture, that's the only way I can describe it. The buildings encircled an immense green campus flowing over with old, interesting-looking trees, purple and red flowers, and water fountains. Threading through the scene were squirrels, white squirrels, gray squirrels, black squirrels, prancing from one clump of grass to the next while begging for food. As soon as the squirrel got hold of an eatable, it would shimmy up the nearest tree with it. Then, I remember the pigeons roaming everywhere, waddling up to me, clucking for some bread crumbs. Little girls, little boys, grown boys, grown girls, would oblige the pigeons appetite and spread out crumbs everywhere. Every now and then, a sparrow would swoop down from a nearby tree and steal the meal away. And between the old trees and the purple and red flowers and the squirrels and pigeons were muscular young men, shirts off, playing soccer to the beat of distant orientation which was being piped over hidden loudspeakers.

KABIR, THE VERY, VERY, VERY AMATEUR POET.

"Kabir, stop," scolded I in exasperation. "Enough of this nonsense about squirrels and pigeons. My readers aren't interested. Get on with it, will you!"

Okay, sure, fine, yeah, that's fine with me. Now, here goes, contact, as I was strolling the campus thoroughly enjoying myself I spotted the guy I had been seeing all morning. This time with hammer and chisel in hand, he was attempting to dismantle a campus bench. Why haven't they locked him up yet? I questioned. Why haven't they put him in a psycho ward instead of letting him roam the streets destroying valuable property?

My watch indicated that I had two hours before the orientation meeting. What to do? It wasn't natural for me to exist beyond some schedule. But I'd make the best of it. Nothing to do but enjoy the campus and take a leisurely stroll. That's when I heard from behind me the patter of huge running feet. Quickly, I looked back. The guy with the hammer and chisel was springing towards me at a phenomenal speed. What could I do? No use in fleeing. It was too late. Stand my ground and fight the madman off as best I could. He came like an oncoming train. I clenched my hands into fists. This is it, I thought. But no this wasn't it, no. About six inches before me he came to a dead halt.

'Oh, I'm glad I got you before you left, so glad,' he exclaimed before reaching for something in his raincoat, which I thought was a gun. But again, my judgment was wrong. He pulled out a piece of paper and explained, extending his arm to me. 'This paper fell out of your pocket back there. Would you like it back?'

'Yes, ah, yes, thank you for retrieving it for me, ah.' I took the paper and put it in my pocket.

"One major characteristic of this big guy I hadn't mentioned before was his big eyes which were frightening. A brilliant orange in color, they shined like the sun and burned so hot with intensity that I could feel the heat generated on my face. Those eyes were piercing, delving, and absorbing my soul. This guy just made me so uneasy. He looked, walked, talked like he had came out of the nineteenth century, a Russian novelist perhaps.

'You're new to this university, aren't you?'

'Yes, but, but how did you know?' asked I worried that maybe this bizarre-looking guy could have supernatural powers.

'You look like a scared rabbit, that's how I knew. Appearances are not always deceiving as the saying goes.'

'You're right. I am scared. I may even collapse. In just a little while, I got to be at my department's orientation meeting. Oh God, I wonder how it will be. I'm a nervous person. Anything makes me nervous. I wish it was over all ready.'

'What department are you entering?'

'The Department of Middle Eastern Studies.'

Vladimir's face dropped to his feet. He began to spit everywhere, everywhere except in my direction. He threw the chisel and hammer, held in his hand, into the nearest tree and pulled so violently on his beard that he pulled out large clumps. Then he started muttering something in a foreign language.

'Is there something the matter?' I asked. 'What is it?'

'"You're entering the Middle Eastern Studies Department is that what you said? I wasn't hearing things, was I?'

'"Yes, that's what I said."

He began violently shaking his head.

'Have you anything against the department?' I followed up.

'I don't know. Why should I know?'

'Are you a student?'

'I guess you could call me that.'

'What department are you in?'

'"I'm in a general department, but I'm working towards a solitary one.'

I felt like making a fast exit. He introduced himself than as Vladimir and I reciprocated with my name.

'Glad to meet you, Joseph Kabir, very glad. Fate has ordained for us to meet. You need me very much,' said Vladimir as he played with his ear. He seemed particularly curious as to why I had picked the Middle East to study. I told him my reason was instinctual, a feeling. He told me that was crazy, that it was impossible to feel anything for a region. He urged me to forget about the Middle East, forget everything he said and just remember, 'Yourself and myself and our feelings for each other.' Vladimir asked me what my ambition was. I said I wanted to be a Professor of Middle Eastern History and also work as a researcher and writer on the subject. He became red in the face, grabbed hold of his raincoat and ripped its buttons off. 'Ambition, that is your ambition. Do not start with that ambition, do not go to your orientation meeting, do not go to your department,' snarled Vladimir. 'Go home where you belong!'

'Ah, yes, well, well it has really been a pleasure to meet you Vladimir. I hope we meet again.'

'Please don't go. I know you think I talk out of place but really, I don't. I am a student in the Middle Eastern Studies Department. I know what's waiting for you. I have seen the great black mass, the malignant steroid. You must believe me. I have proof.' Vladimir pulled out his student identification card which confirmed his statement.

'"Twenty years I have been trying to get my Ph.D. from the department, twenty years. Can you imagine and what I have been met with is one large asbestos blanket that has released its carcinogenic fibers into my lungs. So you see, Kabir, I know what I'm talking about. I am begging, warning, chiding, telling you to never set foot in the department. It's for your own salvation as an individual.'

'Vladimir, you contradict yourself. If the department is so terrible, why then have you remained for twenty years? Now does that make sense?'

'"You are making fun of Vladimir and that is a putrid thing. Twenty years, why? Do you think I had a choice! They planned it so I would stay. In the beginning, they deluded me, did magic tricks before my eyes, and hypnotized me. They waved the Ph.D. degree before my eyes and told me it would be mine soon, just a few more months. I believed. They gave me encouragement. You'll get your Ph.D. just be patient, they kept saying. Everyone is patient. The good things in life don't come immediately. I believed and I stayed and stayed and stayed. And financially, they bribed me, waved dollars in front of me, corrupting me. The department each year awards me a certain sum which is large enough to meet my bills but nothing more. But what price have I paid? My life has been wasted. What have I done with my life? Read lots of scholastic-type books and journals about people, places and things but who cares about those dreadful things. Things, everything is things. The Department, the University specializes in producing things that are then passed on down to the fools out there, the robots who exist for a purpose which has nothing to do with life. Do you understand, Joseph Kabir?'

I nodded that I did but really sought an opening to flee.

'You still do not get it, Joseph Kabir,' he continued to carry on. 'They've destroyed me, finished me now. I'm fifty-five years old and there is absolutely nothing I can do but read and then theorize about what I read. If I'm to put food on the table, I must remain with the Department. However, just because I've wasted my life doesn't mean you have to waste yours. Do you still plan to go to the meeting?'

I began to walk away, but Vladimir quickly blocked my way. 'You must follow me,' he cracked as his orange eyes burned more intensely than ever. 'Follow me and I promise everything will become clear to you.'

I didn't want to follow him but his eyes pulled me along like a magnet. There was no fighting the force. I hung to Vladimir's heels as we zigzagged our way in and around the buildings of the university. Vladimir halted at the parking lot. There he showed a mutilated pigeon which had been run over by a car. 'Now do you understand, Joseph Kabir?' he cracked to me incomprehensibly. 'Are things becoming clearer to you now?'

'I don't understand what a dead pigeon has to do with anything. What kind of logic is that?'

'Hm, I see you are still living in the dark, shapeless mass. I'll have to take you to that other place now. I wish I didn't have to.'

"We were on the march again and circled the campus a second time. Into a tall white building we turned. There was a sign outside with the words *Student Health Clinic*. We entered, turned one corner, twisted about another, until we found ourselves at the head of a long white ward. As we pranced down it, nurses and doctors smiled and waved at Vladimir who returned the greetings with a little bow. Finally, we entered a room filled with television sets and wheelchairs. Vladimir dragged me over to a far corner where a young man was sitting in a dirty wheelchair, holding his trembling left hand over his head and groaning a moooooo sound. By the time we reached him, he was intently glaring at the palm of his hand.

'Hello Cyrus, how are you today?' asked Vladimir.

The young man looked up from his palm to exclaim, 'Vladimir is that really you? This isn't a trick. Could it be you?'

'Of course it is me, Vladimir, your old friend. I can be no other.'

'Vladimir I'm so glad it's you. I've been wanting to talk to you about this superb book I've been reading. It's about the Prophet Muhammad, Muhammad, Muhammad, Muhammad, the bearded Prophet of seventh century Arabia, Arabia, Arabia, Arabia. The author of the book, Harvey Wallbanger is positively brilliant, extraordinary, tremendous, great, hallucinogenic is a better word. Harvey personally knew Muhammad. But you probably have doubts about that; sure, you have doubts, Vladimir. How could Harvey know him, you ask, when Harvey Wallbanger was born in 1930 while Muhammad was born in 570. Well, it's simple you see, our author is thirteen hundred and eight some odd years old. Take a look at this lovely book, Vladimir.' Cyrus showed Vladimir his palm.

'Oh, I've heard, it's a very good book,' responded Vladimir while I hid behind him, not wishing to enter into the discussion.

'"Vladimir, I don't want you to think that I've been wasting time here in the harem of the Shah of Iran. I never waste time. Ask anyone in the Department and he'll confirm the fact. I've been doing a lot. Can you guess what I've been doing? Do you know, already? Of course you don't. Only Allah knows, only Allah, Allah, Allah. But I think I can trust you, Vladimir, I can tell you. You're to be trusted. You've cleared customs.' The guy looked down at the palm of his hand once more, spit into it and then rubbed his palm into his face. 'Vladimir, my comrade,' he continued. 'I've been working on a new theory on the Prophet Muhammad, a theory nobody else has ever thought of. It's my contention that the Prophet was not a male as is commonly thought; he was a female who only appeared to be a male. From intensive reading of the Koran, I can say with some certainty that Muhammad sometimes would walk about the streets of his city wearing low-cut, blue, polka-dotted dresses. This is the plain and simple truth that has been suppressed by pious Muslims for one thousand years. Furthermore, a closer examination of the source material will reveal that Muhammad was born a freak with both male and female sexual organs. Isn't it amazing and I was the one to unearth the situation, me, Cyrus. Now I'll be famous and be remembered for all time, now they'll accept me, now.'

The young man jumped out of the wheel chair, knocking Vladimir over in the process, while he raced for a barren white wall. He pulled out a red crayon from his pocket and scribbled something in funny Arabic letters all over it. 'See,' he yelled to Vladimir who I was slowly helping to pick back off the floor. 'This Arabic saying on the wall proves my claims about Muhammad. I've done it. It's the discovery of the century.' Cyrus took the crayon and started marking up the floors with Arabic letters while Vladimir and I watched, frozen like statues.

One nurse entered, saw, left, two nurses entered, saw and left, three nurses came, saw and left. 'Cyrus is crayoning the television room again,' came the cry. 'Who gave him the crayons, who, who? You know he's not supposed to get any crayons. Who gave them to him?' Four orderlies came flooding into the room. 'Stop you knaves,' yelled Cyrus, jumping to his feet. 'Why do you people approach me, the Prophet Muhammad and a descendant of Jesus, in such a rough manner?' The orderlies rushed him. Cyrus back-peddled. 'Don't touch me you vagabonds. Understand that I'm the great Prophet, the ruler of the Middle East. Bow before me infidels and become true believers in Allah.' Instead of bowing, they chased him with outstretched arms. Over tables, behind tables, under tables, over wheelchairs, around television Cyrus fled. Vladimir, awakening from his stupefied state, positioned himself in Cyrus' line of flight, wedging him in. 'Go ahead you infidels, kill the prophet, go ahead,' yodeled Cyrus. 'Go ahead kill me.' Cyrus charged Vladimir with his head down like a bull. Vladimir planted his feet and somehow managed to survive the collision and take a firm grasp of Cyrus. The orderlies followed, clung, and carried Cyrus to another place.

Vladimir shook his head and looked at me mournfully. 'I have an errand to run upstairs,' he said to me then. 'Come with me?' He pulled out an old pocket watch and eyed its face. 'Doesn't worry, Joseph Kabir, you still have a good hour before the meeting if you choose to attend. What I ask of you will not take more than a few minutes.'

I followed him again to the building's sixth floor. Once off the elevator, we entered the nearest room, which was dim and had a huge brass bed in the center of it covered with a satin sheet with a design of a large red heart and two red devils suspended above it and sticking pitch forks into it. The room's window overlooked the entire university and by it sat a young man who on our approach turned his eyes toward us. His face, now clearly visible, was a sight; it had absolutely no eyebrows; a smidgeon for a nose, his mouth that was unusually large with thick lips surrounding it, and teeth that were long and dagger-shaped. He had a long black beard whose tip was a bright red. A long white bedspread covered him from neck to toe. His head was covered by a black beret with a red feather sticking out of it. Saying nothing, he quickly rose and rushed for the adjacent bathroom. Returning, he was now wearing a towel tied around the lower part of his face.

'Have they sent you Vladimir?' he mumbled to Vladimir through the towel. Vladimir shook his head no. 'They were all here yesterday, you know, stood outside on the ledge watching, checking to see if I'm doing my work. Vladimir have you seen Cyrus?' Vladimir shook his head yes. 'What a mind that Cyrus has. It is so comforting to know him.'

"Gently I whispered over to Vladimir. "This is another Middle Eastern Studies Departmental mental case, huh Vladimir?' He nodded yes while keeping his eyes focused on the funny looking guy.

"'I am happy to report to you, Vladimir that my research is coming along fine. It's all falling into place, a place that is somewhere in the center of the universe. Yet, I am sad to also report that I still feel I am no good, not worthy of respect from anyone or anything. In fact, both of you should not be casting your eyes upon me. I possess the evil eye, the ability to turn happiness into pure vinegar with just a passing glance. But I am trying to correct this, to change my ways, to reverse the process. I must become a specialist, an expert in my field, a total professional man of letters. That will remove the curse, which will make me worthy. Until then nobody should look at me, this ugly person.' The guy rose from his chair again, went over to his bed, reached under its cover, and pulled out four drawings of old, fat ladies. He went over to a wall with the drawings, and attached the drawings to the wall with band aids produced from under his beret.

Back to the bed, he produced a ruler from under the mattress and pointed to one of the drawings with it. 'This is the Ottoman Empire in the nineteenth century,' he explained. 'As you can see by this drawing, it was in a much weakened state then, just ready to crumble like a decayed apple eaten by flies.' Pointing to another drawing, he explained, 'This is Austria, a mortal foe of the Ottoman Empire, and this drawing, emaciated Persia, another foe. Oh, and here this evil looking one with the apple in its mouth was the Ottomans fiercest foe, Russia. Russia was always so mean and nasty to the Ottoman Empire, wanting to eat the flesh off its bones. Just look at the Ottoman Empire. It was innocent and pure, too innocent and pure to be ravaged by the likes of these creatures around it. Oh, why is life so cruel? So that's it, all of it, the terrible view of the history. Vladimir and his friend, I hope you have enjoyed the presentation. Are there any questions you have about what I just showed you?' Vladimir shook his head no. 'How about you stranger, do you have any questions?' I too shook my head no.

'Vladimir, have you brought what I asked for?' asked the guy.

Vladimir reached into his back pocket and pulled out a number of brown paper bags. The guy's eyes lit up and hustled over to the night table adjacent to his bed and removed from its top draw chewing gum wrappers, old magazine ads, old soap box coupons, old buttons, and various other multi-color bits and pieces. His research material he called the debris and 'My most prized possessions.' Putting it in the brown paper bags, he cackled, 'Fantastic. Now I have a place to keep my research notes. Thank you ever so much, Vladimir. You are a great scholar and intellectual. With you around, the world will be safe for democracy for centuries to cone.' That said, the guy no longer paid us any heed. As gently as a saint, he glided past us to his bed, reclined, and pulled the cover over his head. 'Vladimir, you and the stranger must leave now,' he crooned from under the cover. 'I am at a critical stage in my research and have no desire to be disturbed.'

Vladimir looked at the lump the guy's frame made, said goodbye and departed. All the way downstairs, neither Vladimir nor I said a word. But downstairs, Vladimir pulled from his pocket old newspaper clippings and handed them to me. They were obituary columns about students in the Department of Middle Eastern Studies who had killed themselves. There were five bizarre suicides. One column read, 'Paul Krausse a young Ph.D. student took his life by ripping out the pages of his favorite book and eating them.' Another read, 'Lawrence Farsi a man of twenty-six noted for his courage proved it today. First, he smashed through a glass showcase which housed a gold, Arabian sword that the Department of Middle Eastern Studies had on display. Then, despite bleeding profusely from the arm, he took the weapon and with one thunderous swing, chopped his own head off.' Another obituary stated, 'Harry Abdu dead at age twenty-eight. Abdu a promising student, noted his Professors, suddenly went crazy during a seminar class and began banging his head against the desk hard and fast. Before anyone could restrain him his desk was covered with blood and he was under his desk as dead as a doorknob.' My personal favorite was the fourth suicide, 'Carlos Harperoni, aged twenty years ten days last night was found dead in the office of one of his Professors. Mr. Harperoni it seems snuck into a Professor's office, removed notes from his desk, notes that were to be used for a book the Professor was writing, and then laid flat on top of the Professor's desk, piled all the notes on top of himself, spread gasoline on top of himself and his notes, and lit. The fire department later found the body burned beyond recognition. When the newspaper contacted the Professor in whose office Harperoni committed suicide all he could say was, *I want to be at his funeral, I want to get my hands on that body of his and then slice it up into little pieces and feed it to the sharks.*' The last suicide was a plain and simple hanging and doesn't deserve specific mention here. When I finished reading, Vladimir shot, 'Now I will ask you ask you again not to go to the orientation meeting. If you do, I warn you it'll come to no good.'

'I don't care what you say or what you show me. You're crazy if you think I'd drop out even before I begin. Why would I give up the greatest opportunity I ever had? You parade a lot of lunatics before my face and then expect me to obey your commands. You haven't proved a single thing to me about the Department. You just showed me losers, the ones who weren't intelligent enough to make it, the ones who could never make it as scholars.'

"I'm warning you!"

I now felt a sense of outrage against this man. 'Vladimir, to be honest, I believe there is something really wrong with you and your friends. Twenty years you have spent in trying to earn your Ph.D. degree, twenty years and have failed. Doesn't that say something?'

'Joseph Kabir you are sick, dead, finished, suppressed. Go to your department. Let them give you hell, let them crush you, let me them make you cough blood, let them make you be.' Vladimir bent down and picked up some stones. Thinking they were intended as weapons against me, I took off running. Turning my head back to see what was happening I discovered it wasn't me but the *Student Health Clinic* that was Vladimir's target. Up and down Vladimir ran in front of the building throwing stones at the windows. He had a good aim, too. Bang, one window shattered, bang, two windows, key-yang, three windows, rip, four windows. Windows shattered at a increasingly fast rate. Then Vladimir's attention was diverted by a passing plane over head. One stone, two stones, three stones he threw into the air and laughed and threw some more and then set off in active pursuit of the plane. Soon no trace was left of Vladimir to the eye.

I stood before the *Student Health Clinic* stunned, shocked, and sick to my stomach. What a way to begin my new life. There were doubts forming too. Was there an element of truth in anything Vladimir said? How could there be? It was so absurd. But while standing there debating these points, there was stirring from the Student Health Clinic. Uniformed guards came running from the Clinic out to get the guy who broke the windows. I hid behind some nearby bushes while they searched. Luckily, I escaped detection. Since I was a little kid, I've always been a champion hider.

When the coast was clear, I set out for the orientation meeting with the Department. Suddenly, I was fearful of what the future might hold. Was the world not a perfect place? Was the world flawed? Was there such a thing as the world? Question and more questions and no answers right then.

CHAPTER 5

The story continued despite interruptions from Decarrie who decided it was time to eat the peanut butter and jelly sandwiches brought from home with Kabir joining in the feast. I could swear that at this point for a second Decarrie turned into Kabir and Kabir turned into Decarrie. Oh well, that's getting away from the point. Talon, meanwhile, had begun pacing up and back across the room, muttering something incomprehensible. Every so often, he'd go to the door, begin to open it and turn back.

Minutes passing. I was getting impatient. But finally, Kabir, having digested his meal, was ready to begin again.

The orientation meeting, my first day. I was late. I tore away from the *Student Health Clinic* at top speed to make it. On the way, I narrowly missed being run over by a tow truck. Frantically, I zoomed into the appointed building, of the appointed room, of the appointed meeting. But, I couldn't find Room 101 no matter how hard I tried. I queried one passer-by. He didn't know. I asked another, another, another and another. Nobody knew. I eventually found the janitor.

'Pardon me,' said I, 'do you know where Room 101 is?'

"'Sure, gent, sure, I know everything about this place. I worked here years. Don't you think I should know? Room 101, huh, well walk up to the second floor, make a right, walk another twenty feet, make a left, then walk straight ahead of you and you can't miss the room.'

"'May I ask you why Room 101 is on the second floor? Shouldn't it be on the first floor?'

"'Why do you ask me that? I'm not the architect who built this ugly joint,' he growled as he walked away from me.

I followed his instructions and arrived at Room 101 about fifteen minutes late. I just touched the door and it swung open to reveal a five hundred seat assembly hall encircled with flags of all nations and a theatrical stage. There was nobody there yet. I couldn't understand it. Could I have wandered into the wrong room? Could I have misunderstood the time of the meeting? Could I have gotten the days mixed up? No, not at all. I would wait, then for as long as it took. Towards the middle of the hall, I seated myself so that I was directly behind the speakers' podium. Nothing to do but wait. Ten minutes, twenty minutes, thirty minutes went by but not a soul appeared. I was just about to set off for Department headquarters to investigate when I heard what sounded like a buffalo stampede coming from outside. The buffalos banged against the door. The assembly hall shook. The door opened with a bang, the buffalos in the shape of people, charged into the hall. Small people, medium-sized people, huge people shoved inside, shove, shove, push some, kick, go a head, give her a kick, how dare you, tug, unfortunate. They were unusual people wearing turbans, fezzes, Arab head-dresses, veils, long white robes, long green robes, saris, mini-skirts, blue jeans, gray suits, black suits, white suits and came with cameras, with books, with briefcases, with tape recorders, but I honestly can declare none came with a smile. They now jostled for position to find the best seat.

At first, nobody made a sound and everyone ignored each other. The silence was broken when a young man, upon entering the hall, yelled, 'Get off my foot you Muslim freak. Why must you climb over me? Where's the hurry creep.' By the luck of the draw, I was sandwiched in between two very different men. On my left, a short squat little fellow with gold-framed glasses, who had this tendency to pick his nose when he thought nobody was looking. On the other side of me was a middle aged man with pitch black skin wearing a red velvet suit with a red silk handkerchief protruding out of his jacket pocket. He had a worried look on his face and the habit of constantly wetting his lips with the top of his tongue. 'Is the Middle East Studies meeting?' the black skinned guy asked me then, tapping me on the shoulder to get my attention. I noticed that as he talked his head bobbed up and down like a chicken. 'What did you say?' asked I. His accent was almost incompressible

'Yes, yes, that's nice. Thank. You.'

'You're welcome, for what you're welcome I don't know, but you're welcome.'

'"Is Middle East Studies meeting?' he repeated the phrase but this time to my understanding.

'"Yes, it is, yes,' answered I slowly.

'"Good, nice, very nice. I worry in wrong room. I new. No speak English good. Spanish speak well. Hungarian speak good. Albanian speak good. Arabic speak good, but English speak not so good.'

'My goodness, you speak a lot of languages. You're a real scholar.'

'Nice, nice, good, good, nice, very nice, very good. My name is Abu Lulu. Your name?'

'Joseph Kabir.'

'Nice, very good, very good-nice. Me come Senegal. I come learn. I want be big ambassador, big, ambassador. I like, I like.'

'Sounds like a wonderful idea.'

The little squat fellow, who sat on the other side of me, had fastened his eyes on my shoulder as soon as my conversation with Abu Lulu began. As I talked, I could see him making disapproving faces out of the corner of my eye.

Abu Lulu examined his wristwatch and exclaimed, 'Time come. Must call up Senegal Consulate. I promise call. Important business.' Abu Lulu fought his way through a row of pointed feet and tramped out.

The short, squat fellow had his eyes glued to me, but every time I turned towards him, he would quickly shift his gaze away. The game gnawed on my nerves. I had to break the silence between us or I'd go crazy.

'Excuse me,' said I, tapping him gently on the shoulder. 'Do you have the time?'

"Time, time, oh I see you desire time,' he sloshed out in a slow, British drawl. 'I don't keep a watch, my good man, but I imagine it must be at least twenty minutes past the hour.'

'"Hm, the meeting should have started by now, don't you think?'

'"Probably so.'

'"My name is Joseph Kabir, what's yours?'

'"My name, you desire my name, which is a legitimate request, my name is Zeno Beneen.'

'"Aren't there an awful lot of people here, Zeno? I'm surprised. I thought our department was smaller. Have you any idea of the actual amount of students enrolled?' No answer. 'How many professors does the department have?' No answer. 'I'm new. Have you been here long?'

Now he answered. 'Ha-ha-ha-ha-ha-ha-haha-hold-it, my good man, how can you expect an answer when you throw one question after another into my face, not allowing any appropriate response. I tell you, my good man, you must learn to structure your thoughts into a more coherent pattern or otherwise you'll never make it as a tried and true academic.'

My face sagged with hurt. Zeno noticed, turned his eyeballs in, and then changed his tune completely. 'Joseph, my dear boy, I have excellent news to report to you. I am as new to this department as you. So Joseph I know just as much as you as to the in and outs here. Well then again, I probably know a little more. That accent of yours, Mm, I shall venture a guess and say you must come from that huge city down south. Am I correct?'

I admitted the truth of his supposition.

'Yes, I knew it. I've visited your fair city many times so I therefore am able to discern the origin of your accent. Can you tell me what type of accent I have, my dear boy?"

'No, but it's very interesting.'

'Quite, quite. I cultivated it during the two years I spent in Oxford attending university. I have managed to totally submerge the common accent I formerly had, the accent everyone in this city has. My accent is one every scholar should possess. I can't tell you how many doors it can open that lead to high-status positions.'

'Zeno, did you say you attended Oxford University?'

'Yes, yes, quite true, quite, absolutely, quite, true, I did attend that masterful university in merry old England on a Rhodes Scholarship, a R-h-o-d-e-s S-c-h-o-l-a-r-s-h-I-p, a scholarship awarded only to the most brilliant. Like my accent, just the mention of my scholarship appearing on my record opens innumerable doors. It is the way of the world, a world I am so keenly in touch with. I am a sophisticate, a man who knows his own destiny. That is why Joseph, I think I am bound for enduring success.' In another tone, Zeno belched, 'Oxford, Oxford, Oxford, sweet, dear, old Oxford. Oxford was simply a delightful experience, an intellectual awakening in the very least.'

'Hm, if you were at Oxford, why are you now enrolled in this department as a new student?'

'You know the area around Oxford is simple breath taking,' yapped Zeno, ignoring my inquiry. 'England, all England is quite, quite, divine. And London, oh lady London what can I say about her that hasn't been said before. London, without a doubt, is the finest city in the world, a world in which I've traveled quite extensively.'

'"Yes, but why. . . '

'"Oh and Europe, that grand old continent, how exquisite it all is. Barcelona, Madrid, Amsterdam, Paris, Berlin are all flawless diamonds. Someday I hope to write a book on my various journeys. And, I can tell you it will be quite enlightening. I'll call it, Voyages of a Sophisticate in Europe. I can see the common flock of people forming lines at their bookstores waiting to get the opportunity to buy my volume. How divine, how marvelous.'

'"Zeno, could you answer my question, why are you here if you were studying at Oxford? Did something happen?'

'"Oh, well, it's an interesting story, a very interesting one indeed. To tell you all the details would be too time consuming. Putting it simply thought, it was just a matter of me finding Oxford University ultimately not to my liking. It is very poorly organized, a disgrace for an institution so highly regarded by the world. However, I must admit all European universities suffer from the same disability. The educational system there is quite detestable; horrid might be even a better word. Their system is so bloody selective, atrocious really and ultimately ghastly. We North Americans who attend universities here have it so bloody easy.'

'"In other words, Zeno, dear fellow, you dropped out of Oxford, right or wrong?' I questioned with venom.

"'Yes, yes, quite. I really had no patience for Oxford. I was left with no choice but to terminate my association with that mediocre establishment.'

"'May I ask you Zeno, what kind of student you were at Oxford?'

"'I know what you're getting at, my dear boy. You surmise I exited that institution of higher learning because my academics were not up to par. Well, let me state for the official record that is utter rubbish. To be quite blunt about it, at Oxford I was at the head of my class academically, and in fact, I was honored in every way. I was the conversational piece on campus. Whenever, I'd pass in the hallways or in the cafeteria, comments would fly to the effect of, there goes the genius, or, there goes that amazing young man who, or, there goes the most intelligent student Oxford ever saw who. . . . My credentials were utterly impeccable. I was the head of the debating team and won trophies for my oratorical brilliance. In my spare moments I was the editor of the university newspaper whose distribution included the entire British Isles. Whenever my esteemed Professors felt unsure of material they would be teaching, they would consult me and I would always be of service. So you see, Joseph to think, even for a moment, that I fell short, in any way, at Oxford is inane. And, to be quite honest with you, my good man, when I made the official announcement to my superior that I would be leaving Oxford, they literally got down on their hands and knees to beg me to reconsider. However, my mind was made up and nothing could change it.'

The girl sitting in front of us with the long brown hair, which hung down the back of the chair touching my knees, began to squirm like a worm melting away in the sun. While she squirmed, I distinctly heard her say, 'Should I or shouldn't I. Maybe or maybe not. Possibly or possibly not.' She rocked her body in half way turns towards me and then back. Finally, she made a complete turn so that in full view I could see she was a young girl with hope glittering in her eyes. She had a milky white complexion, pink rosy cheeks, a small button of a nose which pointed upwards at the tip, tiny little buck teeth, and gold rimmed glasses. She looked as angelic as a saint.

'Well hello there, you two fellows,' she greeted us in a soft, silky voice. 'So you're new students. So am I. Isn't that quite a coincidence. The Lord works so wonderfully sometimes, doesn't He.

Do you two love the Lord?' We nodded our heads affirmatively. 'That's good, we all must. It's as simple as that. But not everyone does and there are grave consequences. I mean most people do not truly love the Lord and that is why most everyone is a fool. Read the newspapers, and see the fools. Ha-ha. I can only laugh at them. Why can't everyone act civilized like myself; I am a very pure person, pure and simple who knows the right way to achieve salvation. I understand more than ninety-nine percent of the population, and do you know why that is, does either of you two young fellows know why?' Quickly intrigued by her beguiling enthusiasm, we quickly indicated a NO with a shake of our heads. 'I understand more because I'm a follower of Abu Ketab, the founder of the Divine religion. Abu Ketab such an inspirational man, so beguiling, so courageous, so utterly fascinating. I can go on for days telling you about the good deeds he performed. Let me just say that I love Abu Ketab as I love God above. Are either of you members of the faith by any chance?' Again, we shook once to indicate NO. 'Oh, that's too bad. I'm so sorry. But it's never too late to reclaim your soul; it's never too late to right to discover the path. The light is yours, yours is the light. Divines know, we know all. God has personally sent down His messenger to tell us. It is only through the Divine faith that world peace will ever be achieved. Divines believe in world peace, and in general, looking at the world. The goal of the faith is world unity. To achieve this, we campaign against nationalism, the end of all separate countries, and the end of all religions except the religion of Divine. We desire a new order in which nine wise men rule the world in the name of our great prophet, Abu Ketab. Once this is in place, no longer will there be individuality to speak of for as Abu Ketab once said, *For a beautiful world of one paradise after another what is needed is death to the individual and life for the community of all.* In the new Divine world, there would be a world language, a world dress, a world foods, and world ways of thinking. I cannot wait when it shall all happen, when there will be no differences, when we are interchangeable parts in one mechanism. Then, only then will there be fulfillment of man's earthly existence.'

A guy sitting behind us, who obviously had been listening, joined in at this point. 'Marvelous, you have a marvelous religion there. I must compliment you on it.'

'You're not a Divine are you? Asked the girl as if she had been expecting him to interrupt all along.

'No!'

'Would you like to become one? We always graciously accept newcomers.'

'Well, I don't know,' said he evasively.

She dug into her skirt pocket and pulled out a purple pamphlet which she gave to him. 'This little leaflet,' she explained, 'will tell you all there is to know about the us.'

'Will the pamphlet tell me how the Divine religion views the Third World?' asked the guy behind us.

'Of course it will and you'll be delighted to discover that we Divines are seeking to alleviate the plight and misery of Third World peoples by sending missionaries over to them to provide them with food and health care. Our long range goal is to put the Third World on equal par with the Western world economically, socially and politically, and then to fuse both worlds together to make one world. All these Third World people have to do is accept the teaching of Abu Ketab and all their misery will be at an end. It is very simple really.'

'Interesting, it's about time somebody addressed Third World needs,' said the guy. 'Tell me, where was the one you call your prophet, Abu Ketab born?'

'Iraq.'

'In Iraq, oh my God, in Iraq. Iraq is a Third World country so the Divine is a Third World religion. The Divine must be fine since it has such wonderful roots.'

'I am glad you are so enthused," the young girl answered. "But I must clarify one point. The Divine faith provides a universal theme and is not one based on particularism, such as, Third World chauvinism. 'But God be with you because you're heart is certainly in the right place. Abu Ketab loves those who love Him.'

'Thank you ever so much,' replied the Third World guy. 'I will seriously consider becoming a Divine then. But first things first.' He now addressed all of us, myself, Zeno Beneen and the young girl included. 'I am a little apprehensive today for I too am a new student here. I just hope this endeavor to study here turns out happy, though frankly, I have apprehensions. A friend in my Third World country told me about this department and recommended it to me because he said it is fair in its treatment of the Third World. But I have grave doubts because the Department is located in a Western institution in a Western nation and, as we all know the West is imperialistic. All the West seeks to do is exploit the Third World, inducing it to give up all its natural resources and to keep its peoples in serfdom. Will this department teach from a Third World perspective or will it pound into its students heads more of the imperialistic, capitalistic, exploitive mentality of the West? If this Department does not take the proper attitude towards the Third World then I assure you, I'll leave. We Third World people will no longer allow ourselves to be used as punching bags.'

'I quite understand what you're saying but remember we must love our fellow man no matter where he comes from,' the young girl lectured back while she starred into the face of Zeno who at that moment was shaking his head, muttering ah-ha-yes, and playing with his ear. 'We are all brothers and sisters,' she went on, 'so says Abu Ketab. All cultures, all worlds must combine and rejoice to the heart-felt music of unity.' Up she popped from her seat and over to the Third World guy she went, declaring, 'I think you need guidance. I'm here for you, to show you the true way to work for goodness.' She plunked herself down next to him and soon thereafter they both became embroiled in a heated debate over the role religion and God plays in within non-Western societies.

Zeno's mouth, now properly rested, came back to life. 'You know,' he softly whispered to me, 'there is truth in that young man's oratory. As any Marxist knows, Western affluence is based upon the vilest form of exploitation. Yes, indeed, my dear fellow, but not simple exploitation of the Third World, but the exploitation of the proletariat as well. The rights of the proletariat everywhere, and not just in the Third World, are being trampled upon by the petty bourgeoisie and their masters, the large industrialists. It all comes down to one word, capitalism, plain and simple. Capitalism is the enemy of us all; it destroys and impoverishes the earth through its exploitation of resources, encourages the construction of factories housing the underpaid, undereducated, slave laborers. It's capitalism which implants greed within men's souls and teaches them selfishness instead of working toward the common good. The only alternative is

Communism. It must be established before equality and fair play can be instituted. Do you understand? Do you?'

'Su-sur-sure, of course.'

'Wasn't that a fine speech I just made, Joseph? Wasn't it fiercely fanatical? You see my dear boy, I'm a Communist, a real hard-liner. My life is devoted to fighting the free enterprise system. Do you find that peculiar or too radical?'

'No.'

'Smart man. I'll tell you something in the strictest confidence that you must make sure not to divulge to anyone at all; basically, I'm a Communist because of the personal rewards that accrue to one who associates himself with such a wild philosophy. A helpful tip for you, Joseph; it is always important for one to have some iconoclastic ideology, which will make one distinctive. I'm a Communist not because I believe in such nonsense but because I've calculated that here in this Department a Communist will go a long way.'

'Interesting.'

'Another tip for you, Joseph. To be an intellectual you must have an ideology. Observe me this year and notice how I apply the rule. By the end of the year you'll see that I'll be the most respected student in this Department.'

'I don't know. I somehow think it's always better to be yourself.'

'Oh, what a dreadful thought, my good man. Please don't ever say that when there are a lot of people around you or you'll be a laughing stock. Aren't you cognizant of the fact that it always is quite harmful to reveal your true self? The why of it is simple; your true self is horrid and boring. Nobody wants to be around someone who is acting under his own impulses. To be successful in this world, one must be whatever people want.' Zeno struck a pose, then, putting finger to lips and raising his eyebrows. That done, he was ready to shovel more advice. 'Joseph, as a very, very good friend of yours. . . .'

'A very good friend. Zeno, we've just met. What do you mean very good friends? Let's know each other a few minutes before we say that.'

'Joseph as a very good friend to you I must advise you to adopt some ideology you can call your own. How about telling everyone you are a fierce believer in democratic capitalism, free enterprise, supply and demand, the three branches of government, checks and balances, judicial bodies, and all such rubbish.' Zeno stopped to take a breath and to thoroughly scratch his scalp. 'Mm, perhaps such an ideology doesn't fit you,' he continued. 'Perhaps it's too conservative. Mm, what, what, I've got it, by Jove; old Zeno has done it again. Tell everyone you're an atheistically-inclined anarchist bent on destroying all the governments of the world. Oh, that'll go over big.'

'No, I couldn't do that. It's not me.'

Zeno shrugged his shoulders and grinned. 'That's your immaturity talking. 'All I, Zeno Beneen was trying to do was lend Joseph the knowledge that all of Zeno's experiences have brought him. Joseph forgets that Zeno knows best. But Zeno is a fair man and if Joseph doesn't want to follow Zeno's advice and wants to be foolish instead, Zeno most assuredly won't stop him. Ah, but despite Joseph not listening to Zeno's wisdom, Zeno still considers Joseph a good man.'

*　　*　　*

"Without any forewarning the crowd let out a loud 'oooooooo,' which shocked Zeno and I out of our isolation and made as aware of the assembly hall around us. What was it? What was going on? The crowd of people in the hall had taken on solemn faces. Some folded their hands, some fixed their hair, some played with the buttons on their shirt, and some took out hidden notebooks, while the rest just pointed straight ahead of them. I followed their fingers and saw a fat, pot-bellied, pink, balding, middle-aged gentleman come waltzing into the assembly hall flapping his hands against his thighs. The gentleman wore a tweed, green suit, loose baggy pants which had a tear in one of its knees and a purple tie. I couldn't believe that this Humpty-Dumpty shaped man could set off such a reaction. Who was he?

Zeno solved the mystery. 'Dr. Jefferson, Dr. Jefferson,' yelled Zeno as the one he called Jefferson approached the speaker's podium. 'Dr. Jefferson it's me Zeno. I'm back here, in the middle, Dr. Jefferson, right behind the guy with the fat head with the big fancy headdress on top of it.'

Jefferson heard Zeno, searched the crowd with his eyes, spotted him and then waved acknowledgment. Zeno beamed. 'Oh, do you know, my dear boy, I was just at Dr. Jefferson's house for dinner two nights ago,' Zeno yakked, poking me in the ribs. 'Joseph, let me tell you Dr. Jefferson's house is simple a masterfully constructed palace. Oh, and what a delightful conversation we have after supper over brandies. We somehow became embroiled in a debate over the possibility of a Communist takeover in Saudi Arabia. Jefferson took the capitalist approach and declared such an occurrence an impossibility. I, of course, argued that it would only be a few years before Saudi Arabia turned Communist. On and on into the night we debated, on and on. It finally ended in a draw. I, of course, could have won but how would that have looked. You know Joseph, my good man, I think I made a very admirable impression on Dr. Jefferson. He was overwhelmed by my knowledge, as he should have been. I think I now have an important friend who will prove useful.'

My eyes riveted away from Zeno at this point. I was tired of his talk and trying to send him a message. Unfortunately, the message wasn't received.

'Oh yes, a lovely night. The only downside was the meal prepared by his ebullient yet quaint wife. My good man, it was a gastronomic nightmare. I do believe it was Chinese food that was served, though I still cannot be sure. I possessed indigestion all night from that bloody meal. But then again being fair as I usually am, it may not have been the meal that made me sick. The problem may lie with my physical condition. There is something quite wrong with my digestive track, though the doctors have tried to tell me differently. You see, nothing goes down my gullet without later acting up. I am at a loss; it seems to be my bloody fate. I've just been cursed with bad health all my life. Would you believe this young man sitting beside you already has had two surgical procedures performed on his virgin body. Four years ago, it was a hernia operation; my scrotum was most inappropriately coiled around my anal aperture. It was strangulation of such an extent that I would often cry out in pain and walk about like a dog searching for a tree. And then, only last year I underwent bloody surgery for painful hemorrhoids. What a bloody mess.' Zeno began unbuttoning his shirt. 'Now, my good man, I have a new problem. I want you to take a look at my dreadfully misshapen abdomen. I think it's stomach cancer. Wouldn't that be my bloody luck?' I managed to keep Zeno from unbuttoning.

As Zeno continued about his ailments, I could only recount my experiences of the last few days, from Vladimir to Zeno. It was like being part of a carnival and surrounded by clowns parading about with monkeys while I was the ultimate outsider. But thank goodness, the proceedings now seemed to be getting under way. Dr. Jefferson stood up at the podium, staring straight ahead. Every so often, he'd sniffle and cough. Before he could begin, the young girl and adherent of the Divine religion strode up to the front of the hall before the assembled, carrying in her arms, like a newborn baby, a bundle of purple pamphlets which she proceeded to pass out. 'There will be a meeting of the Divine club tomorrow in this hall at eleven o'clock,' she boomed as she stood in front of Jefferson. 'All those who believe in God, in love, and in man as a universal creature of goodness, must come. The topic of the meeting will be *Conversion Plain and Simple*.' Like an angelic saint, she then retook her seat.

Finally, Jefferson was ready to let some words fly from that mouth of his. 'Hello, hello, hello all you people out there,' he began. 'Welcome to the finest, finest department in the finest university this side of the border, or any border for that matter. My name is Dr. Jefferson for the few who already don't know and I am the illustrious head of this illustrious Department. Before I forget, I want to welcome back my dear faculty and my dear students. I 'm glad to see you all smiling. That is a good sign. So we are back together once more for another fine academic year of highly sophisticated learning. I can't tell you how thrilled I am to see that most of you all have returned. Bravo, bravo. I hope you all had productive summers doing lots of reading and researching. I must admit, though, this enormous turnout today puzzles me. Somewhere a mistake has been made. There are just too many of you. For those of you who possibly might have wandered into the wrong assembly hall, let me state and state quite unequivocally that this meeting is for students in the Department of Middle Eastern Studies only. Everyone else please clear out immediately.' More than three quarters of the people rose and charged out of the hall. The few of us who remained found ourselves sitting in isolated pockets.

"Jefferson remained undaunted. 'To all you newcomers I want to say a personal hello,' he continued. 'What a great opportunity you new people have been blessed with. Let's only hope you don't blow your chance. The time you spend with us will enrich and transform you. As I like to put it, this Department is like a potter's shop; it takes filthy, formless clay, cleans it, shapes it, and bakes it, until it produces an intellectually breath-taking work of art. Mm, I seem to have run out of words to say. Mm, what to do. Mm, oh yes, I'd like to give all of you one word of advice. In recent years, a few of you have disobeyed your Professors and have done things in your own way. How utterly stupid, I must say. My advice to you is, always listen to your Professors, imitate them, honor them, obey, obey, and obey them some more. Then, with their guidance, you can read and research, read and research, research and read, investigate and read, perform and investigate, read and perform. You'll notice that in the end you will be rewarded by becoming marvelous scholars. Well now, let me think, what next, yes, I remember, it's time now for Dr. Warly's annual speech. From the back of the hall a man, Dr. Warly cruised up to the front, carrying two large posters. In the meantime, Jefferson sniffed a few times, coughed three times and disappeared into the row of seats before him.

Warly strode before us carrying two rolled-up posters. He had gray, stringy hair which hung down over his face and eyes like a sheep dog. It was a miracle he could see. His body was clad in a light gray suit. That was all one can say about Dr. Warly's appearance. Warly didn't seem aware that there were people in the room. He looked at nobody; his eyes were fixed on the podium to which he now began speaking. 'An innovation this year that I have instituted to raise the Department to greater heights of glory is my design of charts that will be used by the Department's decision makers in evaluating the professional staff and it's future needs.' He raised his posters in the air to indicate these were them. 'We had a problem in the past with uppity Professors who seek their own glory, who maintain their own individuality and attempt to pass it on to its students. We for the most part have eliminated them through purges down through the years but others have come from time to time to replace them. My innovation will put this to an end.' Murmurings were heard in the hall, but Warly didn't seem to notice and continued. 'Now that said, let us begin our explanations of the charts.' He raised the yellow poster while putting down the white one. 'This one graphically displays our Christian Professors. He raised the yellow poster. "It indicates the age, birthplace, childhood, educational background, marital and religious background of each white Christian Professor. The nice part of the chart is it leaves room for comments. I and Dr. Warly will be making the comments which will in effect indicate if our Professors are acting up to our standards. Everyone will be able to see what we write since the charts will hang proudly in the middle of the main office for all to see. If any of you are interested in seeing the posters up close before there are hung, come to my office later. Now I see some worried looks on some of our Professors' faces. But I feel that our white Christians have little to fear.' He went on to relate the many merits of these Professors. Pointing to the chart's purple arrows, he related how all the Professors had published tons of historical articles in the very best historical journals. 'Each of our white Christians is widely known and widely hailed throughout North America.'

Warly put the yellow chart down and picked up the white one, which included an elaborate graph. 'Now, I'd like to use this chart to clarify a number of issues of other issues. This will be of particular interest to our new students who are as yet completely ignorant of the true facts of life. Okay then, let's begin. Do you see this blue line here; it indicates the place of origin of our Muslim Professors: Afghanistan, Egypt, India, Saudi Arabia, Iraq, Iran, and Pakistan. A nice assortment, you must admit, but the cause of troubles in the department. In the past, some of our white Christian students have complained at being taught by Muslims but. . . .'

"'Oh God, I don't want to be taught by any one of them,' whispered Zeno into my ear.

Warly went on to prove through references to his chart that the Department wasn't staffed by ordinary Muslims, but by the finest scholars in North America. He directed us to look at the charts green line. 'This tells us that our Muslim Professors did not, I repeat, did not go to one of those inferior type of schools in their own inferior countries or purchase their degrees through the mail. Where did they go? Well, if you look closely at the pink line you will see they attended such institutions as Harvard, Yale, Princeton, Stanford, and Colombia. Remarkable, isn't it. So you see, we only pick the best."

He paused briefly here to look at his audience for the first time. 'There can be no complaint with any of our Muslims. They are known far and wide in the field and have won various awards. One of them in fact is a celebrity, and would you believe this Professor isn't even a man, you heard right, not even a man. For those of you who are new, her name is Professor R.Z.Z.P. Lunwi and she's an Iranian by birth. Besides being wealthy, she has royal blood in her veins, being the first cousin of the former Shah of Iran. Oh, what a woman; each year she induces the Iranian government to contribute a quite considerable amount of money into our coffers, money which in turn has been utilized in helping to keep up our high scholastic standards of excellence as well as supporting myself and Dr. Jefferson in a style that befits our lofty positions. Yes, our Muslims are top grade so neither I nor Dr. Jefferson wishes to hear any more complaints about them, and, in particular about Professor Lunwi who has been a target of hostile elements in the past. That type of character assassination must end. We cannot afford to hurt Professor Lunwi's feelings, now can we?'

Zeno leaned over to me once more and sang another little melody into my ear. 'I don't care if they received ten degrees a piece from the finest schools in the world, they're still heathen Muslims. There is no getting away from the reality of the situation. I don't desire to be taught by people who believe a dirty Arab vagabond, a fraud, named Muhammad, is the great prophet of our time. These heathens don't even have the decency to call the Supreme Being by His right name. It's always Allah this and Allah that. Bloody fools, that's what they are, nothing more, and nothing less. Why don't they go back to their own bloody, slime-infested countries instead of coming here and taking jobs away from native-born North Americans? Oh, and Joseph I can tell you right now that under no circumstances will I take a course with that any Paki professor. I saw enough of those bloody people in London. Oh, how they're ruining my beautiful London with their dirty habits.'

Meantime, Dr Warly continued his analysis of the department's Muslim professors before switching topics to include a dissection of the student body's ethnic, religious, and racial composition. He apologized to all of us for not having a chart on that subject prepared but promised that by next year's meeting, he would have one made up. On and on he went about the students until he was interrupted. Abu Lulu, finished making his call to the Senegalese Consulate, came marching back into the hall, stopping a minute or two to stare at Dr. Warly before heading back to his seat. Warly became red in the face. 'What is the meaning of this?' he shouted at Abu Lulu. 'What is your excuse for coming to this very important meeting late?'

'Yes, yes, nice, very nice,' sputtered Abu Lulu.

'Don't be facetious with me; do you know that I am second in command in this Department. So I am no person to fool with. Once more I'll ask then, what's your excuse for arriving to this meeting late?'

'Nice, nice, very nice. You speak good English,' answered Lulu while he fell into his seat.

Warly's eyes bulged with anger. He pounded his tightly clenched fist against the podium. The future of Abu Lulu looked bleak, to say the least, when just in the nick of time Jefferson stepped in, calling Warly over and whispering something but in a loud voice. I managed to make out four of the words Jefferson spoke, 'Senegal has connections, contributions.' Jefferson's words had a calming effect on Warly almost immediately who returned to the podium then. "Well let's forget this incident for now. We must all be tolerant. Everybody is late for something now and then. Even I've been late for a few public functions so why should I single out this dear man for castigation.' Warly concluded his address by switching topics from the Department's faculty to himself. He did about fifteen minutes discussing his accomplished career that included published books on every facet of Egyptian cultural life in the fifteen century. He then went on to explain that he'd been with the Department over twenty years and that he was the real power behind the throne. When he'd gotten there, the Department's academic standards were lone, morale was non-existent, scholarship was putrid, the quality of faculty and students overall was deficient. He worked with the new head of the Department, Dr. Jefferson to change all that by organizing the Department in almost paramilitary fashion removing all elements that were not toughened and mature. "And thus, I created one of the finest institutions of scholarship in the land," Dr. Warly concluded. "And I am very proud of myself. I am a great man."

Jefferson strode before us again, this time looking a bit taller, a bit thinner and a lot happier, and began telling his life story. How he was from a poor family down in Texas, how he was a Baptist and proud of it, how his daddy worked day and night as a gravedigger, oh, he told us, he told and told us until he was interrupted by two small fellows who popped up from their seats with cameras in hand to snap a few pictures of Jefferson. Laughter broke out everywhere. Jefferson, clearly embarrassed, calmly went up to the two little fellows, took their cameras away, brought them to the front and returned to the podium. 'They will get their cameras back at the end of this meeting,' he announced to us all then. 'They are fairly new to our group and still do not know our ways too well. They are two of our nice Muslim students from Indonesia. Yes, nice I say, all the Indonesians are nice. They aren't too bright but they're nice.'

"Jefferson resumed conveying his life story, which included almost a minute by minute account. Near the end of this oratory he exclaimed, 'You see here not only a great scholar but a well traveled man, a man who has been to every land in the Orient, who has seen every hill, every desert, every stream, every oasis there was to see. Only recently have I returned from a two year tour of Afghanistan and Pakistan. My good, devoted, self-sacrificing wife Ethel joined me on the tour. Ethel is in the audience today. Stand up Ethel and take some applause.'

Ethel did stand up but before the clapping could commence, she belched: 'Roderick, must you constantly remind me of that dreadful trip. Roderick, I don't understand you. What other person in their right mind would travel to places where you are constantly surrounded by a lot of half savages all living in putrid-smelling mud huts. I'll never do it again. From now on I stay in my own beautiful house close to my lovely children and grandchildren whom you, Roderick, don't seem to care in the least about.'

Jefferson turned purple. 'Well that's my wonderful wife,' he declared in explanation. 'As you've noticed she has says what she thinks, which is to be admired. Well then, getting back to the topic of myself and my impeccable credentials. Let me state and state quite clearly that during my lifetime, I've received ten research grants and I'm still young. Realize that most intellectuals, during the course of their academic careers, are lucky to get one or two grants. I've also published quite a bit. Many of my well-written articles on Islam have appeared in various children's encyclopedias. And there is the famous book I edited, <u>Christians And Muslims: Two Nice People</u>, which has sold thousands in the four years its been on the market; every student in this Department is required to purchase the book, which when read will lend immense guidance to you for the rest of your natural born lives and that's no exaggeration.'

Jefferson concluded his remarks by announcing he is to be in the upcoming <u>WHO'S WHO'S</u> in the world reference book, introduced the next speaker, a heavy-set man with coffee complexion and thick-lens glasses, identifying him as Yusuf Jabarti, the head of the library of the Department of Middle Eastern Studies. Jefferson warned Jabarti to keep his talk brief because he wasn't the finest speaker in the world and would put us all to sleep.

Jabarti removed an old, yellowed piece of paper from his pocket, held it in his trembling hands, and began to read from it, every now and then looking up at Jefferson. 'Dear students,' read Jabarti. 'You sit before me with smiles upon your faces, and your smiles will only be broadened when you see the fabulous Department library. But before I describe it to you, let me pay tribute to the man who made the library and for that matter the department possible, none other than our Dr. Jefferson. So many things have been said and written about this great man that's its very hard to add to what's already common knowledge. Let me say, however, that I have known Dr. Jefferson personally for fifteen years glorious years and I have been extremely privileged.'

"Dr. Jefferson sat in a relaxed, stretched-out position with hands resting on his belly and a smile on his face.

"'I owe my great success entirely to Dr. Jefferson. What a man he is.' Tears rolled down Jabarti's face and he folded up his little speech and put it in his pocket. 'It was hard for me at first to find a job as a librarian, very hard," he spoke extemporaneously now. 'I had a prison record, you see, and one potential employer after another turned me down because of it. Through the grapevine, I happened to hear that the university had just opened a new department and that librarians were needed to build it. I went directly to Dr. Jefferson and practically begged. I told him I was desperate and that he was my last hope but without really believing that he would give me a chance. To my great surprise, he offered me, a young inexperienced librarian, and the position of head librarian. I accepted his offer immediately and so here I am fifteen years later a wealthy man living in the loveliest part of town with my wife and two little children. What can I add to what I've just told you about this magnificent man; there are more stories I could tell, a hundred which show this man's good heart but I don't think it's necessary. We all now understand the outstanding man he is. I would kill for Dr. Jefferson if he asked me to, and my hope is that everyone who comes to know him would also kill for him.' Jabarti paused and then resumed along a different track. 'I would like to take the opportunity now to inform all new students in the Department that Dr. Jefferson's book, Christians And Muslims: Two Nice People, is on sale in my office. IT IS A REQUIRED ITEM. A record of who buys it and who doesn't is being kept and those who fail to produce the required funds will face evil consequences.'

Dr. Jefferson and Dr. Warly followed by the entire faculty rose as one and cheered Yusuf Jabarti who bowed from the waist before saluting each and every member of the faculty. Then, he resumed, 'Now let me speak about our library and try to describe it. What can I say except it's magnificent, one of the seven wonders of the world. Books, we have five thousand all catalogued and neatly piled in proper order. New books, we constantly buy all new books which concern the Middle East. Old books, we have volumes dating back to the sixteenth century. Any book you want, we have, any. Sometimes I just wander through the stacks and stare. I'm so proud of the collection. I really am a very talented librarian. Now to address another point, if you're worried about our books being dusty and getting you all dirty when you pick them up, stop worrying. Our books are taken off the stacks and properly bathed and manicured at least once a month. I treat them like my children and they are very happy. The primary reason my books are in such great shape is because they feel they're wanted and this slows down the aging process. Have you ever noticed that when a book is placed on a shelf and forgotten, it invariably rots away? I love them so much. My favorite thing to do in the world is filing my books, classifying them, and giving them a proper home in the stacks. I do have some reservations about stamping them I must admit; stamping is like branding and who really can fully enjoy that. This year is going to be my year of decision concerning my children. I have seriously been thinking of a new cataloging system. My idea is to arrange books by color. Why shouldn't books with red covers, green covers, blue covers, and black covers have the opportunity to live side-by-side? I'm a segregationist; I'll admit it. The colors must be kept apart. Each color has its own life style and needs its own space. Call me what you want, but I truly believe this. The new system will be put into operation by the middle of the year.'

Dr. Jefferson called over to Jabarti and then pointed to his watch, indicating that the librarian's time was up. Jabarti stopped. 'I know I have gone over my allotted time, Dr. Jefferson, but I need to say one more thing. May I?' Jefferson nodded his approval. 'My books,' Jabarti continued then, 'have been telling me many wicked things about all of you out there, rotten things. They're dissatisfied with all of your students, terribly dissatisfied. Why they ask me do you borrow their friends and never return them to their homes after you finish using them? That's kidnapping you know, kidnapping plain and simple. Why do you do this? What have my poor little books ever done to you? Must you take them from me? Well I and my friends have had enough. If students this year persist in borrowing and never returning, they can expect a police officer knocking at their doors in the middle of the night who'll haul them off to jail and possibly scourge them with boiling oil. Dr. Jefferson's Department will no longer tolerate thieves and kidnappers in its midst. Does everyone understand?'

"Jabarti left the podium, walked over to Jefferson, kissed his hand and thanked him for everything. Jefferson frowned at the display of emotion and then physically took hold of the mauling Jabarti - still shaking his hand - and led him to a seat in the back of the auditorium. Everyone could hear as Jefferson ordered him never to make such a display of himself in public again or otherwise he would strangle him with his bare hands and leave the body dangling from the tops of the library stacks. Returning to the front and escorted the next speaker to the podium. The speaker, a grossly ugly women, about thirty, well over six foot tall with washed out blue eyes, a hideous pink-white complexion, and deep crimson-colored nose. She wore a plain white sweater, brown slacks which were so short that they reached only to her upper ankle, a red and white flowered shawl and a gold medallion depicting two old men with long beards holding books in their hands. The woman looked close to being on her deathbed.

'Hello, hello everyone here right now,' she began in a deep baritone voice. 'Hello to all of you. I hope this goes well. I need to do well. I need Dr. Jefferson's approval. If it doesn't go well, I will fall to pieces. This is my life.'

Jefferson smiled and nodded at her. This seemed to give her the courage to continue.

'Hello, hello, hello,' she repeated, then. 'I want all the attention you have to offer me. There must be no delays. I have a tea party with the girls from my educational resources club. Saaaa-saaaaa,' she sniffed with her nose. 'Oh dear, oh dear, somebody's smoking in here. I can't see who it is but my well-trained nose says someone is. Oh dear, oh dear, whoever the culprit is please, for my sake as well as for the others in the hall, please put out the cigarette immediately. I don't know what's happening in this day and age; people just don't show any courtesy any more, do they? Anyway, cigarette smoking anywhere at any time is such a frightfully appalling habit.' She proceeded to make a lot of stupid faces, to wave her hands in front of her face, cough a few times, shake her head back and forth, before eventually exclaiming, 'Thank you for putting out the cigarette.' In another vein she uncoiled, 'I don't believe in fooling around so let me say straight off that my name is Betsy Smith, an excellent Professor of Islamic Education in this Department. I make up the curriculum and the rules of conduct for the Department. Rules of conduct include the proper way to dress her, to think her, to exist here. If you desire a list of these rules, you may contact me and a copy will be provided for your convenience.

'Now, about myself, I live alone in a boarding house with a wonderful family called the Ivies. Papa Ivie is a business man and he always discusses his business with me. I am a member of various women's clubs. I am a fierce defender of women's rights; I possess two cats, both Persian. I love books, education books and books about war. I love researching in the library. I write a lot of letters to my friends. I knit. I crochet. I do needlepoint. I never watch television. I read a lot. I sleep a lot. My professional credentials; I speak Arabic fluently although I detest Arabic and all Arabs, except very young Arabs. I taught for two years in a little school in Damascus, Syria.

That experience was good. I taught little Muslim children. They were poor but I didn't mind. They were ignorant but I didn't mind. They were rowdy but I didn't mind. They were dirty, physically dirty and that I did mind. I hate dirt of any kind. For ten years, I have served on the educational censorship board of this city. Presently, my day is consumed most delightfully doing research on the different educational systems and programs being applied in various countries of the Middle East. Next Spring my new book on Cairo University will be released by my publisher for public consumption. My beliefs, I am totally Western in attitude and orientation.'

The Third World guy sitting behind now clearly muttered, 'An imperialistic hussy. I knew I shouldn't have enrolled in this racist anti-Third World department.'

'Betsy Smith hadn't heard and continued on. 'I am a liberal reformer. It's my feeling that the educational system in North America needs revision, and, specifically, I believe a modern educational system needs to be implemented in this town. The Klemperer Report released a month ago upholds my beliefs. Did you all read the article in <u>The Star</u> yesterday that discussed how down through the years this town's educational policy has become less and less innovative and more restrictive and is quickly falling into anarchy? I do wholeheartedly concur with this estimation, speaking from experience. I taught in the system and have devoted years of study to it. Well I guess that raps up the general overview. Now for some specifics.'

But something was wrong with Professor Betsy Smith. Her teeth began chattering and she rubbed her hands together briskly before folding them across her chest and snorting, 'Oh-weeeeeee.' What was wrong? What was going on? 'My God, my God, Lord have mercy, my God,' she cackled at the podium. 'There is a draft in here, cold air, a draft, oh, oh,' she finally explained. 'Please someone, somebody, anybody, anyone; close the window in the back, please. I'm catching a cold and getting a backache. Please close the window.'

Her command was quickly obeyed. She then resumed, tell us about the courses offered by the Department. 'This Department's curriculum is the finest in North America, and one that has been designed to achieve the maximum in student interaction.'

Out of nowhere, came the voice of a heckler. 'That's a lie,' he cried, 'a dirty lie. All the fuckin' Professors around here lock themselves in their offices and never come out. They see no one; those bastards don't even see themselves.'

Warly rose and searched the assembly hall for the culprit but was unsuccessful. The heckler's voice seemed to come from everywhere and nowhere.

'"Our department is small,' Betsy plowed on, 'only fifty students, which means, in layman's terms, that our people receive individual attention. This enables us, the educators to carefully observe all of you and spot the incompetent ones right away. By a special program I've developed for these incompetents, we pull them out, train and retrain them, drill their heads with the proper attitude, and by the end of the indoctrination period, turn out the desired product. We have a ninety-five percent success rate with the incompetents.'

'"You're an inhuman leper,' cracked the heckler. 'You're an old maid with a dead cunt and shit for insides.'
Betsy turned a nice pale green while putting hands to chest. Answering the heckler now, she exclaimed, 'Whoever you are, you are a fool. I can take all the comments you dish out. Comments such as yours don't bother Professor Betsy Smith, a woman who has been trained a teacher to handle put-downs by the mentally deficient. What do these stupid remarks actually illustrate? To me they illustrate a baboon who fails to understand the reason there is a Department of Middle Eastern Studies or even a university for that matter. I'm afraid there are others like this heckler who do not understand that the Department is not here for anyone's pleasure. It is here to mold all of you emotion-crazed creatures of the street into proper historians, historians who are thinking specimens of rationality, historians who can properly theorize about people and institutions, historians who are credits to the intellectual community.'

'No, that's not why the department should be here,' answered the heckler. 'The Department should first teach us students to forget everything we ever were taught, and second, it should teach every individual to strive in their own particular God-given way. The Department's obligation is to make each student shine and be a star in their own right. That's what the Department should be doing, but isn't. The question then becomes, why does this department insist on butchering its students, breaking their spirits and turning them into common fodder?'

'How dare you," Betsy shot back.

"How dare you!" the voice back. "And while you're at it, why don't you tell the newcomers the truth about what is in store for them."

Everyone turned toward the voice in the attempt to spot the heckler, but there was no heckler to be seen.

'You cannot listen to his words,' Betsy answered. "They are pitiable. And what he is implying are just ugly rumors. They are utterly, utterly false, utterly and totally.'

'They're all true you bastard, they're all true. It's you and your existence that is false. Tell them of the plot.'

'The rumor he refers to is that the Department plots to keep all its student here forever, that it promises degrees but never delivers. How paranoid can some people be? Let me say right off that it is not impossible to receive a degree from this department. There have been some M.A. and Ph.D. degrees awarded in the past. So what if the department doesn't hand out degrees loosely? So what if the Department makes you stay a few years longer? Not everything in life can come easy. If the department is not bothered by your spending more time here then why should it bother you?'

'Why don't you tell everyone the real truth, Professor Betsy Smith,' the heckler returned. 'It's such a small, inconsequential Department within the university that any drop in the numbers could mean the university might disband it and throw your ass out the door. You can't afford to lose anyone. That's right, and how many students actually enter this Department each year, a few. How many young people in their right minds actually choose to pursue Middle Eastern Studies? What can they do with your degree, that is, if they manage to get one? There are no jobs for your graduates. There is nothing. But that you never reveal because you need the warm bodies to take prisoner. The Department doesn't care if the student wastes his life away in empty pursuits. Departments don't care, universities don't care, institutions don't care, we think they care, we honor them, we take on their characteristics, we die a thousand deaths, and finally we don't care as much as they don't care.'

'Oh you have nerve, more nerve than brains, who ever you are,' answered Professor Betsy Smith now visible unnerved. You're a coward, too scared to show your face publicly. Ha. What kind of man are you? You yell about wasted years here, maybe you've wasted your years here but not everyone else has. The years here are spent in valuable studying, reading, writing, and most of all researching. In this Department, the young man or woman is given the opportunity to learn about important things such as the political, social, economic, and historical aspects of the medieval Muslim world. Now there is nothing, nothing I say, more rewarding than spending your time doing that.'

"'That's all shit, garbage, unimportant trash which belongs in a waste dump. Ugh, it stinks like you, Miss Virginal Educational System, System, System.'
She bit her lip so hard that a little blood began spurting from it. 'I don't have to take this, no, no, no.' She ran over to Dr. Jefferson and standing before him moaned, 'Dr. Jefferson why don't you stop him, please you must? Why do you let him defame the Department like that?' Jefferson simply looked away. She cried louder and harder and burst from the hall.

Jefferson now took command. To each of us he gave a packet filled with registration information, forms and an advisor's name that would help select the courses you would take. I think Jefferson was about ready to dismiss us all when all the lights in the hall went out. For ten minutes, nobody moved or talked.

"We were jolted from this suspended state by one huge explosion followed by another, followed by another. The heckler between explosions yelled, 'You all look so perfect in the dark, so handsome, so beautiful. Let's all sing, on second thought, let's sing one at a time.' The voice of the heckler frankly scared everyone more than the explosions overhead.

Someone amongst the assembled crowd then yelled out, 'It's all the hecklers doing. He's a fiend. He plans to blow us to smithereens, butcher us, to slice us up and burn the remains.'

'Yes, you should all blow away in the darkness, ha-ha-ha-ha,' churned the heckler ghoulishly.

A panic ensued. All got up from their seats and rushed in search of the door. Some tripped over seats, some tripped over others, and some just found a corner for themselves and lay on the floors. The explosions kept coming, plaster kept falling, and people kept screaming and crawling. It was all a mess. Meanwhile, the heckler cheered from the sidelines.

I don't know how it happened but very soon fists started being thrown and heads got knocked together. Someone picked me up and threw me against a wall or a chair, or whatever it was. I hit my head. I was dazed. What did I hear? All I could hear was metal clanking and scraping together. It was a good sound, a nice sound. Then the clanking stopped and the chant of, 'Jefferson you stink, you stink, bastard. The Department stinks. Dr. Warly stinks. Jabarti stinks. Smith stinks. Jefferson stinks. It all stinks. Rip their arms and legs from their body, rip them off and feed them to the birds. Jefferson you stink, you stink, the department stinks.' That song soon subsided to make room for a chorus of, 'My name is Jim, Jim who loves trees without bark and their sap melting down; my name is George, George who loves the smell of Jasmines and the smell of bees when they're pollinating; my name is Zaine, Zaine who thinks she is the most beautiful person that ever lived.' They chanted, everyone except Dr. Jefferson who demanded it all stop, stop, stop. Jefferson screamed for it to stop, stop, stop. Everyone sang, sang, sang one improvised song after another.

Outside the explosions stopped and all grew calm. I was happy even though I had a large painful lump on my head. But then it happened. Lights appeared, candle lights, flashlights accompanied by voices, 'Folks, don't be frightened, it's only the campus police. There's been a blackout in the building, that's all. We come to escort you all out.' What about the explosions, someone asked.

'The explosions, don't worry about the explosions. It's okay, the construction crew dynamiting a new site where they're to build a gymnasium.'

We were instructed to line up single file and follow the men with the lights. I refused to leave. I was threatened. I still refused. Finally, one of the rescuers gave in, told the others to let the kook stay if he wanted, and gave me a flashlight. Jefferson stood at the door while everyone filed out. As each member of the department clanked past, they gave him their personal apologies about what was said about him. Jefferson nodded his head in acceptance each time saying,

'Thank you but if it happens again next time, I'll personally supervise become destructive.'

'No, no, no,' cried the mysterious heckler from somewhere in the dark. 'Don't go out there to look at yourselves. Don't you know, you're all ghastly? You must stay.' But the heckler's pleas did little good. Soon they were all gone.

Jefferson yelped with laughter, 'Heckler, hey heckler, do you see who wins in the end, heckler? I win, we win, we always do, always. Heckler, give up, you and your kind, you always lose. Ha-ha.' Jefferson waved the flashlight he held over his head and said, 'This meeting is now over,' and departed with the rest.

I sat in the last row wondering if I would catch a glimpse of the brave heckler but that did not happy. I fell into a trance-like state thinking back on Vladimir, the Student Health Clinic, and the heckler's comments. I was shatteringly awakened by a trapping on my shoulder.

'Joseph, my dear friend, we must go,' came the familiar voice of Zeno out of the darkness. 'Aren't you coming? Why do you sit like that? There is nothing more for you in this room. Let us go.'

'Nah, I'd sort of like to sit here by myself for a while. Okay?'

'No, no, no, it's not okay, my dear fellow. We must leave this room immediately. That maniac heckler might still be around someplace. I'm here to see that you leave. Why don't you come to my apartment? I'll brew some mint tea for your pleasure and serve some very tasty vanilla biscuits. I believe in the privacy of my apartment we'll be able to have a very productive chit-chat. Come, come, we'll just have a perfectly exquisite time.'

'Zeno, I'm sorry but not today. I'm not in the proper frame of mind.'

'Oh, you're making a mistake. Will you come tomorrow?'

'I'll see.'

'Gooooooooood, quite, goooooooooooood,' twanged Zeno as he took out a piece of paper, scribbled something on it and passed it to me. 'That's my telephone number. Call me before you come over tomorrow. Please Joseph, if you won't come home with me now, at least leave the hall. Staying here alone won't be good for you.'

'I'm staying Zeno and that's the last time I'll say it.'

'Oh, that's quite all right, quite, quite. You're a good man, a good man. Well tata Joseph, I must be off to bigger and better things.'

He was off and there I was alone. It'd been an interesting meeting. Never attended anything quite like it before. New experiences can be exhilarating sometimes.

*   *   *

Well Kabir can tell a story, can't he? Decarrie believed every word out of Kabir's mouth and seemed to sympathize with him. What kind of precinct captain was he? He even called Kabir a great butcher for butchering and masterfully filleting all of those bastards, as Decarrie so quaintly put it. Talon didn't like Decarrie's attitude and liked it less because it was voiced in front of me, the leading journalist in the town. When Kabir stopped talking, Talon calmly rose from his seat, walked peacefully over to the pool table, smashed a pool stick against the table breaking it in half, and throwing the remaining parts of the stick at Decarrie's head, missed him by not more than a couple of inches. "This is it," Talon yelled. "You've gone too far, made a mockery of everything. I don't care who you know, I'm going to make sure that others hear about this and that you're fired."

"Go right ahead," Decarrie answered. "Do as you wish, wish as you do. You must follow the way of your internal clock. It is the way."

Talon completed his rebellion by walking out of the Officers Lounge and never returning.

I could understand Talon's rage. What is Kabir other than a louse? His story to me is libel. Kabir is a slanderer pure and simple. He takes ordinary good people and turns them into caricatures with only shreds of truth in them. Yes, his world revolves around the creation of caricatures. He sees not the human but only the outward shape, and mistakenly he calls this creation of his an individual. It's all an excuse invented by Kabir to attack society with a clear conscience. Oh, he'll argue that most of us out there in the world are caricatures or barbarians as he likes to call his caricatures, and it is only these barbarians that he attacks. Ha, but our Kabir never will even imagine himself as being the supreme caricature, the supreme barbarian, which I must tell you he most certainly is.

A little while ago, I called Kabir a slanderer. Why have I called him this name? What else can you call a man who slanders the great name of Dr. Roderick Jefferson, a local celebrity in town who is best known for his well done local radio show and his generous philanthropy to the underprivileged of our community? Everyone who knew him loved him. What a fine, soft-spoken person he was, so intelligent and wise. Ah, the justice of it all; a man like Dr. Jefferson being slain by the likes of Kabir and then on top of that having his reputation smeared by Kabir after his death. But I won't let Kabir get away with it. My next book, done entirely by me, will expose all.

Kabir does have a good imagination, wouldn't you say that? Oh and how he does like to tell fictional tales of the supernatural. He should really have gone into that line of work instead of becoming a bomber. Personally, I thought his character, the invisible heckler was original, and isn't it something how the heckler's ideas are so much like those of Kabir himself? It's like the heckler was Kabir, strange huh? But there's more, Kabir has more and better stories for us. Ah, wait till you hear his slanderous account of the meeting he had with his advisor that first day. Marvelous, the work of a creative genius.

CHAPTER 6

The orientation meeting was over but I, Kabir sat silently in the darkness of the assembly hall. Lights went back on. A cleaning man wandered in and ordered me to get out and get out I did. If he hadn't shoed me away, I think I would have let my body totally decay there. A terrible uneasiness swished around all the pink crevices of my stomach. A horrible feeling it was, a feeling like I didn't belong anywhere or to anyone and that I never would. I fought the feeling, I fought the depression; I fought it by throwing myself into activity. I decided to go see my Department advisor immediately, work out my course schedule with him, and ask his help in filling out my registration forms. I would go; I had to go; I would force myself to go.

Up to where the department was located, I marched. The closer I came to it the more jittery I became. I found the Department, like Christopher Columbus I found it. The world famous Department of Middle Eastern Studies was one entire floor, containing a long line of Professors' offices, plus two classrooms that had a conference table and chairs rather than the traditional desks, and a large student lounge. Connecting the diverse elements was a dim tobacco-smelling corridor.

My destination was the office of Professor Majnoon Jazzar, the man elected as my advisor. Majnoon Jazzar in Arabic means crazy butcher, unbelievable but true. Through the corridor, I traveled searching through the maze of offices. Every office door was tightly sealed. The more I walked the corridor, the longer it seemed to grow in the opposite direction, making my walk through it endless. The knock on my head, received at the orientation meeting, really started hurting about now; a large lump was forming. I plowed forward anyway even though I felt dizzy and began seeing talking red lips on the corridor walls. The walls groaned to me that there were bodies encased within them, bodies that longed to get out. I must help get the bodies out, they said. I must get pick axes and shovels and help. I ignored but the lips wouldn't let me ignore. I explained to them I didn't have the tools and even if I did, I wouldn't know how to use them. They muttered. They conferred. I wasn't ready yet, that was their final verdict, not yet, but soon I would be. The lips disappeared into the walls.

I looked and looked yet I couldn't find Professor Jazzar's office. I heard a door creaking in the distance and rushed towards it like a shot. There, a door opening, one inch, two inches, three inches. An eye appeared in the space made by the opening, a blue eye which twirled around and around in its socket. Now, according to the tradition of the East, a blue eye cast upon someone means that person will receive many years bad luck. An omen, an evil sign. The eye blinked once, twice, three times. I stood before it a worshiper. Suddenly, a bell rang out. It came from one of the offices. The eye disappeared. The door began closing again. I dashed for it but I was too late. The door slammed in my face and was securely bolted from the inside. I knocked on the it without result. I listened. At first nothing, but then I heard someone or something on the other side was panting. I banged on the door again, why I can't explain. The panting stopped and was replaced by the sound of rain against a tin can. The door shook. I stood back and noticed a giant Z scratched into the wooden door. I could no longer stand there. I had to leave, I had to.

I wandered the corridor and while I did, passed another interesting office door. Printed in letters on it were the words *Hans Svelter* and under that, *Expert in Islamic Mysticism and Occult. Please Do NOT Enter.* I was drawn to the door like metal to a magnet. I drummed on it with the base of my palms. No answer. I twisted its doorknob and heard a slight click but that was all. I twisted and turned the doorknob again. A louder click but with the same results. I repeated the process over and over again until the door finally opened before me. I saw. Unbelievable. I closed the door in fear. Thought about it. Regained my courage. Opened it again and stared. Why was there was a bare-chested man sitting cross-legged on top of his desk with pink cushions underneath. One of his eyes was closed while the other was open so wide that the blood vessels were all visible. The one opened eye stared off into limitless space or off into another world, I don't know which.

I greeted him with a hello, not expecting a reply and was right. The guy was too far gone. I stood in the doorway while he began chanting something or other in a foreign tongue. Continuously he moved his upper body up and down while repeating the strange words. I became engrossed in his rhythm, hypnotized you might say. The guy all at once stopped his rocking motion, reached down under one of the pink pillows he sat on, and pulled out a large metal knitting needle which was sharp at its tip. Still chanting he stuck the needle clear through his cheek, and would you believe, showed not one sign of pain. Nor was even one drop of blood spilled. What the hell? His chanting continued at a faster and faster pace now. With the knitting needle still lodged in his cheek, he grabbed at a wine glass he had beside him, picked it up and looked at it upside-down, right-side up, sideways, front-ways, and all ways while his chant turned from a soft cry into a loud shriek. Then, putting the glass to his mouth, he bit into it, broke off a piece, ground it down with his teeth, swallowed and then repeated the process over and over again. As he ate, he remained perfectly erect with his opened eye continuing to stare off into limitless space. Finished devouring the glass, he began the chant of 'Allah, Allah, Allah.' I reached for the doorknob, preparing to make a speedy getaway but then was frozen to the spot watching his next action. The guy was slapping himself in the face with the utmost ferocity and then taking his nails and ripping at his neck. That was it for me. I had to get out. No telling what he'd do next. I quickly closed the door on the man and set out again on my desired destination.

At last, I found Professor Jazzar's office. But I couldn't work up the nerve to knock. I froze, still shaken from what I had seen and too afraid what I might find behind this door. I couldn't go in just then. I decided to leave and return in ten minutes, time enough to compose myself. I wandered into the student's lounge where I planned to look over my registration forms. The lounge had one large storefront window overlooking the whole town, one beat-up, dirty, yellowing couch which rocked back and forth on four shaky wooden legs, two purple upholstered benches which flanked both sides of the couch, and one kitchenette off to the side which contained one miniature sink and stove on top of which were two antique silver coffee pots. The floor was decorated with yellowed Arabic and Persian newspapers and pistachio nut shells.

Entering the lounge, I encountered two young fellows with legs crossed and coffee mugs in hand. They looked like identical twins. Both had long shoulder length brown hair as straight as strings, both were as skinny as rails, and both wore gold rimmed glasses, white shirts, gray pants having red cuffs and blue bow ties. I never learned there names and never did I desire to know them. To me, they were just Mutt and Jeff, Mutt and Jeff forever. I sat down on one of the purple upholstered benches closest to the miniature kitchen. Both stopped the conversation they were having to glare at me. They glared, stopped, huddled, glared, stopped, huddled, whispered, glared, stopped, huddled, whispered. I meanwhile took out my registration material and began examining it.

'Excuse me,' meowed Mutt. 'You're new here, are you not?'

'Ah, what? I didn't catch what you said,' I responded, looking up from my materials.

'I asked you whether you are a new student.'

'Yeah, I am.'

'See, I told you, I told you,' cried Jeff to Mutt.

'Are you new here also?' I asked Mutt.

'Meeeeeeee, meeeeeeee, new here, meeeeeeee, no way. I and my friend we're second year students.'

'I'm curious, are you brothers?'

Mutt and Jeff looked at one another and grinned.

'No, not in the least bit,' replied Jeff. 'We have no genealogical affiliations whatsoever. However, it is utterly perplexing how many people think me and my friend are twins.'

'"You do look like twins. Anyway, so you two are second year students. How do you like the Department?'

'Like it, us, yes, everyone likes the department. It's marvelous, simply marvelous and very energizing as well,' beamed Mutt.

'Agree, agree,' chucked Jeff.

'What wonderful stimulation you will find here,' chimed Mutt. 'I've visited many Middle Eastern Studies Departments in a lot of universities and so can forthrightly declare that this Department of Middle Eastern Studies is most probably the finest anywhere. When it comes to the critical analyzes of historical texts, there is no finer place. The Department fosters the uncanny knack of probing below the surface and successfully discovering the underlying factors in the rise and fall of the historical process. That's what makes being here so utterly electrifying.'

'"Yes, yes, agree, agree,' joined Jeff. 'The possibility for human awareness is quite extraordinarily heightened here. One's mind is simple dazzled by the infinitesimal road of organized facts and figures one is sure to encounter in a single day. But let us not be mislead, information is not conveyed in some vacuum. What makes this Department great is its Professors. Let me speak quite plainly, the Professors one intimately comes into contact with are true giants in their specialties.'

'"Agree, I agree quite profusely,' clapped Mutt with his mouth. 'All our people are quite accomplished researchers who have worked in the archives of Egypt and are true technicians in the world of academia.'

'Wow, that's great and a relief to hear,' I responded. 'By the way, could you tell me something about Professor Hans Svelter. When I entered his office before I saw some weird goings on.'

'You should never talk about Svelter,' bitched Jeff. 'Dr. Jefferson has ordered us to say nothing about him. Anyway, I'm the wrong person to ask. Like ninety-nine percent of the other students in the Department, I have rarely even seen Svelter. But let's change the subject. It is not permissible to talk about it." There was a brief pause before he resumed along another path. 'So you're a new student, Mm, interesting. It is odd but you are the second new student me and my friend have been fortunate to make the acquaintance of today. What was the other new student's name? I've forgotten.'

'Zeno Beneen,' answered Mutt.

'Oh, yes, Zeno Beneen, riiiiiiiiiii-ghhhhhhhht. Quite a young man, an intellect like that I haven't seen in many a day. His theories on Communist movements in the Middle East, of which he amply provided us, are extraordinary.'

'Agree,' blew Mutt. 'You should meet Zeno, ah, what's your name?'

'Joseph Kabir.'

'Yes, you should meet him immediately,' Jeff chimed.

'I have.'

'Then you should become close friends with him and listen and learn from him,' advised Jeff.

'Kabir, Kabir, Kabir,' beeped Mutt. 'Since you are a new student and quite young, let me give you advice I received when I was a new student. You have entered an important field, a field which deals with a region of the world that is of universal importance. Once you graduate, you'll be an important man, more important than nine-nine percent of the trash out there in the vulgar world. Don't louse up your opportunity. Work hard and long. Research, research, and then do some more research. The effort you put in will be rewarded.'

Jeff nodded in agreement. Yes, you're extremely fortunate.'

'Fortunate is not the word, privileged is a better word,'' added Mutt, 'privileged to have entered the field of Middle Eastern Studies, a field where specialists are in demand especially now what with the KLLP alliances breaking down and the increase in weapons shipments to oil exporting nations which is destroying the block of RCC nations both financially and psychologically.'

'I disagree wholeheartedly,' countered Jeff. 'The KLLP alliances seem to be in the process of revitalization of their essential mechanisms. Since the twenties of this century, there have been enormous fluctuations in the KLLP figures of growth. So one must always be careful when using these figures.'

'Mm, Mm, Mm,' sang Mutt in reply.

'And another thing, I must take exception to your comment that the RCC block is being destroyed. My dear fellow, why do you constantly put forth such preposterous hypotheses. If you thoroughly scrutinize the growth ratio figures of the RCC block in the last couple of years, you will clearly see that your statement in essence, is erroneous. Professor Boriskovesky, that brilliant social scientist from Stanford, has proven, and proven conclusively, that as things stand now, and if the factors affecting growth don't change within the next five years, then the RCC nations will survive till the year 2010.'

My eyes shifted from Mutt to Jeff and back about ten times as they conversed. I couldn't help staring at their craniums, wondering what the hell was inside them.

'Mm-eh-Mm-eh,' repeated Mutt to Jeff's comments.

'Don't you know,' continued Jeff louder than before, 'that last year the RCC nations grossed an incredible sixty-six billion in export-import surplus materials. New trade agreements were signed between the RCC member nations which lower tariffs by a remarkable percentage. I must say from all the collected data so far accumulated, it seems to me that theories connecting the RCC nations are getting stronger rather than weaker."

'All good points,' returned Mutt. 'However, I do feel your perspective is somewhat amiss. Have you forgotten about the Alhambra talks. . . ."

They quacked on while my attention returned to examining the registration materials. A few seconds later, I felt a tapping on my shoulder and looked up to see, standing before me, was a little man, midget-size, balding, with dark bushy eyebrows and mustached wearing a little green sweater and holding in his hands a jar of instant coffee, a spoon and a coffee mug. He stared into my face, with perspiration dripping down from his big, floppy ears. Continuously, his eyes kept scanning the lounge.

'I am a little worker in the library, only a little worker,' he belched in my face bizarrely. 'I work in the airless room with the other workers. I stamp books. I run errands for our head librarian, Jabarti. I work like slave. I need break. You better not tell on me, you better not.' He waved his silver spoon in my face.

"'Tell on you about what?'

"'That I take a break. Jamila, Jamila the bitch she will tell Jabarti on me. She can't stand me because I Muslim, oh God. She always beat me over the head, beat me, and beat me. I can do nothing about it, nothing. You better not tell on me. I warn you.'

The little fellow turned away, finished making his instant coffee and stole away from the lounge without looking at me again, and disappeared into the hallway. I was about ready to leave also when Mutt and Jeff's eyes found me again after completing their discussion. They started to nod at me for whatever reason. Self-consciously I said, 'Isn't the weather nice today. I've heard tell though that the weather isn't so nice like this all year round.'

"'Oh, so you're not from around here,' said Jeff. 'That's too bad. Mm, oh yes, oh yes, Zeno told us you are from that large town down South, yes, I remember now. He did.'

"'Kabir,' exclaimed Mutt. 'Since you haven't been around here, you don't know how horrid the winters are and it's intriguing. The topic of weather is intriguing in general. Don't you concur Kabir?'

'Naturally, I concur, naturally.'

"'Good. Most people just don't realize how intriguing and important weather is. Did you ever once realize that the success of Communism can be attributed to the weather?'

"'No, to be honest with you, I never did'

"'Most people don't. Weather, without the slightest doubt, is a political determinate. Climatic conditions effect economic enterprise most profoundly. I, for one, believe Communism is best propagated in colder climates and for proof, I give you the Soviet Union. If you'll recall Russia was facing its coldest winter in years when the Communists successfully staged their revolution. Of course, there are exceptions to my rule, numerous exceptions, but all in all, I do believe my hypothesis holds up. I really should explore the subject with Zeno. I'm sure he could shed some well needed light on my theory.'

On and on he cackled about his brilliant theory. 'You know Frankel and Smith, those pioneer explorers of the Political Science field, have drawn up a magnificent chart which illuminates just what I've been talking about. Oh, you should see it, ah, tremendous, exquisite, beautiful.'

"'Really,' popped Jeff as his eyes bulged from their sockets. 'Why haven't I seen this chart of theirs. Do you really have a copy of it?'

"'It's in my apartment. Come over tonight and I'll show it to you. There are a few problems Frankel and Smith illustrate which I'd like to discuss with you.'

Around the merry go round, they traveled about the weather, forgetting about me again. This time, though, I took the opportunity to flee, or at least I tried.

"Tell me Kabir, what position do you hold on the Middle Eastern situation?' asked Mutt, catching me in mid-flight.

"'Well, it-it-it-it-a is-is-a certainly a-a situation,' hammered I like an inconsistent drill. I was standing in front of them looking the dope. 'It certainly is a situation. But to be honest, I usually don't concern myself with politics much.'

'Oh, I see,' said Jeff.

'That's very interesting, indeed you might even say fascinating,' honked Mutt.

'Well fellows if you excuse me, I must be off to see my advisor.'

Already they'd turned from me and were discussing the political ramifications of the government of Turkey's recent acts of violence. I was gone in an instant. But this wouldn't be the last I saw of Mutt and Jeff. During the year, whenever I passed the Student Lounge, they'd be there holding one of their marathon debates.

*   *   *

To Professor Majnoon Jazzar's office I went with my knees shaking with fear. I rapped on his door twice and received no response and I tried a third time. This time I met with success.

'Yes, yes, who is that knocking?' asked Jazzar through the door.

'It's a student here to see you.'

'A student to see me,' yelled Jazzar ridiculously through the door. 'A student. You joke. A student. Are you sure? A student. Allah preserve me, there is a student here to see me. This is nice. Come in student. Oh student, please come in!'"

I sauntered into his office and immediately a powerful odor of whiskey smacked me in the face and almost tore my nostrils off. I must admit it was a wonderful odor, so warm, sweet, and invigorating. Jazzar launched himself out from behind his oval, black desk, grabbed my hand, tugged, tugged again, tugged a third time, and then released. I was stunned by the friendliness of this man, this Professor who taught in a Department I so far had found quite cold and inhuman. Jazzar was a heavy man, with dyed black hair and a sandy-colored, acne-scared complexion. He wore a gray suit and sunglasses.

'Hello student,' he shouted to me in an oriental accent while he pointed to a chair he desired me to sit in. 'How are you today?'

'Fine.'

'That's fine. It is fine when all is fine.'

'Yeah.'

'Would you believe you are second student come today for visit. Young man name Zeno come see me before. He nice. He show me proper respect. He bring me big box of cigars. I like cigars. Zeno nice young man. He listen when I talk. I like that. I like also having two students visit on same day. Never happen to me. I never get respect from students. Students no respect learned men anymore. In old country, at least, still bow before learned man. But here no respect, no respect at all.' Jazzar reached into his opened file cabinet and produced a bowl of pistachio nuts which he set before me. 'Eat, eat, have some, they good for you, eat!'

'Thank you,' said I as I reached for a couple of nuts.

'This is what you call Arab hospitality. I am Arab man and follow custom of making guests feel comfortable. You come home with me one day. My wife cook you Arab dishes. We give you everything. You will be treat like Sultan. We will show what meaning of Arab hospitality.'

I munched on some more nuts while attentively listening.

Off the top of his mind, he shot, 'I love camels; do you love camels?' I shrugged my shoulders meaning I didn't know. 'Camels are wonderful creatures. I don't like when I see in zoo. They must be allow to roam. My brother Ismail, a half brother, he agriculturist in Kuwait, has ten camels. He use their milk. He use their skins. He use them for transport. When I visit my brother I ride on his camels. Camels have spirit. Camels spit if no like. Camels are sturdy. One of few animals can survive in desert. Can survive in cold also. Camels can go a week without water. I love camels. They are symbol of noble Arabs, excellent symbol.' Them, off in another direction, he churned, 'Talking of camels, my great-grandfather leader of nomadic tribesman in Arabia and his tribe own fifty camels. He tribe rich. His tribe best warriors in Arabia, everyone fear even Sultan. Tribe over five hundred years old. Great grandfather always rode on camel.'

Jazzar's face became red and his fat cheeks puffed up like balloons. 'Great-grandfather,' he continued, 'famous man. Known as best lover in Arabia. He had one hundred concubines along with three wives. Satisfied all of them, always busy. Ha, ha. Great grandfather had one hundred and fifty children. All women see him, fall in love with his beauty. He irresistible. Grandfather had reputation as honorable man, the most honorable in all Arabia. There is story about him. One day he catch man with his daughter, a man not from his tribe, and they lone in desert and she wore no veil. Great grandfather knew honor of whole family at stake. Great grandfather took out his gold sword and chopped strange man head off with one swoop and then go to daughter and do same thing. He saved honor of family. He cheered by the rest of tribe for his quick action. From then on they call him Abu Sharif or father of honor.'

"'Woo, my God, Arabia back then must really have been something,' said I as I grabbed a handful of pistachio nuts and stuffed.

"'Yes, and my grandfather something too. All Arabia knew of his daring. Once while his tribe in war with another tribe he storm the enemy lines with his camel and sword in hand personally killed fifteen of enemy, chopped their heads off and wiped their blood all over himself as a gesture of pride. My grandfather do one daring deed after another. Grandfather didn't care who or what he attacked.' "He told me one unbelievable story after another about his grandfather and then skipped to vivid tales about his father in between chewing a few nuts himself. 'My father, assistant foreign secretary of Yemen. Man of wealth and learning who travel everywhere and given gifts by everyone including Sultan.' Professor Majnoon Jazzar reached down into his desk draw and pulled out a diamond and emerald decorated sheath which held a long handled dagger. Swiftly, he unsheathed the dagger and waved it under my chin. 'Nice, nice. You see how sharp it is, see.' The blade came dangerously close to my neck. 'You may hold it for a second, only second though.'

"'Oh, it-it-it is really beau-beautiful,' said I flustered as I held the heavy thing in my hand carefully. Hurriedly but politely, I handed the thing back to him.

"'Dagger priceless,' Jazzar explained while he re-sheathed it and put it back into his draw. 'I always carry with me back and forth. Would not leave in office. Priceless. If you buy it would cost twenty thousand dollars. But I no sell. Sell it would be like selling my father.

I love it. Arab craftsmanship, example of. Praise be to Allah. Student, now student, tell me what can do for you, student?'

'You've been assigned as my advisor and I would. . . .'

'Are you Muslim?'

'No, why do you ask? Must I be a Muslim to have you as an advisor?'

Jazzar ignored my inquiry and made a little one of his own. 'Student, I don't remember have I found out your name yet?'

'It's Joseph Kabir.'

'Noooooooooooo, an Arab name. Ah, goooooooooood, that is goooooooooooooood. You are an Arab and a believer in Pan-Arabism. You smart young man to me. I glad I made your advisor, nice. Lucky for you. I am big man at university for Arabs. I am head of Arab club here. We need member. Membership only 15 dollars. Would you like join?'

'Well I don't. . . ."

'Oh, Arab club, you must join Arab club. We have big dance coming up and you meet nice Arab girl make you happy, very happy. Join, join now.'

'Would you let me think about it?'

'Give me telephone number. I call you tomorrow for decision. We need Arab people.' I wrote my number down on a piece of paper and passed it to him.

'Ah Professor, Professor,' I tried to get his attention while he analyzed my telephone number. 'Professor, the reason I'm here, oh Professor, the reason I'm here is to find out if you could help me with. . . ." Professor, Professor Jazzar, can you hear me Professor?'

"Jazzar was gazing up towards the plain, dull white ceiling with his hands raised straight above his head. Bizarrely he was chanting, not chanting like mysterious Professor Svelter before him, chanting in a serene manner, 'Allah,' he sang. 'Allah, thank you, thank you for permitting me to be born an Arab gentleman. Praise be to Allah, Lord of the universe and master of us Muslims, and even master of those who have gone astray from Your teachings, the Christians and Jews. You are so wise, Allah, so merciful, so compassionate, so bountiful. Allah, You are great, Allah, Allah, Allah!' Jazzar, finishing by touching his forehead to the desk three times, then again looked me straight in the eye.

'Professor are you better now?'

No reply.

'Professor, my courses, I've come to ask your help in selecting the courses I should take.'

'Your courses, Mm, courses are being offered. What are courses being offered, Mm, what's your name?'

'Joseph Kabir, Kabir. The courses I am talking about are the courses the Department, the Department you teach in, are offering this coming semester.'

'Oh, oh, I see, yes now I understand,' said Jazzar as he tore off a sheet of paper from the notepad on his desk and quickly jotted down the courses he had deemed fit and proper for me to take. I scanned his list and found there was one course he left off the list that I wanted to take, that being Persian. I'd always wanted to learn to read and write the language, a language which had charmed me with its beautiful sounds and history. Instead of Persian, Jazzar put me down for Arabic. I carefully explained my desire for the other language. Jazzar eyed me a minute or two and then vehemently advised the taking of Arabic instead. His words soon grew into a tirade against the Persian language and everything Persian. I carefully held to my conviction. He now took a different tone. He went from attacking Persian to attacking me, criticizing the way I spoke, the way I looked, the manner I conducted myself, and mostly he criticized me for being disrespectful to an older, more learned man. He as much as called me a fool and I sat there listening to him insult me so I guess in one instance he was right. I should have walked out but instead I sat and listened like a dutiful young lad. To the ceiling he moaned, 'Allah, Allah, give this young man guidance. He needs to be rightly guided so desperately. He does not know the true way of Allah, compassionate and forgiving Allah. Instruct him in your way, teach him, show him.'

With these words, Jazzar rose, stared at me with a cold bracing stare, and rubbed his hands hungrily together. This is it, thought I, get ready to defend yourself. Jazzar turned, but not towards me but away from me. He bent down. He was doing something, lifting something, what, what. Up, up, up from a large brown paper carton he produced a red and black water pipe with its long stem hanging limply down. He planted the thing victoriously on his desk right and exclaimed, 'Pipe needs water. Must run to bathroom to get some.' And run he did.

"In two minutes, Jazzar returned with a jug of water in hand and promptly loaded his pipe. Ah, but the pipe needs tobacco and so Jazzar like a swan glided over to his bookcase and pulled out, from behind a giant volume called, <u>The Arabs, A Contribution To World History</u>, a plastic bag containing some sort of finely ground tobacco. I watched as he scientifically loaded his pipe and lit the whole thing. Waiting until the pipe properly warmed, he carefully placed the long stem in his mouth, puffed once, puffed twice, and puffed a third time. Almost magically, the tension on his face eased and he leaned back in his chair, adjusted his sun glasses, and let his big belly sag out. In that condition he exclaimed, 'I sorry the way I talk to you Kabir. I was a little harsh. I should not be harsh on young who still not know a lot.'

'It's okay, but can we find a solution to the. . . ."

"'Smoking relaxes. I know you yearning for puff Kabir but I sorry. I can no offer you one, I sorry. I smoke a special blend of tobacco which no good for anyone not used to it. Only can give puff to regular users. I sorry.'

'No need for apologies, Professor. I understand.'

'Then Kabir, if you understand, you take Arabic like your Professor directs. Arabic great language. You should be eager to take. You know lot of English you speak come from Arabic. Example, yes, good idea, I give you examples. Word algebra, word admiral, word nadir, all come Arabic. Word, coffee, word, assassin, word, check, word, alcohol come from Arabic. Amaze you. Word, macabre, Arabic. In Arabic mean tomb, grave, interesting, huh, Arabic interesting language. You take.'

'Well, I don't. . . ."

'Still not convince. Arabic, holiest language on earth, did you know? Arabic language of Islam, the Koran, the holy bible for us Muslims written in Arabic. Allah, God, speaks in Arabic.'

'Well I don't. . . ."

'Kabir, Kabir,' Jazzar quickly took a few more puffs from his pipe, and calmed down once again before proceeding to recite twenty Arabic poems learned in childhood. "Beautiful yes? Lovely yes? Seeing that didn't convince me, Jazzar decided to take the historical approach. He told me about the birth of the Arabic language in Arabia and how it spread through the Middle East in the seventh century, he told me how it then rubbed out all previous languages, he told me, he told me fifteen hundred years worth of history of the Arabic language.

When he finished I cranked defiantly, 'I still don't want to take Arabic.'

Jazzar took more puffs from his pipe and commanded, 'You will take Arabic, you will take Arabic. I can have you expelled from the Department. I have influence here. I bring in contributions from countries of my friends in the Middle East. Dr. Jefferson likes me, always bows to my judgment, always. You watch your step Kabir, you take Arabic.'

'"But can I take Persian at the same time I take Arabic?'

'"A problem. Hm, this Department has rule, students not supposed to take two languages at same time. You make problem for yourself, Kabir. If you follow advice and not take worthless Persian, you be all right. Hm, problem. Mm, I have it, if you get special permission from Professor Lunwi, she teaches Persian, then you can take both. I'll talk Dr. Jefferson personally about it. Go Professor Lunwi. Tell her problem nicely. She'll understand. I sure. She nice Muslim woman. I like her, I like her so much. After you finish with her come back, finish filling out registration forms, we have nice talk and we enjoy. Oh, that right Kabir, I must remind you not to forget about Arab club. You think about joining and I call you about decision. You need to become member to help you with Arab heritage reaffirm. You must be made to feel pride in ancestry.'

Jazzar rose and saluted me in the customary Arab way, then walked over to me and personally escorted me out and over to Professor Lunwi's office while giving me Allah's blessings as I left.

*   *   *

I knocked on Professor Lunwi's door. In a deep voice, through the door, she questioned, 'Who-is-there? Quickly, tell me-who-is-there?'

'One of the new students.'

'A new student. What do you mean new?'

'I am a first year student in the department.'

'Why are you a first year student?' came her query through the door.

I was stunned by her question and didn't know what to say.

'Why are you a first year student?' she repeated.

'Time has said I should be a first year student and not a second, third or fourth year student, I guess.'

Those words of mine worked like magic. Slowly her office door opened and Lunwi stood behind it. As I entered, she came up from behind and machine gun-like asked, 'what do you want?'

'I-I-I-I, j-j-j-just wa-wan-want to a-a-a-ask you about the per-per-Persian language course you teach.'

Speaking loudly to herself as she journeyed over to her desk, she raved, 'It's Dr. Jefferson's doing. He makes all the Professors here see students. Ah, all that Jefferson is interested in is public relations. If Dr. Warly was in charge, things would change for the better and quickly. Dr. Warly would handle everything well.' To say the least, the meeting went down hill from here.

My eyes now fixed on this huge picture that hung on the wall behind the Professor's desk. In it, Lunwi stood staring expressionless straight ahead of her between two men in some jungle area. All were wearing brown safari suits and hats. Above their heads hovered a multi-colored bird. Ah, but the weird part was that both men held four shrunken heads a piece.

'Don't daydream in my office,' she berated me as I sat still staring at the picture. 'State your business immediately or out you must go.'

I told her everything that had passed between myself and Professor Jazzar and explained the reasons I desired to take Persian. She just sat and stared. I grew nervous and that triggered me to talk and talk and talk. For some reason I began telling her my experiences with Vladimir, how mixed up I was about the Department, how confused it was all to me, on and on. I had to tell somebody, I guess. I was so sick inside, so depressed. Throughout, Lunwi just stared. In the middle of my talking jag, she broke in saying, 'Okay Kabir, I've heard enough now. I've had time enough to judge you and to label you. Now I shall speak frankly. You will not take Persian with me, you will never take Persian with me until you become something different than you are. I am sure Professor Jazzar knew how I would react when he sent you here. I will allow no one in my class like you who stand outside us all, who threaten our existence. I despise you Kabir and have sworn to destroy all of your type wherever I can find them and I shall, as I shall destroy you, we shall destroy you, we shall, we shall.'

I rose from my seat, burst out of her office, and ran back to Professor Jazzar's to whom I explained what transpired. All he did was laugh and exclaim, 'I knew that would be, ha, ha. Kabir, such thing would never happen if you not deny your Arab-ness. You must say and be Arab and then your trouble are over. You then find acceptance here.'

Well that was the end of that and if I had been more aware of the world of costumes on parade and men wearing costumes and humans seeking to put others in costumes that would have spelled the end of my days in the Department. But no, I was the fool, the idiot, a young man who knew nothing about the true reality. And I was prideful too. I couldn't go home. I couldn't go back a failure, I didn't want to go back a failure. Anyway, the study of the Middle East had become my life. Leaving the Department before I began would be like slicing out my heart, or so I mistakenly thought at the time. Frankly fellahs, I was stuck. And very, very, very soon I would start sinking."

CHAPTER 7

Frankly, Kabir's story reveals quite clearly part of his sickness. Kabir is an interesting case, a case of a man who believes the world is out to get him. What can I say, you heard, you read, and honestly, I don't think there is anything I can add.

Precinct head, Detective Decarrie craved for more of Kabir's lies. "Joseph, Joseph, could you tell us more about the students in the department. Were they as sick as the Professors?"

Kabir needed little inducement to slander the dead, little inducement whatsoever. He told one tale after another about his fellow students, making each and every one into a ruthless caricature. In the interests of good taste and because of space limitations, I will venture to repeat only one story he told of a fellow student in the department of Middle Eastern Studies named Stan Lord.

"Stan Lord, now there was an interesting bastard," Kabir began. "Like me he was a new student. I met him that second day in the Department. I was in the General Office handing in my registration forms, yet dizzied by my surroundings. The Office was a large but sterile one dotted with small, black metal tables that matched metal floors and metal mirrors that passed for windows. On top of the metal tables were metal statues of groups of men and women posing. That wasn't as odd to me as the metal heads of young boys and girls hanging as plagues from the walls. What did it mean? I had no idea nor did I ask. I went directly to the women sitting at the desk at the front of the room. She was blond, blue-eyed and as pale as a ghost. I addressed her but she did not reply. She simply took my forms, stamped them, put them in a folder and waved me away with her hand. I noticed that behind her desk was the office of Dr. Jefferson. It was closed and on the doorknob was the sign, 'DO NOT ENTER AT YOUR OWN RISK.

As I was leaving the General Office, I crashed into Zeno Beneen in the doorway; he was headed inside. He looked at me curiously, then slapped me hard on the back while whaling, 'Joseph, Joseph, Joseph, my good man. How are you? I'm surprised to see you in the office. Why are you here?'

'Oh, oh, I don't know. I was just taking a walk and somehow, I really don't know how, I wound up here. Isn't that something. It's really funny how some people wind up where they do.'

'Ha, ha. You are a good man Joseph, a good man,' pooh-poohed Zeno. 'You're terribly humorous. And to tell you the truth, Joseph, I knew it the very first time I saw you. You know I am quite enamored to funny men, quite.' I blinked and he continued. 'I am here to do some business with the Department, and frankly hoping to see my good friend, Dr. Jefferson.' I blinked again and I might have blinked a third time if an ugly-looking character hadn't come walking up to us, and when I say ugly, I mean it. Not only was his milky white skin grotesque with its crystal-like pores, but there was that beard, misshaped so that one side of it was two inches longer than the other side while over its entire circumference were bald spots. A nasty sight! Stan Lord wore beat up glasses which were held together by white adhesive tape. He wore a red and white hunting shirt with a bundle of papers and pens stuffed in its front pocket - incidentally, he had this shirt on every time I ever saw him - and a pair of jeans three sizes too big which sagged in his derriere and ballooned out in his groin area. He had one front tooth that stood out before the others and grew down toward his lower lip.

Zeno gave the guy a big hello and introduced him to me as, "that very descent, good man Stan Lord.'

'What's your name?' inquired Stan of me.

'Joseph Kabir.'

'Gee whiz, gee whiz, gee whiz,' sang Stan in a soprano voice. 'Perhaps, perhaps, perhaps if I might inquire, if I might, are you Persian, Joseph Kabir, Kabir, isn't that a Persian name, yes, perhaps.'

'I don't know,' smacked I innocently. 'Kabir is just the name I was born with. Nobody ever told me the derivation of it.'

'You must know. It is an impossibility. The answer has to be here, somewhere,' Stan further annoyed. 'You look like you are of Persian stock. I can tell stock.'

'Stan, I'm sorry but as I already said, I don't know.'

Stan frowned and then pouted like a child.

I changed the subject. 'Stan, you do come from around these parts?'

'Oh, no, gee whiz. Can't you tell from my accent that I don't come from around here. I was born in a beautiful little town out West. My father ran the local post office there. There was nothing there, gee whiz, only sagebrush and gophers. Hardly any people.' Stan Lord then became quiet. He kept checking the papers in his shirt pocket and eying me strangely. I was very uncomfortable, not knowing what to say or do next while Zeno was shaking his head back and forth and repeating the words to himself. 'Yes, blood good, yes, I need to do that.'

Zeno finally broke the silence between us. 'Joseph, Joseph, Stan over here has been quite upset these last few days. Stan tell Joseph why you've been upset since it concerns him also.'

'Ah, gee whiz, I really don't want, ah, well, I've been agitated because they're making us new students take those worthless introductory courses which cover the most rudimentary material any grammar school student would know. They must be making you take those courses also Joseph, right?'

'Yes.'

'Isn't it ridiculous. Gee whiz, I'm going to protest. I think each student has the right, as a mature adult, to pick and choose his own courses. At Harvard, my former school, everyone had the right to choose. Why should it be different here? Has the department not heard of the right of self-determination? Has the department not heard of the word democracy? Where is democracy? Why doesn't this department have a student representative committee? I propose that three committees be set up to act as a check against the arbitrary abuse of power by the administration. Why don't I see checks and balances? Can there be real democracy without checks and balances? Well I tell you, Joseph, my voice will be heard, and it will sound the signal of freedom throughout the university. I've made an appointment tomorrow to speak with Dr. Jefferson, and speak I will. Everyone here shall hear the voice of Stan Lord.'

'Good, you're right, good, yes, yea,' dribbled I. What I really thought at that moment was, well Joseph you've now met another Department freaks.

Zeno meanwhile had shuffled away over to Dr. Jefferson who just had made his way in to the General Office on his way to his office. Zeno could be heard meowing to him, 'You know Doctor, the other night at dinner it completely slipped my mind that my chief mentor at Oxford, Dr. Hair Saghir, when I last saw him told me to convey his best wishes to you. He tells me you two encountered one another in Egypt while studying in the archives there. Oh, what a scholar Dr. Saghir is. He's almost as brilliantly insightful as yourself. How I miss the good man, how I really, really do. Dr. Saghir and myself used to get into many long, arduous debates on Islam and enjoy every moment of it. His primary thesis, the religion of Islam sanctions capitalistic exploitation was always countered by myself who holds that Islam and its holy Koran explicitly preaches the communist idea. What's your opinion, Doctor?'

Dr. Jefferson smiled and invited Zeno into his office. They soon disappeared.

My attention was now riveted on Stan. It seems besides democracy, Stan had a great love for the country of Iran. Maybe love isn't a strong enough word, maybe fanatical devotion would be more appropriate.

'Did you know the Persian nation this year is two thousand five hundred years old, Joseph?'

'No.'

'You didn't, gee whiz, you should. Okay, okay. That's okay. Here's another one, tell me all you know about these three ancient Shahs of Iran, Cyrus, Darius, and Xerxes? Be precise now.'

'To tell you the truth, Stan, this is the first time I've ever heard those names.'

Stan shook his head disgustedly. 'That's the problem, and I am really bothered by it. It all points to what I am always harping about to anyone that will listen, Iran is always being overlooked as a historical force in this world. Why is that? It's just terrible.' Stan took out a handkerchief and blew his nose. Thus refreshed, Stan continued clucking, 'I can't wait to hear from the bureau of records, you know Joseph."

'Okay, about. . . .'

'It will probably be another month before I hear anything.'

'"Anything about what?'

'"About changing my name. I am thinking about officially changing it to Cyrus, Cyrus who was the greatest King that Iran ever saw.'

'Stan, how did you develop such an interest in Iran?'

'It happened during the time I spent digging in Iran.'

'Ah, Stan, could you explain that?'

'Oh, gee whiz, of course you don't understand. What a dunce I am, really and truly. So let me explain. Until quite recently I was a student of paleontology and one of my duties was digging for fossils and one of the places I did my digging was Iran. I wandered over the whole country with my pix and shovel and just plunged into the dirt."

'Okay, I see, you were in Paleontology. Interesting.'

'"Yes, isn't it. A-hum, and I was doing well in the field and had just another six months to go before I would have gotten my Ph.D. from Harvard. I was at the top of my class too and already had published. Five of my articles appeared in the <u>Paleontologist Quarterly</u>.'

'And then what happened?'

'Well, I just got tired of studying layer stratification, old bones, rocks and all such unexciting things. I found something which fascinated me much more. During my digs in Iran, I became enamored with the customs and the history and the politics of the country. Gee whiz, what was I doing with some old bones when I could deal with living, breathing people. Now for the rest of my entire life all I want to do is read about Iran, write about Iran, and live Iran. That wonderful nation is my soul, my life.'

I want to stop my narration here to make a brief editorial comment. Stan Lord was one of the greatest barbarians I ever met. Who else but a barbarian would claim a nation as a soul, who else? Soul, Stan completely lacked it so how could he talk about it, how? Can you believe that? Stan didn't understand that the nation destroyed the soul or maybe he did understand. Maybe I didn't understand then either but at least I didn't feel comfortable equating my self with some nation, which exists purely in the mind and on paper. There is no such a thing as nation; the reality is false. Maybe I didn't understand that then, but I had an inkling. That's probably why Stan Lord sickened me even then. Now I know better, I know he nation as the destroyer, but it is only now that I know it, and only after last night that I fully understand. A man must perceive the one, the individual for total fulfillment, and not perceive some vague general term such as nation. He must not let the general block his truly seeing himself and others. Now I can return to the narrative after venturing into my polemics. But it was necessary to maintain my sanity.

This would not be my last encounter with Stan Lord. For some reason, he dogged my footsteps, came to believe that he must instruct me on Iran, and with the knowledge he imparting, save me from myself. Every time I'd see him, he'd hit me with a barrage of facts on Iran, past and present, and ever time he would ask me if I would like to visit his home for a bit of imported wine he saved for special occasions. I always told him I couldn't, giving some excuse or another. For almost a month, this went on until the guy literally started begging. He explained how nobody ever wanted to be friends with him and come to his house. I must come over to his house and meet his wife Bertha whom he met on a dig. Eventually I broke down and agreed and soon thereafter Stan and I went steppin' on over to his apartment. Along the way, Stan took delight in ramming it into my head of how delicious the wine he was going to serve me, repeated it at least fifteen times. Yeah, and the guy got to talking about his apartment building. It seems it wasn't properly painted in the lobby and Stan said this was in violation of a stipulation of his lease agreement and he'd already scolded the landlord about it but that it brought no results. This wouldn't be tolerated and if need be the fight would be taken to the town's housing bureau, and if that didn't work, the neighbors would be organized into a protest group and would set up pickets in front of the building. Democracy would win. Autocracy would fail. The people would never accept tyranny or tyrants. 'My lease is like a sacred constitution to be venerated in the highest courts of the land.'

As we reached the apartment, from inside I heard ching, chang, ching, chang, chang, ching. My imagination, possibly. Stan opened the door to reveal a remarkable interior. The ching-chang sounds were real and were produced from a little tape deck; Stan explained that this was classical Iranian music. The tape deck worked on a timer; at certain times of the day, the music played. Why he did this, was not explained. The apartment itself was lined with wall to wall posters of Iran, posters of the shepherds of Iran, posters of the camels of Iran, posters of the foods of Iran, posters of the politicians of Iran, posters of the common people of Iran, posters of the mosques of Iran, posters and more posters. The hallway leading into the living room was covered with linoleum tiles, each tile being part of a puzzle which covered the whole living room and was a perfect recreation of detailed map of Iran.

"Stan's living room was a sight. Old and rusting Iranian rifles, pistols, and sabers were suspended everywhere from the ceiling by steel cords. Small pink pillows were sprawled erratically on a floor covered by an exquisite Iranian carpet and two green, wooden snack tables were stationed there on top of which were two worm-eaten Persian manuscripts, rare collectors volumes of twelve century Iranian poetry worth plenty of money. There were a number of chairs, positioned at which male and female mannequins were dressed-out in traditional Persian garb. Meanwhile, each door in the apartment had a miniature Iranian flag flying above it. In Stan's den were bookshelves of Iranian books and collections of Iranian stamps and coins. There was also the collection of rocks he'd collected during his excavations in Iran. The den also was cluttered with Iranian carpets, Iranian caftans, Iranian pottery, Iranian tiles, piled up, lined up and hung up. My God, this was better than being at a museum. I stood with mouth ajar taking it all in.

'Come into the bathroom with me, Joseph,' Stan Lord suddenly declared. 'There is something that you really need to see, which I hope will trigger within you a sense of your own tradition and history.'

I followed Stan into the potty room. There I was faced with another extraordinary sight. Lining the entire wall opposite the toilette was an enormous poster of the Shah of Iran waving to a crowd with lips puckered and eyes turned towards his nose. There were also Iranian puzzles, games, wind-up toys in baskets beside the bowl. 'I picked them up in Iran,' he explained. 'They come in handy sometimes when I'm in here for an unusual amount of time.' I did not ask him to explain that.

"'Isn't that a marvelous picture of the him,' beamed Stan with pride, pointing to the poster. 'Although he is unquestionably an undemocratic tyrant, a true opponent of democracy, the democracy of the little man and the little woman, I still love him because he represents Iran; he is Iran. And I must say in the Shah's favor, he has promised Iran democracy as soon as she is ready for it, yes, he has. Oh, and you must admit, he has done great things for his country. Why just last week he christened a new dam.' Stan went on to enumerate other wonders produced by the great man. Once finished with the bathroom, he took me to his favorite room, the bedroom. Surprisingly, the only thing unusual about it was the picture of the Iranian royal family, the queen, the little princes, and the little princesses, hanging on the wall above the bed. There was a work bench near the window and something on top of it covered by a blanket. Stan took me over to it and removed the covering to reveal an incomplete wood carving of an ornate oriental building with a water fountain surrounded by a large square. This was a replica of the building housing the Iranian parliament or Majlis, Stan explained. He'd carved the whole thing himself, a craft he had learned from his very accomplished mailman father. While in the midst of showing off the carving, Stan suddenly dashed over to his bed, dived for the floor and crawled beneath it.

'Stan,' screeched I, alarmed 'What's the matter? Staaaaaaan.'

My query though met with no reply and I paced in front of the bed not knowing what to do. Shortly though, Stan reemerged into the world of light, holding a brown, vinyl book. 'Let's have the wine now that I offered you offered you,' he suggested. I followed him into the kitchen. He was still holding the book. 'I'm sorry my wife Bertha wasn't here to greet you,' he apologized, rummaging through a kitchen cabinet to produce the bottle of wine. 'Most probably she went to the supermarket to buy carrots. We're having them for supper tonight you see. Bertha and I are strict vegetarians, you know. It's interesting to note that Iranians for the most part eat mainly vegetables also, although they do eat quite a bit of lamb.'

We sat at the kitchen table while Stan poured the wine and opened his vinyl book. The book turned out to be a album of page upon page of pictures of angry men. As pages were turned, Stan explained who the people in the photographs were. 'You see this man, Joseph, this man, yes, yes, the dark faced, sinister looking one in the middle of the crowd, yes, yes, right, he was the last chief treasurer under the old Iranian dynasty.' A few pages later. 'This man standing under the roof with the pigeons perched on top of it, is Salih Darvish, a famous man in Iran. A few years back Salih tried to assassinate the Shah by throwing a brick at his head, but luckily was caught before committing his dastardly act. The secret police tortured him and before an assembled crowd of thirty thousand in the new Olympic stadium in Tehran, removed his eyeballs. Nobody knows for sure where Salih is now but there is rumor he's imprisoned in the basement of the imperial palace.' Pictures, pictures, pictures and more pictures I was made to peruse of cabinet ministers, former Shahs, former eunuchs of former Shahs, former concubines of former Shahs, wives of former Shahs, palaces and mosques of former Shahs. The ocular tour only was halted by the ringing of the doorbell. Stan opened the door and in trudged a little weasely-looking wench. She was wearing a frayed wool coat and had large brown hiking boots on her feet. There was a green kerchief tied around her head; her glasses was so thick that you couldn't see her eyeballs.

'Hi Bertha, look who I brought home,' jabbered Stan nervously. He used his nose to point to me.

'Stan, would you please get out of my way,' returned Bertha, carrying a shopping bag filled with carrots. Rapidly, she hauled her bag into the kitchen, Stan following closely behind. She glanced back at me at the table, her eyes bulging out of their sockets. On the kitchen counter, she let her bag fall before heading straight at me and wearing a fierce expression. In front of me she stood, for a minute or two, then put her nose to the glass of wine I held in my hand. Becoming red in the face, she pulled the glass of wine from my hand, rushed over to the sink, and promptly spilled it down the drain and threw the glass shatteringly into a garbage bag nearby.

'Sttttttttttttttaaaaaaaaaaaaannnnnnnnnnnnnnn, why Stttttttaaaaaaanleeeeeeeey?' she shrieked. 'How dare you allow this to happen. You know liquor isn't to be touched in this house until after dinner, and that rule must not be broken, not even for guests.' Bertha rushed into the bedroom then and slammed the door while Stan stood dumbfounded before me looking like a recently castrated gorilla. I didn't know what to say or do, that's how uncomfortable I was. I really wanted to leave then, but didn't want to hurt Stan's feelings.

The door of the bedroom opened now and Bertha reemerged into the kitchen attired in a purple and yellow house dress with the kerchief still tied securely over her head. Stan hovered around her like a mosquito hovers around its next victim. The uncomfortable silence particularly annoyed me so I addressed Bertha, who at that moment was at the stove chopping up carrots into a pot.

'Stan's told me that you met him on a dig. He didn't say but I imagine you are a Paleontologist, either that or you are somebody who likes to dig. Ha-ha-ha.'

She didn't look my way, didn't laugh, and didn't do anything except continue chopping while her husband grinned.

'Stan has a wagging tongue, I see' Bertha suddenly addressed me. 'What's your name by the way? I do dislike involving myself in conversation with people whose names I don't know.'

'Joseph Kabir,' rattled Stan answering for me. 'I think he's Iranian but he won't admit it. I'm working on him, though.'

'Are you in the Department of Middle Eastern Studies like my Stanley?'

'Yes, Bertha he is,' Stan chucked again in my place.
'Stanley, why don't you shut your mouth. When a question is addressed to you then answer but when one is not then shut up.' Bertha gave Stan a piece of raw carrot which he proceeded to chomp on.

'Well Mr. Kabir,' Bertha rolled on, 'I am a Paleontologist. If the big mouth hasn't told you yet, Stanley met on a dig and it was quite fortunate for Stanley that we did. God, what a mess that man was when I first encountered him, myyyyyyyyyy. Oh, he was so lonely like a little lost sheep. But thanks to me Stanley is just fine now as you can see.' Stan munched his carrot. 'I am a Paleontologist, yes, Mr. Kabir, a quite exceptional one, one of the best in the country. I'm totally devoted to the profession. I am not like some others who go about their field work half-hearted or still others who abandon Paleontology because they say it is not rewarding enough.'

I nodded and said how good that is.

Bertha's eyes now fell on Stan once again. 'How could you touch the wine at this time of day,' Bertha was once more bitching at Stan. 'Don't you have ears. We've been over the rules time and time again.'

I thought it was time to say goodbye then. Politely, I excused myself only to have Stan grin and block my path while Bertha returned to the sink to drain her carrots. Stan made me wait while he rushed to the bedroom, returning seconds later with a rolled-up poster which he presented to me. 'Joseph, it's for you. I give it to you as a token of appreciation for your being so nice enough to come today.' Stan unrolled it, revealing an aerial view of the city of Tehran at night. 'I want you to hang it up in your living room so everyone can see it. It's about time your Iranian roots became apparent to the world.'

I gave the required thank you and charged for the door. Bertha ignored it all and didn't even say goodbye.

'"Bi-u-mide-didar, Khuda-Hafiz,' yapped Stan to me at the door. 'That's Persian for goodbye if you don't know it already. I do hope you'll come back to visit, I do hope so. Perhaps next time I can take out my projector and show you my film footage of Iran. Wouldn't that be nice!"

'Sttttttttttttaaaaaaaaaaaaaaaaaanleeeeeeeeeeeeeeeey,'   oh Staaaaaaaaaaaanleeeeeeey,' yelled Bertha from the kitchen. 'Your carrots are waiting for you on the table. Come and eat them at once before they get cold. Staaaaaaaaaaaaaanleeeeeeeeeey.'

Stan shook his head nervously. 'I must go and eat Joseph. Bye. Bye.'

I departed but the encounter with Stan Lord had left me baffled. What a strange man. At the time, I thought he was harmless enough, a bit of a fool, that's all. But I have subsequently come to realize that I was wrong, that Stan Lord was a robber, yes that's right, a robber. He robbed me of feeling, robbed me of the pleasure of sense, robbed me of the pleasure of unity with him. Stan was a pane of glass with sharp corners that cut passers-by. Stan was evil. Oh how glad I am that I had him blown up, oh and how gleeful. And I am delighted to that in the end I didn't become like him when it would have been so easy."

CHAPTER 8

Back at the officers' lounge and back to the world of reality, this drama now turned. As Kabir finished telling me - remember I am Bombser, the reporter from The Star - about Stan Lord, he slowly closed his eyes, slowly. Soon he was asleep. It being three-thirty in the morning who could blame him. Decarrie was sitting there but wasn't asleep. He was in a trance of sorts and when I tried to rouse him by tapping him on the shoulder, I failed miserably. I was getting a little nuts, being alone in the basement of the Precinct. I'd had enough of Kabir and just wanted to get through with it. It was impossible, though for me to sit there watching Kabir sleep without winding down myself. Maybe I was more tired than I thought because soon my eyes had closed too, soon I was unconscious to the world. But this state did not last long. All at once, I awakened to the sound of a yell coming from Kabir. He'd literally gone off his rockers.

"Ugh-ooooooooooow, there she is," yelled Kabir, "she's coming out of the wall, oozing out of the way with her gang, with her gang behind her. Ugh-ooooooooooow, it's Jamila's mother, no, no, I see her, I see her. Someone, someone get her away, away, away.'

I looked around the room but saw nobody but Decarrie who'd finally awakened from his trance. He rose pale in the face too, but to my astonishment, he was yelling like Kabir, "Yes, yes, yes, I see her, I see her Joseph. She's the one in the black shawl. What's that in her hands. Oh no Joseph, Joseph she carries a dagger."

Even though I was scarred out of my pants, I remained seated with my notepad and pencil taking notes and observing. What was going on? I didn't know. I didn't know.

'Decarrie, don't you see the mob she has behind, a mob that is pointing at me?'

'Don't panic Kabir," cried Decarrie. 'That's the worst thing you could do.'

'Decarrie look now, they're moving towards me, they're moving. How can I not panic when they're coming at me with their evil looking faces?'

Decarrie ran this way and that, back and forth through the Officers Lounge. 'Hold on Joseph. Be brave,' he belched. 'Don't let them do this to you.'

'Decarrie, they're getting closer,' screamed Kabir shrilly as he stood petrified in the middle of the floor. 'Do something, do something. I feel breathe on my face. Save me, please.'

Decarrie, his indecision over, took decisive action. Over to the pool table he raced, grabbing pool balls off the table. One, two, three, he let them fly, bash, bang, they smashed against the walls. I ducked behind my chair with notepad and pencil in hand, peering at the action from time to time wondering what the hell was going on.

'No good Decarrie, no good, they're still coming,' Kabir yelped. 'I can feel their saliva against my face now they're saliva. And ohhhhhhhh, look how the old woman is playing with the walls.'

Decarrie grabbed some more balls and threw them but with the same results as before. "My god, my Lord, my Existence!' Decarrie picked up a pool stick and with it ran up in front of Kabir using his body to shield him.

'Decarrie, Decarrie, what the hell are you two doing?' I yelled out from behind my chair.

'There's a crowd circling, a crowd nearing, a crowd closing in, there's a crowd out for Joseph's blood,' spurted Decarrie as he stood alongside Kabir swinging his pool stick back and forth fiercely through the air. 'An old lady, oh God, with a dagger is leading the vicious assault. Take that, take that bastards. They have stopped, the old lady has stopped, and I have stopped for the time being. Ah, the old lady laughs at us now. Oh no, oh no, she comes again, she comes again with her crowd and this time she will not stop.' Decarrie swung the stick more violently then ever while Kabir ran, Kabir hid, Kabir wiggled under the pool table.

'Why, why is the crowd clapping, why is Jamila's mother chanting? Yes, yes, yes, yes, ha, yes, ha, yes, yes." Kabir asked while stretched out under the pool table.

'I have no idea, no idea,' answered Decarrie, retreating a few steps. He broke his stick in two against his knees, and threw both pieces down. 'I have it, I have it Joseph." Decarrie extended his arms affectionately, lovingly, seeking an embrace from the invisible demons. There was a grin on his face. Now this was a ludicrous sight, I must admit.

'Come out from under the pool table,' Decarrie announced to Kabir. 'You must come and join me or you'll be dead within a matter of minutes, Joseph. Come, please, join me, come, please, let us face this together and bare our souls for them to see. Look, they don't harm me. See, they don't approach me. They stare. They remain like stone figures, but they don't hurt me. Come out Joseph or they will have won.'

Like a frightened child, Kabir arose from way down under with tears in his eyes. He stood before Decarrie and imitated his bodily form exactly.

'Wh-wh-why is the crowd circling us?' chattered Kabir. 'Wh-wh-why is the old lady jumping up and down whooping and hollering in some unknown language?'

'Be quiet Joseph and keep that grin on your face.'

'Decarrie,   working,   they're   stopping, Deeeeeeeeeeeeeeecarrrrrrrrrrie. What are they doing now? Oh God, God in heaven, this is it, this is it, they're all pulling out their daggers. Arms back, they're all ready to bye. . . .'
'Keep your chest out, don't be intimidated, that's it, that's it. Don't be afraid to fear, fear is good for you.'

'Nooooooooo, Decarrrrrrrrrrrrrrie, myyyyyyyyyyyyy. But look. Amazing. I can't believe it. A miracle. We're saved. They've all plunged the daggers into their own stomachs, and the old woman is retreating to the wall. Myyyyyyyyyy God thank you.'

'Joseph don't turn your head away. Look at how their blood flows. Now, now, now we have witnessed a true act of creation.'

Kabir and Decarrie both took a deep sigh of relief.

'Thank you Decarrie, thank you, thank you Decarrie,' yapped Kabir like a repeating rifle. 'You saved my life Decarrie, do you realize that?'

Both returned to their original places, the lounge chairs.

'Don't thank me Joseph, never. You saved your own life. You did it last night when you blew up your Department with everyone in it. You saved your life from wickedness and evil and at the same time may have saved others also.'

Decarrie glanced around the room while I peered out from behind my chair where I had been in hiding throughout the ordeal. "Hey Bombser," yelled Decarrie at me, "the coast is clear. You can come out."

*   *   *

I came out, yes, from hiding wanting explanations. But wanting and getting are two different things. I asked them if they had just staged the scene described above for my benefit. Were you deliberately acting mad, I asked Decarrie, to prove something to me? To prove what? Why? I deserve to know. The public deserves to know. But no answers were produced from their mouths. All either of them did was smirk back like two conspirators. I tried to use reason, explaining that they're never had been a crowd of old ladies in the room attacking them. What really had happened?

"You did not see them Bombser because you are not ready to see them. That is because you are one of them, one of them," Decarrie answered like a spook. He and Kabir now were perfectly serene. That angered me.

I wanted answers and answers quickly. I pumped them for straight answers but all I received was some mystical bull shit. Eventually I managed to hit upon a question which garnered something. It was in the form of another of Kabir's stories.
"Kabir," said I, "while you were screaming about the crowd, you mentioned the name Jamila. Does the name bear any significance?"

"Ha, ha, does the name have any significance did you say? You must be joking, Bombser?" cracked Kabir. "Jamila is the one who launched the conspiracy against me in the Department, the conspiracy that if it had succeeded would have blotted me off the face of the universe, of God's universe."

"Who exactly was Jamila?" I asked.

"Jamila was the assistant librarian of the Middle Eastern Studies Library, a harmless position yes, but one made deadly by Jamila, deadly and vicious.

The plot against me began on the third day of the term and third day in the Department. My classes had begun, one with Dr. Jefferson, another with Dr. Warly and another with Professor Majnoon Jazzar and in each of them, I was lost. They talked and I understood little. And I always had this feeling they were staring at me and secretly disapproved of me. Zeno Beneen was in all three of the classes but that didn't help much. The other students, they sat with hands folded glued to the words of the Professors. Heads were nodded occasionally but that was it; they never looked sideways, never looked at me, never looked at the windows or to the outside world. Questions were not allowed, questioning the world was not allowed, questioning facts was not allowed. You sat and accepted what was told to you; you sat and became what they told you to become. Of course, I knew something was wrong with this picture but I didn't care. My idea, I had to get through it, I had to succeed.

On this third day, I got a chance to visit the Department Library after my last class. It was located on the top floor of a building devoted to the university's science and medical departments. Why it was located here, I can't tell you. Anyway, journeying there I was filled with enthusiasm, that is, until I got out of the elevator. The floor, the hallway leading to the library I mean, was shrouded in darkness. There were no lights, there was nothing except the fierce odor of ammonia pervading every patch of darkness. No way could I see where I was going, But, I walked using the walls to guide me, a mistake which left me in no where land. This way and that I wandered with futility. Nothing to do then but go back downstairs and report the blackout to the janitor. Slowly I made my way back taking the same route as before, but when I reached the spot where the elevators had been, they were gone, disappeared. I was trapped, a prisoner. Terrified, I searched for the missing elevators only to find walls and emptiness.

I panicked which I shouldn't have. I ran. I smashed into one wall, then another, then another. I crawled and prayed for deliverance. That's when the yellow fireflies shining their yellow lights appeared to light my way. Above me they flew, showing me the way. I picked myself up and banged viciously on the row doors that now showed themselves before me. Nothing happened. For a while, I imagined my mind was going. Going crazy, was that it? The fireflies danced and flew over me giving me as much light as they could. But I wanted more light, I wanted more like a greedy slob. I wanted my own personal light so I grabbed up at the flies hoping to catch some. The flies stopped buzzing and flew up, out of reach of my greedy hands and disappeared, leaving me without any light at all. Out of sickness, out of loneliness, out of isolation, I laid myself down in the middle of the hall and cried and prayed once more, hoping, hoping.

Another miracle appeared before my eyes, this time in the shape of a ray of light. The ray pierced the hallway and cut my body in half. Where was it coming from? I scanned the hallway. There, I found its source, there. A round door with a square knob was opening with a growling noise. A foot wearing a white shoe slowly crept out as if to test the ground outside to make sure it was safe. I crawled towards the door on all fours. A young man belonging to the foot emerged from the door. He came with flashlight in hand. I yelled at him. Quickly he slammed the door behind him and turned his flashlight on me. I rose heading straight towards him while I shielded my eyes against the intensity of his light.

'Please, please help me, I can't get out of here, can't get out. Please could you either direct me to the Middle Eastern Studies Library or the elevator which seems to be missing.'

'What the fuckin' hell yah doing on this floor?' he shouted in inquiry. 'Nobody but a select few is allowed up here, and you ain't no select person I can tells. I never seen yah, youse a stranger to these parts, an outsider. But howse yah know the ex-is-tence of the library?'

'I'm in the Department, I'm one of the new students, really I am. So now, will you help me? Is the library through the door you just came out of?'

'I feel like spitting on yah pig. Always your tricks. I'm young, yes, but no fool. What's the real purpose of your visit?'
'What the hell are you talking about?'

"ZZZZZZZZZZZZZZZ, don't play dumb with me pig, not with me. You and your gosh-darn comrades have sought to destroy the Middle Eastern Department and its library for a long time. Well, you can't trick us. We knows youse guy, we knows your phony tricks.

Ha-ha, you go and tell the people who sent you, no wait their people, their animals, but tell them we can't be fooled. Now you get the heck out of here before I beat your face in with my flashlight. I might even kill you if I'm in the mood"

'Wait, I, I don't understand what you're talking about, but, I can prove I'm a student in the Department.' Hurriedly, I pulled out my student identification card and showed it to him. Thankfully, that convinced him. And he began to smile.

'Can you help me, direct me to the library?' I repeated my former request.

'Why sure partner,' said he nice and friendly-like. 'You're right in the immediate vicinity. It was the library I just came out from.'

I tried to push past his frame but it blocked the door. He wouldn't budge.

'You can't just go in there. You got to signal first before the door will be opened. Now here's what to do. You first kind-of easy-like knock on the door three times. Stop. Yell Allah three times. Stop. Give it a knock three more times. Stop. Say the name of that Dr. Jefferson twice. Stop. And finally, you got to knock on the door four quick knocks and wait. You gonna hear bells, then, and three seconds later the door will open slowly. Now you gotta quickly rush in and never look back or these evil consequences will follow you through the door. Now have you got it new student?"

"Yes, ah, I think. . . ."

"Gooooooooooood, good. Oh yeah, one more thing I gotta tell yah, never, under any circumstances, tell any non-Department people about the signal I taught you. You do that and I gots to hunt you down like a dog and kill you till you're dead as a doorknob. You understand?'

'Of course.'

He was off with that word, off down the hall. The only thing I could see of him anymore was the light emitted by his flashlight. Soon I heard an elevator slam and even the light was gone. I was rapped in a cloak of darkness once more.

*   *   *

The door loomed large before me, a door which was my salvation. Through it, I would leave the darkness far behind me. I performed the signal as instructed by the strange guy, heard the bells, watched the door open, and I flew in quickly without once looking behind me. Now that I was in, in, there standing before me was this smiling, gray-haired women with silver-framed glasses and a pointy nose. Her eyes shined, shined like a cat. Her head twitched, a pity inducing twitch. In her hand, she held a cup and saucer, the cup being filled to the brim with tea.

'My name's Alice,' she explained. 'Nice to see you, Mr. Kabir. We've been expecting you I think, I know, yes, I do believe you were expected. I should find out about that, yes. Ah, Mr. Kabir this tea is for you. Here. Why are your hands shaking. Come sit at the desk. You can sit alongside the desk and keep me company, yes, I think I'm supposed to keep you company but I'm not sure. It's too late to check it out now.'

I carefully looked around this small room which had maybe a hundred books suspended from hanging bookshelves placed here and there.

'Mr. Kabir, I see your eyes wandering. In explanation let me declare, this is the reference section. All your encyclopedias are here. Do you like it?'

'Ah, yes, nice.'

'Our library, yes it's ours, or does it officially belong to the University, Mm, I must check into that, our library with its one hundred thousand volumes, Mm, maybe it's two thousand, Jamila would know, she knows everything, well our library is through that white door in the back. Yes, it's through there, of that I'm sure.'

'Alice may I ask, how do you know my name?'

'Know why when someone knows it's really nice. I like to know when I can see, but why should I, it's Jamila's job not mine. Right or wrong?'

I just stared and opened my mouth and closed it.

'The library, big metal desks in there, cold to sit on when you wear a short skirt in the winter time. Everyone has there name on their desks, nice name tags. Jamila assigns the desks, and if you don't have a desk assigned to you then you can't go in, yes, yes, that's how it works I think but I'm not sure. All I know is that Jamila told me don't let Kabir enter the library, that's what she said exactly.'

'Who's this Jamila?'

'I like toast in the morning, toast while I read a book and drink down a nice glass of milk.'

'Yes, that's good. Who's Jamila?'

'Jamila is the assistant librarian, my boss, everyone's boss. Dr. Jefferson's boss. She's an important lady. I don't like plain tea, I like my tea with cream, two teaspoons of sugar, and a tablespoon of honey.'

'That's nice. Is this Jamila around?'

"My name's Alice."

"You already told me that."

"I work in the library as a helper, worked here ten years. Been a Ph.D. student here for fifteen years. Yes, I do believe fifteen. Have I really, Mm, really have I? Isn't that interesting."

Oh boy, how off your rockers can a person get.

'I always thought that the species of flowers they have in the Middle East are beautiful,' cracked Alice off the top of her head. "But one never knows why things happen like that now do we? If it is done right, wrapped tightly and securely, why then can't the Turkish peasant bring home Tulips to his wife, why can't he? I always have been a great believer in living and living well. It's fantastic.'

She now shut up for a second, staring at me with those shiny eyes of hers. Suddenly she cackled, 'Jamila, why Jamila, hello Jamila, yes Jamila.'

I twisted my head around and saw a middle-aged woman in a black satin dress with a yellow flower design emerge from behind the white door. This woman had long black hair twisted in a bun on top and a brownish-yellow complexion.

'Ooooooooow, look who's here, look who's here. Mr. Kabir, welcome, welcome. I'm sorry I wasn't here to greet you when you arrived but I was busy in the back dealing with two disruptive students. My name is Jamila.'

'Hello. How do you know my name?'

'Alice, would you go into Mr. Jabarti's office. He wants to see you,' said Jamila.

'Oh, that's nice,' answered Alice as she scampered out the door as quick as a flash.

Jamila sat herself behind the desk next to me. 'So Mr. Kabir how do you like the tea?'

'It's excellent.'

'Splendid, splendid. I'm glad you could make it, very glad.'

Interestingly enough Jamila pulled out a notepad and pencil from her desk and began to sketch me. When I bent over to get a closer look she cried, "No, no, Mr. Kabir, no peeking is permitted."

Finishing the sketch quickly, Jamila then carefully scrutinized it. 'Mr. Kabir,' said Jamila, 'would you allow me to run my hands along the contours of your face. It is important for me to determine your facial dimensions and bone structure.'

Before I had a chance to answer, she had her hands all over my face, running them slowly over my eyes, mouth, chin, neck, nose, forehead, and hair. Next, she grabbed my hand, examined it, examined my wrist, and examined my arm. When that was done, she took another look at my sketch, tore off a piece of paper from her notepad and wrote a lot of figures down on it.

'May I ask, what you are doing?' inquired I.

'Of course, asking is free like the air is free, you may ask. I've been jotting down figures here based on observation to determine your race type, and I must say I have very good news for you.'

'Huh?'

'Hm, I see you are somewhat perplexed. I shall explain it to you. For years, determining a person's race type has been a hobby of mine. I've studied and read all the books on the subject. I am one of the greatest authorities on the subject of face type in this university. Now, race type can be determined by measuring the person's bone structure, cranium size, body build, and various facial characteristics. And now for the good news, I have determined that you, without a doubt, are of noble stock. Now tell me how you feel about this? Please be concise!'

'Well, to be honest, I never believed much in racial theories. If a person has a good heart, that's what is really important to me.'

Jamila made a hideous face. For a minute there, I thought she was going to scratch my eyes out.

"Jamila, why are there no lights in the hall and why, may I ask, must one use a signal in order to gain entrance to the library?" questioned I, changing the subject.

Jamila played with her pencil while a young girl with red hair, red shirt, and red jeans skirted out of the white door, smiled at me, said hello to Jamila and soon was out of the main reference room door.

"My Kabir, let me tell you the girl that just left is such an atrocious person, so vile. A horrible student also, just horrible. Would you believe she received two C's last year and one D. How embarrassing it is for the Department! I've talked to Dr. Jefferson about her. Something will be done about her, you can be assured of that. When another term rolls around next fall, mark my words on it, she will not longer be with us, mark my words."

Jamila unbelievably began talking about me, about anything and everything that ever happened in my life, about my schooling, my parents, my sister, about all the part-time jobs I ever had, about past girl friends. My God, she knew more about my life thank I knew. I asked, and asked, and asked how she knew so much about me, but Jamila just ignored my questions and then rattled off a few more intimate details about my life. I was getting very mad, but alas, my fear of her and the power I felt she had in the Department held me back.

'You are a Christian, Mr. Kabir, I know this also, marvelous, marvelous,' blew Jamila from out of the woods. 'There are many of us here, nineteen at the last count. We are catching up to the Muslim population in the Department. Not that I have anything against the Muslims, but, I must be quite forthright and say that they do stink. Take it from me who has been around them. Yet, we must deal with them as best we can, try to tolerate tem because they are in the majority here. It is upsetting. We live in the realm of Christendom and yet we are surrounded by Muslims who line the halls of the Department. It is unbearable. These lower-class Muslims, who are nothing less than Gypsies, ruling over us. I fear them, their numbers, I fear that they will overwhelm us; they come in bunches and swarm. They took Spain and the Middle East away from us and if we are not careful they will take North America away.'

About then a small, dark-skinned man came strolling out through the white library door carrying two books in hand. 'I wish to take these books out of the library,' said the man as he approached the desk.

Jamila took the books from him, stamped them, noted them, gave them back to him and then exclaimed, 'How is your head Hasan? A little better, I hope? Has your wife left on her vacation yet? You'll miss her, won't you, Hasan? What a beautiful lady you married. What intelligence. What charm. I have no doubts that she could win any beauty contest she entered.'

'Yes, yes, yes, that's true,' grinded out Hasan. 'Thank you very much, thank you. I shall tell my wife what you said. Thank you.'

'Hasan, I want you to meet Joseph Kabir, Joseph Kabir I want you to meet Hasan.' Hasan extended his small hand in greeting.

'Hasan, Joseph is a Christian,' swiped Jamila.

'Nice, nice,' answered Hasan.

'Joseph, Hasan over here is a Muslim from black Africa'"

'Mm, yes, Mm, yeah,' said I with profundity while Hasan collected his books, nodded, gave Jamila a long flashy smile, and departed.

When Hasan was no longer any where to be seen, Jamila took out her tongue which substituted as a knife and cut, 'What a dumb Muslim that one is. Now you see first hand what the Department is faced with. The quality of these people is so very low that it is appalling. What a pity how our once magnificent Department is being infiltrated by the likes of them. Maybe it wouldn't be so bad if they were white Muslims from semi-civilized countries. But a lot of our students are black Africans, black Malaysians, and Negroid Pakistanis and Indonesians. The Pakistanis are by fare the worst of their lot. Oh, whenever they come and talk with me, I can just die, they all suffer from bad breath, all of them. I was talking with a new student yesterday, Zeno Beneen by name, and he just told me one horror tale after another about what those people are doing to London. How dare they attack such a Christian enclave! It's just terrible.'

I was upset by her words and attempted to voice an opinion, but she stopped me even before I began.

'Would you like more tea, Mr. Kabir?'

'Ah. . . .'

Bursting through the white door at that second was a balding young man with pinkish complexion, long pointy nose, and plump rosy cheeks. To Jamila's side he rushed with a crazed look in his eyes. He had his derriere in my face as he spoke.

'Jamila, Jamila,' he shrieked with urgency. 'I'm hungry, famished, dying for a bit to eat. Will you call up Barney's Diner and ask them to send over two peanut butter sandwiches, two packs of French fries, and a vanilla milk shake?'

'Oh, so you're hungry. Why don't you eat properly. Haven't I warned you time and time again, what can happen when a person eats junk foods, haven't I warned you. You don't want to die at forty now, do you? How long has it been, how many days on end, have you enclosed yourself in the library doing research? Twenty days, isn't it?'

'No, it's only been twelve since I visited the outside world, but who's counting.'

'You should go out a little bit. A little air is always good. Go to a nice restaurant and stuff that face of yours. It will do you a world of good. Listen to Jamila.'

'I can't Jamila. I have no time, no time, no time for that. Please, won't you call up Barney's for me?' As he said that, he shook his behind in my face, forcing me to lean as far back as I could to avoid catastrophe.

'Of course I'll call for you. Doesn't Jamila always do everything for you. Mm, and I tell you what, I will order an extra milk shake for you, my treat. You must eat, eat, eat to keep up your strength. So now go back to your studies and let Jamila do the rest.'

He turned, turned, turned and whizzed by me as he was off to the library once more. Jamila placed his order as promised. 'Isn't he a nice young man,' yapped Jamila to me. I nodded affirmatively. 'Very well behaved and respectful. He's been in the Department working on his Ph.D. nine years now. I can remember when he first joined us, a child then like you. But the years, the passing years, have done him a world of good. I like him, I like the Jew. We have three with us now. Like the Muslims, they're on the increase. Time was when he was the only one here, but gradually, they have crept in. I don't really mind them. Usually, they don't give me much trouble. But I teeeeeeeeeeeeeeeeeeeeell yoooooooooooooooooooooou, they are bossy, bossy as can be. Ah, and what big mouths they can open when they don't get their way. It's. . . .'

A baby began crying in the hallway. Jamila rushed to the door, listened with ear to door, opened, and then zoomed out. From where I sat, I could hear Jamila trumpet, "Oh, Sayyar, what a beautiful baby you have. Kutchy, kutchy, kutchy-coo, baby, kutchy, kutchy-coo." Jamila reentered the reference room holding a chunky black baby with big puffy cheeks in her arms. The baby's father followed two steps behind pushing the baby's stroller.

Jamila set the baby on the desk and began tickling it. 'Isn't baby cute,' dribbled Jamila sweetly and with lips puckered. 'Give me a smile baby, give auntie Jamila a big smile.' The baby sucked passively on Jamila's finger.

'What's his name, Sayyar?' asked Jamila.

'Muhammad,' answered Sayyar.

'You gave him a Muslim name, how nice,' responded Jamila as she gave me a quick, sinister look of disapproval while I played with little Muhammad.

'Isn't he some boy,' burst Sayyar. "Look how big, bigger than most baby's his age. See how large his hands and feet are. He's going to be tall when he grows up, aren't you little fellow. Oh Jamila, I must tell you what a good boy Muhammad is. Never cries. My wife and I are so happy.'

'He's one in a million, one in ten million,' shoveled Jamila. 'And such a beautiful child. Mr. Kabir, just look how big his eyes are. Gorgeous, absolutely gorgeous. And, oh how I love those wonderful cheeks of his, love-love-love. I could eat them all up. Yummy for the tummy, yummy for the tummy. He's just darling, just darling.'

'Jamila would you watch my son for a minute?' Sayyar asked. 'There are some books in the library I must get.'

Sayyar took leave of us while Jamila watched Sayyar's retreating movements like a cat. When the coast was clear, Jamila hurriedly pulled down the baby's shirt, and pointing to his uncovered back, explained, "I wondered, Mm, wondered, Mm, I've been studying up on it, studying up, Mm. Look how dark the skin on his back is compared to the color of his face. It is very strange. To be frank, it bothers me to see such black skin as this, Mr. Kabir. I never have trusted anyone with skin as dark as this. It is a know fact that the darker the skin, the more Godless a person is, unless, of course, they accept Jesus as their Savior.' Jamila remove the rest of the baby's outfit and examined the rest of his body, particularly his genitalia. 'He's going to be a big one; but they usually are,' she cracked. 'Christianity is the only faith that can tame their basic inbreed needs to fornicate.'

Why didn't I say something, do something. Ah, today, the Kabir of today would have done something. But then, I was like a little mouse and let things happen, let people be people, I let Jamila be a monster and just sat and smiled like ass hole.

Jamila began feeling around the baby's head. 'A very small cranium like most Africans. The child will never be bright, his brain is too small I'm afraid.' In preparation for Sayyar's return, she quickly redressed the baby and just in time as he returned with books.

'Have you been a good boy for Jamila?' asked Sayyar of his son. The child wheezed, sniffled, and burst into a sobbing wail. 'That's funny,' exclaimed a startled Sayyar. 'He was in such a good mood a few minutes ago. Mm, I wonder what's the matter?'

"Who knows what makes a baby cry, Sayyar," cracked Jamila. "You shouldn't analyze such things. He could be hungry, he could be coming down with a cold, he could be a wet. But I wouldn't be concerned. Babies cry that is what they do. You must accept this and listen to wise, Jamila.'

'You are right, yes, yes,' answered Sayyar as he picked his son off the desk and fitted him into his stroller. With his books in one arm and the stroller in the other Sayyar said his goodbyes and was off while Jamila ran behind and yelled down the hallway, 'you're son is such a love. Please do bring him up to the library again.' Returning to her desk then, she started talking to me again, 'I lived in Spain for some years pursuing my studies. On those Spaniards are so exquisite, so exquisite indeed. They have manners; they know the proper way to act. For a year, I was there before I became bored and moved on to France where I dabbled with higher education at the Sorbonne for a time. I became cultured there, and in fact, I can say without a doubt that Paris made me the sophisticated person I am today. You know that I can speak French fluently.'

In the middle of her banter, she extended her arm to the bookshelf near her and in one sweeping motion, like an avaricious condor, brought down a cake box. 'Doughnut, have a jelly doughnut,' said she, pushing the opened cake box in front of my nose. 'They're good for you, very good. Doctors are now prescribing them for patients with heart disease. Mm. Come, come Mr. Kabir, take one!'

'No thank you, I never eat Jelly doughnuts.'

'You never eat jelly doughnuts. Okay, I see. That's fine. Everyone has his own personal preferences and that's all right. As for me, I simply adore jelly doughnuts. My aunt, who has now passed away, used to come to my house when I was a child. I still remember the greasy brown paper bag they came in. Oh what a lady she was, what a lady.' Jamila strolled over to the white library door, opened, and yelled, 'Jelly doughnuts, I have fresh jelly doughnuts here. Would any of you students in here care for a freshly baked jelly doughnut? First come, first serve.'

Shouts of, 'No thank you. Jamila, no thank you,' reverberated throughout the library. However, there was one exception. A tiny cry of yes intermixed itself with the other declarations. This yes was followed by a pleasant looking lad with reddish, brown hair. Through the white door he came, stopping at Jamila's desk. She reached into the box and gave the lad his doughnut.

'Gee thanks,' cried the lad, looking at her and smiling. 'Jamila you're the greatest. You've been like a big sister to me.' The lad then turned to me. 'I don't know what I would have done without Jamila. When I first entered the Department, I was new in town, all alone, and knowing nothing about anything. But there was Jamila. Right away, she took an interest, helped me, advised me, and listened to my problems. Where would I be today without her.'

Jamila blushed some, said thank you three times and then inquired of him, "Have you submitted your thesis proposal to the board yet?"

'Yes,' responded the lad dejectedly. 'The board turned it down.'

'What was your thesis topic again? I've forgotten.'

'Middle Eastern music. What I proposed was to trace its origins and development down through the ages. I spent months researching the topic. For the life of me, I can't understand why they turned it down, I can't understand. Nobody in the Department has ever written on music so I just took it for granted that it would pass. When it didn't, I swear I almost had a nervous breakdown.'

'Oh my! How could they possibly turn down your thesis proposal,' roared Jamila. 'You're topic sounds quite marvelous to me. I can't believe the board members; they doesn't know what it's doing. What conservative idiots, what incompetent fools. I can't tell you how terrible I feel for you. It's all so horrible, so dreadfully horrible.'

'Yes, yes, yes, yes, it is horrible,' cried the lad, 'sickening, maddening, God damn it. But, there's nothing I can do about it, Jamila. All that's left for me is to some how revise my topic and submit it again.'

'A good attitude to take, I must say, but, I'm still angry.'

"So am I but that's the way it goes.' He looked at his watch, then. 'I have to be running back into the library now. Thanks a million for the doughnut. I'll eat it at my desk while I revise my thesis proposal.'

The guy had begun to open the white door to the library when Jamila stopped him, yelling, "Wait, wait, wait," reached up to the bookshelf above the desk and pulled down a napkin and then gave it to him. 'Take it!' she barked. 'Jelly doughnuts are so messy. We wouldn't want the jelly getting over all our nice old books, now would we?'

The lad did as instructed and then vanished behind the white door. Jamila and I were alone once more. 'Oh what a fool that young fellow is,' cackled Jamila. 'How can anyone in this Department even contemplate writing a thesis about Middle Eastern music. Do you think the board would, for a second, approve an exotic topic like that. I'm beginning to wonder if that young man has any brains in his head. Maybe I've always wondered. Brains him? Do you know what he did? He, of his own free will, converted from the Christian faith to the Muslim one. That was a few years ago and I've never understood. Why would somebody born into a civilized world into a wonderful, true religion, actively seek to become a savage. It doesn't make sense. I lost all respect for him from that point. How can you respect anybody who weakens and demeans our faith.'

'Well it doesn't really. . . .'

I was interrupted by knocking. Someone was rapping out the signal on the reference room door to which Jamila responded. Dr. Jefferson entered. Not even acknowledging me, he grunted something or other in Jamila's ear and both disappeared together through the white door. Before leaving, she instructed me to wait at her desk. For ten minutes, I waited, wanting to leave, to get out of the library and away from Jamila. But, I felt constrained to stay though, fearing getting on the wrong side of that powerful woman. Another ten minutes I waited before I made up my mind to leave. I would say goodbye to Jamila first though it meant journeying into the mysterious library.

Entering the forbidden zone through the white door, I encountered row after row of books stacks along with sweltering heat and a lack of air movement. Between the narrow spaces left by the room were desks with students manning them. Where to begin searching for Jamila? I walked up and down the rows, in and out weaving until I heard her voice. I closed in, stop and listened. She was talking to Dr. Jefferson.

'I am watching the situation closely,' Jamila was saying.
'Good, good,' returned Jefferson. 'Have you compiled the list for me?'

'Of course. Did you even have to ask? Here it is.'

'Mm, Mm, well done Jamila, well done. This list will prove useful. So I think that about does it. Is there anything else?'
'One more thing, that new student Kabir. . . .' I moved closer. 'He's going to be trouble. I am interrogating him now and all I can say is he's different from us. The fire in him burns high. Something must be done immediately. We must build a cell around him to isolate the contagion before it effects the others. Ultimately, we must find a way to destroy the house he lives comfortably in around his fireplace. We must not only make him homeless but destroy the fireplace. We have done it with others. We can do it with him.'

'If you think it's necessary, okay. I trust your judgment on things Jamila. You are generally right most of the time. Okay, then I shall spread the word to everyone and we shall start building on the sight of Kabir. I think we shall turn out a worthwhile product, don't you.'

'Of course, we usually do, well almost always do anyway.'

What was I to think about it all. I was bewildered by their words, stupefied, uncomprehending. What did they mean when they talked about building on the sight of Kabir? What type of mumbo-jumbo is that? And what was that shit about tearing out my fireplace? Symbolic crap, a code, what did it mean? Later I learned it all meant conspiracy.

I was shaking now. I wouldn't let anyone know what I had heard. I would pretend but keep my eyes open. I couldn't face anyone now, not Jamila, not anyone. I felt this uneasy burning feeling in my stomach. It made me want to be alone, it made me realize I had to be alone, alone to sort everything out I had seen and heard. Out of the library, out of the reference room, and out into the dark hallway, I ran recklessly. I charged through the darkness with abandon, not once banging into any walls. And thank God, the elevator was waiting for me. Quickly I entered, quickly and quickly I was gone.

CHAPTER 9

Kabir was visibly shaken by the scene he had just described. Spittle rolled down one side of his mouth as if he were a baby. His face had turned deathly pale and he quivered uncontrollably. Decarrie humanely put his coat over his shoulders and that seemed to help as did the hot coffee he gave him. Notwithstanding Kabir's shaken position, I plowed on with questions while the plowing was good.

"Kabir," said I. "What I don't understand is that after you supposedly overheard the conversation between the librarian and Department head and after facing nothing but bizarre situations from day one, why did you stay in the program? Why didn't you just drop out?"

"I thought about it, of course I did, I thought about it seriously. But something, my fear of failure made me stay. Dropping out of the department my third day, how would that have appeared to family and friends who sent me off like a conquering hero and who expected great things from me. Yeah, but it was more than that, yeah. I think I stayed out of curiosity. Ever since I was a child, people had looked at me differently, always shaken their heads the moment I spoke. It was as if I was a criminal, that's it, they viewed me as some outsider, criminal, enemy of all. Believe me, it's not my imagination. I always ran from them, the people, never tried to understand what it was about me that made everyone react. I decided to stand my ground now and try to understand what I was being accused of, what crime. All my life people had accused me of things with their eyes and actions, things I didn't understand, but now I would solve the mystery. It didn't matter if I would be treated as the social leper. Finding the truth was the most important thing. And I had confidence I would find the truth in the Department, I had confidence that the Department would tell me why, why, why and show me how, how, how to fix whatever was wrong with me and make me a better human being, happy, healthy and accepted by all.

*   *   *

My stay in the Department, time passing, three months, six months, nine months, and before long almost two years. All the time spent were packed, tension packed, incredibly packed until I ended it all with my purifying bomb. The conspiracy against me began the day following the overheard conversation between Jamila and Dr. Jefferson. I became a hunted man, a wanted man. They were out for me, they were out to tear my heart out and replace it with a mold. They were wood carvers seeking to hollow out my insides.

Time passing, me alone, and they against me. Throughout, thoughts of Vladimir and our encounter kept returning. But where had he gone? Vladimir was no where to be seen. I looked for him on the streets but he had disappeared from my life as mysteriously as he had appeared. Maybe he could explain it to me, my life, and the attitudes of others toward me, maybe he could reveal what was hidden. But it was no use. He was gone and I was alone to face the firing squad. Who did I have for friends, Zeno Beneen? He made sure to keep his distance from me throughout the ordeal, although from time to time he'd sit down with me in the Student Lounge to advise me on structuring my future for success. I eventually learned to just keep walking whenever he approached. There was also Stan Lord, but I avoided him too. All this talk of Iran and its wonders and how I should admit my Iranian heritage wore on me to the point where I thought of murdering the guy on the spot. I made no other friends, not really. I couldn't make any friends. I could not reach out. It was not allowed to me. So there was nobody for me, nobody but them.

Everyone was in on the conspiracy, students and Professors alike. My life was made into hell. My classes, ha, ha, were more like courts for witches, with the students and Professors being the judge and jury and me playing the witch. Nobody in class ever took their eyes off me, not even the Professor. From time to time, they would all leave their seats and huddle in the back of the room and whisper about me, or, make strange faces at me behind my back. They made fun of the way I folded my hands in class, the way I got out of my chair, the way I walked and talked, they made fun of everything I did. Pretty soon I began thinking there was something wrong with me, something terrible wrong. I've became self-conscious of everything I did. Oh boy, did I ever get the treatment. It was a regular practice of my Arabic Professor, Professor Majnoon Jazzar to stand me up for the last fifteen minutes of his class and have all the students judge me openly one at a time. At the end of the week, the Professor would then sum up all the remarks of the students and add his professional opinion. Everything said was defamatory, that I was a fool, an idiot, a moron, a worm, a cockroach, etc., etc., etc. And this also took place in my classes with Dr. Jefferson, Dr. Warly and with everyone else on staff. But I received a certain pleasure standing up before them all, pleasure because my inferiority which I had always believed in was being confirmed by them.

What else would they do to me? Professors would interrupt their lessons to ask me these strange questions that for the most part I couldn't answer. Even if I could answer, the Professor would automatically yell incorrect, incorrect Kabir, Kabir you are an uncommon, unintelligent turtle whose answers are inane. Aren't Kabir's answers inane, class? Yes, they would always answer as one. More scolding. Your talk is not becoming to a scholar. You must change your ways. You are no good, no good, not good, I repeat, no good. Got that Kabir? Meekly I would shake my head in affirmation while the rest of the class grinned. I made special effort to avoid walking in the hallways because people literally appeared out of nowhere and yelled from behind me, "Kabir is stupid, Kabir is a criminal, Kabir is a convict, Kabir is a black spot on the lung of mankind. Kabir smells up everything." Professors clustered in groups in the middle of the hallways to discuss my sickness and as I passed they pointed at me, then held conferences about me, plotting, plotting I say, the strategy that was to be used against me.

I should say in his behalf that Dr. Jefferson was a little more straight forward with me. I had been in the Department perhaps six months when he hauled me into his office, demanding I learn every fact there was to know about the Middle East and giving me an end of the year deadline to do so. I would be tested then to see if I had learned all my facts properly. If I, God forbid, didn't, I might just be thrown out bodily from the Department. Not only was I to learn all the facts, but once I did I was to never answer anyone using my own mind but only regurgitate the facts as my reply. I did study, I did obey Dr. Jefferson's demands but I failed. I was tested, got few facts straight, but was never thrown out of the Department. Nobody ever threw me out. I was never failed. I was always passed. Nobody was ever failed in the Department, nobody.

Another time Professor Osman Seljuk, who taught Turkish Studies and one of the new members of the Department, grabbed me, in the men's room no less and physically shook me up. I was taking a course with him on modern Middle Eastern history. He was the only Professor who had not singled me out; one of the few who treated me at all fairly. But now, he was coming at me.

"Kabir, you fool why do you attack all us, why?' he growled at me amidst the bathroom porcelain. 'Who the hell are you man, who the hell? Why don't you listen to all the people who have been here trying to help you. I want you to totally forget about yourself, totally forget. Make believe you have amnesia, that's all you have to do. Then when you are totally free from your stupid self, you'll find it easy to like all of us in the Department. It will then be just a matter of imitation, that's all. Do it, Kabir, do it." Gradually he eased his grip on my arms. "Believe me I am your ally here. I am trying to help you. I understand that this is difficult. Just conform, that is all that is being asked, conform to the wishes of the crowd. Life is majority rule, the sooner you learn this the better." Professor Osman Seljuk then wished me well and departed.

Oh, and there was good-old, Professor Betsy Smith who took a special interest in me. During my second semester, I took a class with her on Islamic Education. Once a week, she'd call me into her office. Like a mother she'd say to me, "There is potential in you, I know it, I know it, it's there somewhere, I know it, I know it. But, I must tell you honestly my son, the path you have chosen is the wrong one, it's archaic, prehistoric, and idiotic. Listen to me, son, you'll never be accepted either in this Department or in life if you don't change your ghastly ways. I am willing to give my time to make something of you, to tutor you. If you agree, we will study together the various educational programs which presently exist in North America and the Middle East. Education will become your life like it is mine, like it is mine. Think it over Mr. Kabir."

I thought it over as I thought over every proposal a Professor made to me. But I never understood and never could agree. There was something in me that made me not agree, as there was something in me that made me never understand the source of my own sickness and criminality. One of the funniest of my experiences came one day when four fellow students - they were all scowling and looking sinister - corralled me in the hallway and demanded I follow them to the gym. One of them was Mr. Outi who was the unofficial leader of the Muslim students in the Department. He was a small, thin and dark man with a thick Middle Eastern accent. He was none for his piety and his hatred of Christians and other non-Muslims. He led his fellow Muslims in prayer five times a day. Anyway, these four fellow approached me led me to the gym, took me to the basketball court and stood me before the net. Mr. Outi proceeded to lecture me on the value of physical fitness while the others man-handled me into doing push-ups and exercises on the parallel bars. "You must develop your body," yapped they in unison. "Your body, your outsides are the most important part of you, the only part anyone cares about, remember that. You must take care of your body. Give it all your attention. Every day you must come to the gym and work out."

Everything considered, the worst part of the conspiracy was the laughing. Being made the butt of laughter didn't help my self-esteem. Everywhere I went they followed, laughing, even to my apartment they followed and laughed. They spread the word about me to ordinary citizens on the street and they too laughed at me, everyone laughed at me, everyone. I was on the verge of suicide, I really was.

*   *   *

"Kabir, you paint a very passive picture of yourself," exclaimed I, Bombser. "But your action last night was not passive, by no means was it. It seems that your seething anger - which had always been directed against yourself - had turned outward against the Department. Up until then you had a classic self-hater, lacking confidence and always feeling inferior. Then, in a flash that all changed. When did this change cover over you?"

"That's another long story, Bombser, a story which I'm not sure you want to hear."

"I've listened to plenty of your long stories so I can listen to this one."

"Yes, tell us Joseph, please tell us," Decarrie sang. He was walking back and forth across the Officers Lounge drinking a cup of coffee. "Please, be frank with the gentlemen, Joseph. That's why he's here."

"Okay, you asked for it. The change started coming over me, the realization of the true state of affairs the last time I went to see my thesis advisor, Professor Osman Seljuk. Let me explain something before I go on about department policy. Each of the Department's new students were required to write a thesis on a topic approved by the Department's Thesis Board first. The thesis was supposed to be completed by the end of the new student's first year in the Department. If not the student would not be granted a degree and would still be required to take the Department's classes. The catch in all of this way that putting together a thesis proposal for the topic you selected often took months of research and then presented to the Thesis Board for its approval. The Board met only twice a year. If it rejected the student's proposal, which it did in ninety-nine percent of the cases, they had wait another six months before it could submit another proposal. Often students could be turned down, five, ten, fifteen, twenty times. Some new students had been in the Department five, ten, twenty years. Professor Osman Seljuk had been assigned my thesis advisor - he had refused at first like every other Professor, but Dr. Jefferson had forced him as fairly new to the Department to take the job. My thesis proposal had already been rejected three times by the Thesis Board. It claimed that they saw little scholarship in any of my proposals.

All this meant, I was completing my second year in the Department and I was no closer to getting any sort of degree or of losing my status as a new student. On this day when all was revealed to me, I went to see Professor Osman Seljuk about my latest thesis proposal, which I was about to present to the Board as well as to voice my ultimate frustration with the entire process. Innocently, I journeyed to Seljuk's office as I had many, many times before, but when I got there his door was opened, which was unusual, and a green light was shining out. What was this? How odd! I walked inside and like a classic horror film, the door slammed shut behind me, and a small dark little man, wearing a green suit, a blue tie, and a beard trimmed very close, very close to his face, appeared from behind the door.

"I've seen you before, sir, I know I've seen you before," he exclaimed to a stupefied me. In appearance, he was not only odd but looked like a little devil. He turned his head peculiarly towards me, then and exclaimed, "I, Mr. Outi, am the leader of all the Muslims in the department."

What? He didn't look at all like the real Mr. Outi. Odd. There was something wrong. What was this imposter doing in Seljuk's office. Was he here to see the Professor also? Before I could ask him anything, he suddenly crumpled up and fell to the floor. I rushed over to his side and tried to help him back on his feet but he refused. Instead, he just lay there staring up at the ceiling.

"Are we stuck?" he bizarrely asked.

"Stuck where?"

"Oh, my, oh, my, we are stuck."

"Stuck where?"

"In the elevator, in the elevator."

I ran straight for the door and twisted and turned it's knob to open but it wouldn't open. The door without a lock was locked, how, how, how? I don't know, know, know.

"Allah, Allah, Allah, forgive me Allah, forgive me," screamed the guy from behind me. "Do not try to press the emergency button. We shall not escape from this elevator, there is no escape for us, for me, none."

I ran back to him, bent down over him, and exclaimed, "What, what are you talking about elevators for? This is no elevator Outi or whatever your real name is. This is a Professor's office, a Professor's office."

"I am being punished, punished, oh Allah, oh Allah, forgive me," said little Outi putting his hand to head.

"What are you being punished about?"

"Punished for straying from the path of Allah. It clearly states in the holy Koran, Allah's book, chapter six, verse twelve that he who shies away from self activity will fall into the deepest of pits, pits filled with the most evil genies and ghouls. Oh, oh Allah, Allah,

Allah, I know I should have taken the staircase. I am a sinner, a sinner."

"Fellah, fellah, you're not in an elevator, fellah please don't say you're in an elevator," I pleaded with him more worried about my sanity than his.

"I am a sinner, a sinner. A true good Muslim does not use elevators, no he doesn't. We shall not get out of here. We shall perish, I shall perish for disobeying Allah's commands."

The little guy started pulling out his hair by the roots and beating his chest with his fists. In fear, I moved as far away from him as I could. Outi soon calmed himself, picked himself up somewhat, balanced on his knees, and did three Muslim prayer prostrations while mouthing something or other in Arabic. Once more, I rushed to the door in hope that it might be open now. But unfortunately, it was not. "We're trapped," I yelled.

Meanwhile, the little guy had crawled over to a large file cabinet at the side of the office and made like he was pressing elevator buttons. I tried to reason with the fellow, and make him understand where he was. "Look see the desk? See the brown wooden desk over there. Now are desks in elevators?" I lifted up a chair. "See this chair. Are chairs in elevators? Are pictures of a Professor's wife in elevators? How can this be an elevator, Outi? Look around. We're trapped inside a Professor's office."

"I have always been a good Muslim, you know."

"Did you hear what I said, Outi? We're trapped."

"Yes, yes, we're trapped in an elevator. But why do you concern yourself with such a thing?"

"Who are you?" I yelled. "Why are you playing games? Are you trying to make me go crazy or what? Tell me the truth!"

"Your anxiety is uncalled for. Our safety as is our faith are in the hands of Allah, and we cannot fight his will. I believe he has ordained that I should die so there is nothing to do now except sit and wait. Allah knows best."

My body shook all over. My head felt feverish. I had a terrible closed in, isolated feeling. Slowly I realized the guy didn't just happen to be here, he was put here, put in the office. This was some sort of attack on me, it just had to be.

"I am a lover of Allah, Allah the powerful. He is a king with a long beard like Solomon. But Allah is more powerful than any king. He is the Lord of the Universe. It states this very thing in the Koran, the holy bible of us Muslims, which I have memorized from cover to cover and can recite. Tell me the chapter you want and I will recite, any chapter."

"Are you a loon or is it me?"

"Allah decides all. Allah guides us through his prophets the greatest of which is the Prophet Muhammad. Allah is so wise, so wise."

I belted myself over the head continuously trying to bring myself back to reality, trying as hard a I could but I was already living through reality.

"No need to hit yourself Kabir, no need," Outi suddenly honked in a very lucid voice. He rose for the first time, opened up a draw in the filing cabinet and took out a big white sack. From his pocket, he pulled out a yellow piece of paper and pen. Then with pen and paper and white sack in hand, he came towards me with such an evil look in his eye that I picked up a chair to ward him off.

"You're an infidel, Kabir, a barbarian, a non-Muslim, a non-Muslim, that has to change now," Outi yelped.

Still holding the chair as a weapon, I ran frantically to the door and used the chair as a battering ram. The door wouldn't budge. Outi got closer.

"Kabir, you don't believe in the Koran, you don't believe in the Prophet Muhammad. You don't believe in Allah. You must die Kabir, you must die." The only thing that was kept him off me was the chair. Outi waved his paper and sack cloth at me then. "Kabir, Dr. Jefferson wants you to convert, he wants you to become a Muslim and you will become one, you will, this elevator won't start again until you do. All you have to do, Kabir, is sign my yellow paper, sign it, that's all and then remove your clothes and put on this white cloth. We will be going on a little trip."

"Stay away or I'll smash you over the head with this chair, stay away. Leave me alone."

"As Allah is my maker, I will not leave you alone. We will never leave you alone. Constantly we will hack at you, wear you down, and seep into your brain."

Outi quickly flung himself at my legs trying to trip me, to make me fall, to lower me to earth. But I outmaneuvered him by hoping on top of the Professor's desk. I still held the chair in hand. Outi wasn't discouraged. He crept towards me. "You shall become a Muslim like me and my father, the greatest of all Muslims. I shall instruct you in your religion. I shall make you memorize the Koran. You shall know every law of Islam."

"I don't want to know every law, I don't want to know any law. I don't want to be like you, a miserable, unfeeling object.' Something was beginning to happen to me, something I knew not what.

"You don't want to be like me, this is a crazy thought. I am the greatest of all Muslims, didn't you hear. I lead all of them in the Department. I know the Koran and all the glorious sayings of the Prophet Muhammad by heart. I am honored by students and teachers alike for my knowledge. I led the prayers at the Friday meetings of all the Muslims at the university. My father, my wonderful father, leads the prayers at the largest mosque in Pakistan. I am very pious. I look down on anyone not a Muslim. I now will make you a Muslim."
Outi tried to scale the desk but I shoed him off with a kick in the head.

"Kabir, you will go on the holy pilgrimage with me to the birthplace of the Prophet, Mecca, the holiest city in the world. You will sign the paper, put on the cloth and come or you will never, ever escape from the elevator. I shall not escape no matter what happens because I have sinned, but you Kabir, you have a chance. Sign."

I threw the chair at him and it hit squarely, felling him. What happened next, though, is very fuzzy. A terrible pain erupted in the pit of my stomach, a terrible nauseating throbbing pain. My stomach was burning virtual fire. I could feel my stomach lining, my liver, my gall bladder, my appendix, being burned away. I felt dizzy, lost my balance, fell from the desk. Bang, but I was all right. The pain remained. It was intense, intense. I rose, banged on all the walls, screamed. Outi began coming around, he began coming at me again with the paper and sack cloth. I couldn't take my pain. I plunged to the floor thinking I would never rise again.

My eyes, they were burning now, my eye sockets were melting from the heat. Outi stood over me in stunned awe with mouth open. My eye sockets melted over my eyes almost entirely obstructing my vision. I could now barely see, but what I saw, what I saw was enough. No longer was Outi standing over me, no, not Outi but billion of cells which squirmed and wiggled like sperm fighting their way through a womb. The cells were flanked by white vapor which looked like smoke. As the cells moved closer, they became more transparent to me until I hardly could see them. My pain kept on increasing and that burning feeling now invaded my brain.

A breeze blew into my face, a cool refreshing breeze, a breeze that made my eyes twirl and my eye sockets return to their normal shape and solidify. My eyes re-focused, allowing me to see Outi and then see his brain which was a gray color and which had green blood pulsating vigorously through its tiny canals which ran throughout. Like a heart, Outi's brain expanded and contracted, pounded, pounded relentlessly never stopping, never stopping. Mr. Outi's face was like a mask tightly secured on his brain. The mask moved, the lips on the mask moved, Outi spoke, and he recited one passage of the Koran after another over me. His brain, in the meantime, expanded so much that I thought it was going to bust while its green blood slowly began working itself down to the millions of cells. Consequently, the cells turned a dark green color and formed themselves into lines and columns surrounding the white vapor. Out's face, his mask simple vanished now. The canals of his brain overflowed with the green blood. Some of it, drop by drop, spilled over on me, slowly at first but then speeding up, speeding up, speeding up. The drops were cold, freezing cold. I couldn't take it, it was pure torture. I crawled away from the brain as best I could, crawled away from the cells, the white vapor, and the green blood. From afar, I watched in sadness as the white vapor slowly was eaten away by the green cells while the brain pounded happily. The room grew as cold as a freezer. My burning reached its crisis point, but then eased considerably. I was left with a peculiar nauseous feeling along with knowledge that I must confront the brain. I had to, I just had to.

With all the power left in me, I managed to crawl back to the cells which were waiting for me. I rose and puked my guts out, puked on top of the gray brain, with its green blood, puked on top of the green cells, puked without end. The cells wiggled, twirled, knocked into one another and circled the brain. The brain meanwhile had contracted until it looked like a plain shriveled up brown paper bag.

All the little cells, jumping in frenzy, dive-bombed into the brain and imbedded themselves within it. The white vapor, little by little, reappeared from the core of the brain till it formed a huge, thick cloud directly above it. For a minute or two, the vapor circled above before it descended down upon the brain, shrouding it in an impenetrable fog. The vapor turned a brilliant yellow, warming the office to a bearable level. The burning on my insides ended as did my nauseousness. I moved toward the yellow vapor, out of instinct I moved towards it. I looked for the brain in the vapor but it was gone, gone without a trace. The vapor floated away from me. I followed behind intrigued and watched as it drifted to the door and sucked itself under. It was gone.

*　　*　　*

The vapor gone, gone, goodbye, gone. I was alone in the office, strangely alone. Just then, the door opened. Professor Osman Seljuk appeared. Putting his hand to hip, the Professor exclaimed, "Mr. Kabir what are you doing in my office with the door closed?"

"I don't know, I don't know, I don't understand about anything anymore to be truthful about it. The door was locked though of that I can assure you. I was trapped in here with this little guy named Outi, but not the Outi in our Department, who thought your office was an elevator. And there was Outi's brain, which was crazy. I don't know, what, and the cells, cells like a million bugs, and the green blood, yes, yes, and. . . ."

"Mr. Kabir please sit down immediately. I believe you are suffering from some sort of mental fatigue probably brought on by the trouble you've had in writing that thesis proposal of yours. Take it easy Mr. Kabir. The Board will pass your proposal eventually. If it takes five, ten, or twenty years, so be it. Time is relative, isn't it. Ha, ha, I'm teasing you Mr. Kabir. Don't look so worried."

"I know you were joking, Professor, I know. Of everyone here, you've treated me fairly, not like some outsider."

"Well Mr. Kabir, I'm glad you feel that way. I take that as a compliment. I pride myself in always being very student oriented," said Seljuk in a nervous manner. "I will add to that it's been marvelous having you to advise. You just can't imagine what it does for a new Professor's status to be able to say he is supervising a student's thesis. Yes, yes, yes, and Mr. Kabir, I am glad you do not take me for granted. I certainly befriended you when no one else would, why I don't know but I have. Whenever you have walked in here, I have tried to forget you're a student and make believe you're an old friend. Mm, an interesting relationship I have with you, one that I wish to explore in further detail with you soon, maybe like today."

I wasn't paying much attention to Professor Seljuk now as he yapped. The Professor was a big talker and often-times I found my mind drifting. Today, I couldn't keep my thoughts away from what had happened in the office with the Outi character. My hands still trembled. Could I have been imagining it? When I finally managed to turn my attention back to Professor Seljuk, I heard him say, "You know Mr. Kabir I've been in this Department only three short years - I am the junior person on staff - but from what I observed I can say honestly that nobody on this staff is a better teacher or scholar than I. Who can equal my knowledge in the field of economics? Nobody. I am a whiz and an absolute magician with figures. I have an advantage over the others, you see, a great advantage. I was not always an academic. For ten long years, I worked in business doing this and that before I returned to higher education. I have seen the outside world. I understand. I really applaud myself, I really do. I am wonderful. Who else can teach higher economics, mathematics, built complex graphs and charts but at the same time teach Turkish, teach modern Islamic history? I am so versatile. I sometimes get up in the middle of the night and just shake my head. My ability is so overwhelming. And there is my mastery of interpersonal relationships. There's no doubt in my mind that I have the best rapport with students in the Department. My door is always open and it will always be open, you can depend on that with your life. You see I'm young and dynamic, filled with innovative ideas, yes, a young, liberal thinker. Isn't that true, Mr. Kabir?"

"Yes, I guess. I don't really. . . ."

"I'm a totally Western man, a Western liberal man. I love the West. I love it more than anything here on Earth, and you can be sure of that." The Professor leaned back in his chair, put his hand to his hip and knit his eyebrows, giving him that earnest, military look. "I was born in the East, Mr. Kabir. Grew up in the foothills of Turkey between two mountain peaks. I'm rugged and tough but also grounded in wisdom. But enough of my Eastern background. I want to forget my Eastern origins and think of myself only as a Westerner. Mr. Kabir look here." Professor Seljuk lowering his head, showed me his hairline while pulling a comb and small mirror from his pocket. I held the mirror for him while he combed his cranium. After doing such, he analyzed his other facial features in the mirror. "Ugh, ugh, damn it, damn it," he moaned. "I'm losing the hair off the top of my head, ugh. It started a couple of months ago, but look how far it's progressed, ugh. My beautiful looks are disappearing. I was always the handsomest man. Hair loss is hereditary in the family; my father, grandfather and great-grandfather all went bald in the same place. But I cannot accept this. It isn't fair. Why must I of all people, who is good to everyone, who gives to charities, who never beats his wife or son, lose my hair. Mr. Kabir, do you think I should have a hair transplant?"

"That's up to you, Professor."

"I didn't really want to have one anyway. What about a toupee for me?"

"That's up to you, Professor."

"Yes, I'll wait and think it over. A very good suggestion, Mr. Kabir. Now, let us go to the restaurant, I'm ready."

"Restaurant, I didn't realize we were supposed to go to a restaurant today?"

"No, of course not, it wasn't scheduled, no, no, not at all, but I am inviting you as a friend, as one of my blessed student. Yes, and there is something I'd like to tell you in privacy."

"Tell me now!"

"Now, not now, not here. This is not a safe environment to speak in. We must always consider ears at doors. In life, it is best to be cautious. So we will go and it will be my treat. I like showing off my magnanimous nature. I like doing things for students. Besides being gratifying, you'll be surprised at the dividends a policy of generosity brings. When people like you, you career advances, your salary rises and you are granted tenure. Now let us go and dine that true gentleman."

Off we went. Professor Seljuk - strangely carrying a copy of the Financial Times of London, a newspaper under his arm - took me to this little greasy spoon in a seedier part of town, down a steep hill opposite and between two green factories. All the way there the Professor =spoke of himself, his brilliance, his financial insights, how he would use his economic background to make a great killing in the commodities market, etc., etc., etc.

In the diner, Professor Seljuk picked out a table next to the kitchen. "Hi yah Joe," yelled Seljuk to one cook. How's the little wife of yours? How's the new baby?"

"Fine Osman, just fine," Joe called back.

"I like to be friendly with everyone, even kitchen workers. It's just my way."

Seljuk rose from our table and snuck up behind a waitress, in a yellow uniform, serving two customers. He poked her in the middle of the back with his finger. She turned, almost dropped what she was holding and said, "Hi Osman, you haven't been here in a long time. What a yah afraid of me?"

"Afraid of you, Mildred? Never. I fear no woman, women fear me, and they love me."

Professor Seljuk returned to the table with Mildred following behind; she took our her order pad.

"Mildred," exclaimed Professor Seljuk. "This is a fellow student of mine, Mr. Kabir. He has created quite a commotion in my department this year. He is not liked very much and is looked upon as trouble maker. I have taken an interest in him, however; I feel everyone deserves a chance, even a common dog. Say hello to Mr. Kabir, Mildred!"

"Hello there Kabir. Osman give me your orders. I have two customers waiting."

"For me you can wait," wisecracked the Professor, winking and sneaking a pinch of her behind.

"What will you have Osman or I'm going to walk away."

"Mr. Kabir, what's your pleasure? Anything on the menu is yours. Go ahead. Don't be afraid."

"I'll just have a coffee."

"That's all you want. I can't believe it. Please order something else, please give me the pleasure of spending my hard earned money on you, please."

"All I want is a coffee, Professor, that's all. And if we could get around to discussing the subject of this meeting, my thesis proposal I would be grateful."

Professor Seljuk frowned and asked Mildred to bring me over a coffee, while he ordered a hamburger with plenty of onions and a nice tall glass of coca cola with plenty of ice and a twist of lemon. "I like to eat Western food," he explained as Mildred retreated. "As a matter of fact, I make it a habit to do everything Western. I wouldn't want to fall back on my old Eastern ways."

The Professor looked repeatedly at his watch. "Where is Mildred with my hamburger. Boy she's slow."

"Professor, ah, could we. . . ."

"I know Mr. Kabir, you want to discuss your thesis proposal, two and a half months we've been discussing your latest proposal so what is another few minutes." Seljuk opened his financial newspaper wide, placed it between us and quietly read. What the hell was this. Is this man playing games with me?

"Professor Seljuk about the thesis proposal," said I through his newspaper. "How did you like the final version I gave you to read? I followed exactly the guidelines you laid down. I don't think there will be any problem of its passing the Board this time, do you?"

Professor Seljuk gave no reply, being too embroiled in his newspaper. Only after Mildred returned with the food did the Professor put it down.

"Okay now Mr. Kabir, what's your problem?" asked Professor Seljuk inanely between bites of his hamburger.

"My thesis proposal, what did you think of the it?"

"Mr. Kabir, your coffee, you are not drinking the coffee I am paying for. Drink it up Mr. Kabir, drink it up, and then I'll buy you another cup."

"Okay." I took a sip. "Now about my thesis proposal."

"Well I read it last night in my den with my son on my lap, we're very close you know, and I see you put a tremendous amount of work in it, three months of work. You have followed my advice about what to include in it very nicely, yes, but, but, and this is a big but, the proposal just will not do. It will be rejected again."

"What?"

"I'm sorry to say it to you, but it's the truth. I want you to go home and do a lot more reading on your topic and then come back to me and then in a month or two we might discuss it some more. Oh yes, when we meet again it will be best if we hold our gathering in my home at a late hour."

"What, I don't understand? What do you mean it will not due. I wrote it exactly the way you told me to write it. And as far as doing more reading I have already read and taken notes from all the books on my topic, I have put in tremendous hours on the thesis. The proposal is as good as it will ever be. Why are you giving me the run around Professor, why? The Board is meeting next week, I have to get in or it'll be another six months."

"So it is another six months. The idea is to get it right."

"The idea is to get my degree. I don't have unlimited resources. My family cannot keep lending me money."

"Is this our problem. We do not concern ourselves with such things."

"Please, I see no reason why we cannot at least submit my thesis proposal."

"I didn't want to say this, Mr. Kabir," cried Professor Seljuk with dark blue veins popping out of his forehead, "but the thesis proposal you showed me is horrendous, simply horrendous, rotten, awful."

"What? That's not true. I can write it no better than that."

"Hm, it's true you have put everything you have into it, Hm, and you have followed my advice about it word for word, yes, yes, then perhaps Mr. Kabir you should choose a new topic and find yourself another advisor. Yes, I think that's the best solution all around."

"No, no, I can't start this whole rigor-mar-all over again," I shrieked. "No, no, no, no, I can't, I can't. Not another topic."

Mildred the waitress and Joe the cook came racing out to see what the screaming was about. "It's nothing," explained Seljuk to them, "nothing at all. It's just a student acting out his feelings of frustration." The Professor took on an icy expression. I had never seen him like that before.

"Professor, please give me a break. I spent fourteen hours a day in the library for three months researching and writing the proposal, I can't drop it now."

"But you must as you must find yourself a new advisor. I don't want to be associated with you any more. You are a fool of great sort."

I sat there stunned. Seljuk was one of the last persons I thought I would say something like that to me. What a nightmare.
"But, Pro-Professor, I thought you liked me, I thought you were my friend. How can you talk to me this way?"

"Your friend, Mr. Kabir, I can't be your friend, it's quite impossible. Do you realize that everyone in the Department, including our leader, is talking about my relationship with you."

"So let them talk! Please don't dismiss me and allow the work I've done to be thrown out the window."

"Did you say let them talk. Mr. Kabir, don't you realize that I'm a recent arrival to the Department. My contract runs out at the end of the year. I must make a good appearance. I can't afford to be let go. Do you know how much it cost me to move to this town, with all the furniture and the wife and everything all the way from Chicago, do you know how much that cost? Half my years salary, Mr. Kabir, can you imagine. I can't afford to be let go. I must become like everyone else. I must become the ultimate scholar. One can find great strength in being such a thing."

"Why must you become anything. Just stay my friend."

"I'm afraid scholars don't make friends. Scholars discuss, thoughts, ideas, theories, books, analyze concepts, but we cannot be friends. Friends are personal issues, and the personal is not tolerated. But, why do you look so shocked, Mr. Kabir? All of us submerge our personalities for rewards, we all become preordained things. Rewards are more important than the self. Who wants to go around being nothing. We all want to be honored in the world, worshiped in the world. It is the way of all men. There's no pleasure in being nothing. Personality, to have one that is distinctive is not the winning ticket. It is the ticket to failure. My personality is too strong right now. It's no good. I hate it. I must become a scholar like another becomes a doctor, a lawyer, a policeman, a fireman, I must, I must."

"Look, I'll do anything you say but please help me with my proposal. I have to get it passed by the Board and. . . ."

"Your thesis proposal is atrocious and will never pass. Your thought is atrocious, your writing is atrocious. Why do you think the Board has rejected you three times already. Do you think for one moment they will pass a thesis proposal composed by a students who has been attacking them the past two years."

"That's not true. I haven't attacked anyone!"

"You have and you just don't know it. Just by exhibiting your existence you have led a campaign of individualism which has effected other students. You're no good, Mr. Kabir. Give up."

"Please, don't say that. You've lead me around all this time Professor, encouraging me to read on the topic, to research, writing the proposal and I think you've done all this just to waste my time. And as far as leading a campaign against the department, that's just not true, not true, not true."

"You see, there's a startling example of your debauchery. You do not understand the proper way to address somebody in my honored professorial position."

"But if I talk in the proper way then what happens to my way?"

"Now there it is. You talk with emotion in your voice and thereby insult my dignity, Mr. Kabir. You insult everyone's dignity by existing on an emotional plane. And you exist there because you belong to nothing, did you hear that, nothing, I said, nothing. You live in your own bubble, a bubble which circles around that head of yours, a bubble which substitutes for the real world. You view each of us separately. What type of nonsense is that? I have tried to be fair with you. I have bent over backward to tolerate you, but no more. You are just no good and there is nothing any of us can do about it. I don't want to see you ever again, Mr. Kabir. If I ever see you in the hall I will walk the other way, and if you try to approach me, I will break your neck in half. Now go, leave my table, go and be gone with you, you piece of filth, you no good bum, bastard, bastard bum. Leave my table instantly."

I left the restaurant, left bewildered, bewildered at the transformation of Professor Seljuk in only a few minutes. What could I have ever done? Was there something that I was missing? What?

CHAPTER 10

After the incident, the catastrophe of the restaurant, I walked and walked and walked feeling sorry for myself. Besides being sick about the conspiracy, which had grown everywhere against me, I wondered about myself. Maybe I was a fool and that's why I was standing out; maybe I was an idiot for not understanding. Everyone was calling me stupid. And if I am, doesn't that mean I have to change? But how? How? I am what I am and I know no other way to be. Oh God, help me, I prayed.

Walking, just walking and not on not knowing where I was going and having my thoughts turn to more practical matters. What was I going to do about my thesis proposal? Was all the work I had done in the Department down the drain? Was I to stay locked into the Department for years like some of the others? Was I to waste my life also? Why don't I just drop out now, thought I, the way I should have a year ago. But no, I couldn't. Something strong still holds me, something about this game of a conspiracy being played against me. Thinking, wondering and then suddenly looking around to find myself sitting on a park bench on campus. I reviewed all that happened to me since that first day I arrived. I particularly couldn't get Jamila's face out of my mind, her evil face attached to her evil body which had initiated the evil conspiracy.

* * *

While sitting on the bench, I was awakened from my torpor by tapping on my shoulder. "Now Joseph Kabir, now I think you are ready to listen to me," came a vaguely familiar voice from behind.

Quickly I turned, quickly I saw. It was, it was Vladimir, the mysterious man I had met my first day in attendance in the

Department almost an eternity ago. I rose like a shot while he came around and we were face to face. His eyes still burned with more intensity than I had never seen in another human before.

"I warned you, Joseph Kabir not to enter the Department, didn't I?" said Vladimir. "You just wouldn't listen to Vladimir and now here you are in mortal danger of dying."

I looked at Vladimir sorrowfully and squeaked, "Yes Vladimir, you were right. But maybe the Department has been a good experience, showing me that I am deficient as a person and that if I don't change, I will always remain an unhappy outsider. But I don't know how to change."

"NNNNNNNNNNNNNNNNN," came the sound from Vladimir's mouth. "I wish to help you, Joseph. First things first, you are having trouble with your thesis proposal, are you not?"

"Yes, more trouble than you can imagine. I don't know what to do about it."

"Then follow me. Vladimir will take you to someone who will solve your problems. Trust Vladimir."

I did trust Vladimir, remembering that the advice he had given me before had been sound and wise. I followed him, block after town block, I followed, never imagining where he was taking me. As we progressed, we became surrounded by little red-brick houses, each with a garden of red flowers out front. Hours we marched. "Can't we stop for a rest?" I inquired of the fast walking Vladimir.

""No Joseph, not yet. Soon we shall reach our destination, and you will find the rest you've always been looking for."

On the outskirts of town, we reached our destination, a spacious brown barn made of decayed wood that had hundreds of rusted pitch-forks balancing against its front. The structure seemed out of place. "Back in the eighteenth century," Vladimir explained, "this is where all the grains for the town were stored."

I was reluctant to enter the barn, but Vladimir was insistent and I followed. Inside I found a huge empty enclosure, two tiers. The upper, was filled with piled up hay, the lower tier was a floor covered with a white gritty material; it had two doors at opposite ends from one another. The barn smelled bad, like a horse stable. Behind the door to the right, a constant banging and hammering could be heard. Suddenly, out of it came Cyrus and Riza, the two mental patients at the Student Health Center who Vladimir had introduced me to on that very first day. "Joseph, Joseph, hello, hello," both greeted before approaching and hugging me.

"It's been a long time," cried Cyrus. "Last time you saw us in sickness but thanks to Vladimir we are well again, well. Now we wish to help you."

Vladimir stepped forward. "I've agreed to help Joseph with his thesis proposal. He has been having difficulty with it, as you can well imagine. But now he is in safe hands. Shall we take him through the left door? Everything might just become clear to him in there."

"Yes, let's," cheered Cyrus.

"Good, idea, nice idea," chucked Riza.

The three of them escorted me to the door before which I stood frozen.

"Bang on it, go ahead," barked Vladimir.

I couldn't. Vladimir banged for me, banged and banged, but there was no answer. He opened it for me and there sitting at a desk in front of me, there was Dr. Warly. With Cyrus and Riza waiting outside, Vladimir pushed me inside the room with him. Dr. Warly didn't see us at first; his eyes were riveted on a book he was reading. Vladimir nudged me over to his desk. "Say hello to Dr. Warly," he urged. "Go ahead. He will help you with your problem. Say hello, don't be shy."

I obeyed. "Hello, ah, hello, ah, Dr. Warly, it's me, Joseph Kabir, hello." Warly didn't hear. He kept reading.

"Breath on him, breath on his neck," said Vladimir. "That should get his attention." I tried but it did no good. Warly didn't feel a thing. Vladimir tapped his feet against the floor loudly, banged on the desk, whistled, jumped up and down yelping and howling, but Warly remained deaf to our existence. "We are not allowed to touch him," Vladimir explained then. "Otherwise, we would be able to get his attention easily. Physical contact is the ultimate sin. Communication through signs and words is the only methodology. We must wait then, wait, till he comes up for air."

Our wait wasn't that long. Warly presently got up out of his chair, still with the book glue to his face, did an about face, and finally lifted his eyes to the bookcase behind him. "I know I have The Political Elite in Egypt by Pilsner. Where did I stick it? Where?"

Warly furiously searched through the bookshelves. "Let's see I remember bringing the book with me from home three weeks ago, Hm, what the hell is this? Why must I waste time on such stupid things. Now where did I put that damn book?" Warly looked for some time before giving up. Doing a full twist around, he now stood before Vladimir and I, gazing straight at us. "What's going on here? What?" Warly shrieked upon seeing us. "How did you get in here? I can't believe this! What nonsense! What insanity! I'm a busy man. Is this some kind of joke? Nobody jokes with me. Why am I the one who is always annoyed? Jefferson is the head of the department; why doesn't everyone bother him? Why is it always me?"

Vladimir sauntered over to the side of Warly's desk and leaned his body against it. Warly strangely didn't notice. He never took his eyes off me. I really felt uncomfortable being there. "Vladimir," said I to him. "Can't we leave. This isn't going to do me any good and it might do me harm."

"You must stay and observe," answered Vladimir sharply.

Dr. Warly began to shake his head. "Who are you talking to?" he asked me. "What are you a nut case, Kabir? Do you like talking to yourself. Why is it that everyone who comes into my office lately is a crackpot?"

"Don't you see him," I addressed Dr. Warly for the first time. "Vladimir is standing right next to you."

Warly looked bewildered. "Kabir, if you don't stop with such idiocy I'll have the janitor throw you out of this office. I didn't realize you were such a maniac."

Was Vladimir a ghost? Why couldn't Warly see him? Why could I see him? I don't know and never found out.

Warly glanced down at the book he held, made a mean face and bitched, "Kabir, you are intruding into my completely-controlled existence and I don't like that. I've been keeping a close eye on you this year and heard a great deal of comments from others. You're quite infamous in our Department. But I'm not intimidated. I am Dr. Warly and I am a legend in the world of academia. I'm not bothered by much. I am tough, strong, and brilliant. But in this instance, I am most certainly bothered and I shall now tell you why. You a new student, a lowly new student, and you're impudent enough to come waltzing into the office of myself, Dr. Donald Warly and you expect me to listen to you. You know something, ever since that first day I became supreme scholar, I could never stand new students. They don't let things churn through their brains, don't analyze, are too instinctive. Swing pigs! Their thoughts are never properly organized and plotted before they let them come out in words. They make me sick with their spontaneity. Throughout my career, I have always been disgusted by them." Warly stopped to scan the room and then asked, "Kabir, did you happen to see a little purple book around here?"

"No."

"Ah, what am I asking you for! You don't know anything." Warly in search circled his office, scrutinizing it before finally finding the purple book in a waste paper basket. "Kabir, Kaaaaaaaaaaaaaaaaaaaaaaa-b-iiiiiiiiiiiiiiiiiiiiiiiiiiiiiiiiiiiiiiiiiiiiiiiiiiiiiiiir, did you throw my book in there, Kaaaaaaaaaaaaaaaaaaaaaaa-b-iiiiiiiiiiiiiiiiiiiiiiiiiiiiiiiiiiiiiiiiiiiiiiiiiiiiiiiir?"

"No, no, Dr. Warly, I swear I didn't."

Vladimir, observing it all, smiled a wide smile while Warly returned to his desk with purple book in hand. With a contented look on his face, Warly sat stiffly in his chair and for the first time looked directly into my eyes while pulling at his earlobe. "So what do you want Kabir? I've a million things to do today, a million, a million. Do you understand what I mean by a million things Kabir? I'm a real scholar, the greatest scholar and researcher in this department. Intelligence runs deep in me. To date, I have published six books which probe the Arab mind, three on the Persian mind, and one on the Turkish mind. Right now, I'm deeply engrossed in research for my new book on the Indian mind. All total, all total I've published seven books, that's two more than Dr. Jefferson. So Kabir, now you see, I am a famous man and famous men are not used to being imposed upon."

Vladimir bowed his head and hissed some words in the background but too low to make them out. There was an empty chair before Warly's desk and as my legs were buckling beneath me, I moved to the chair and began to sit down when Warly yelled, "Kabir, what in the world do you think you're doing?"

"Ah, ah, ah, ah."

"Students do not sit in my office. That chair is reserved for full-fledged scholars only. How dare you desire to sit before me, how dare you."

"I'm so-so-so sorry. I-I-I did-did-did-did not realize it was-wasn't al-al-allowed."

"Stupid-ness is no excuse; educated people need no excuses, remember that. Now quickly, tell me what you want with me? Out with it."

"Well it's about my thesis, I have somewhat of a problem. Some of my friends directed me to you because they thought you just might be able to help me."

"You came about your thesis, about your thesis did you say, your thesis, what about your thesis?"

"Well, I have written another thesis proposal, a really good one I might add, but I find myself without an advisor who will sponsor it and help it pass the Board. If possible, maybe you could read it, make a few comments which I'll gladly listen to, and maybe you then might agree to become my advisor."

"You, you, you, Kabir, you Kabir, want to write a thesis, you? Writing a thesis takes brains and talent, and you say you want to write one?"

"Yes, of course, it's a requirement for all new students in the department?"

"You're serious Kabir. Mm, Mm, this is interesting, interesting. And you want Dr. Donald Warly to read your thesis proposal, and then you want me to be your thesis advisor and sponsor your proposal with the Board? Do you realize that I do not deal with students' thesis proposals, do you realize that I do not deal with students theses? I am an exceptionally busy person who has little time for the minor things in life."

"I apologize then. I didn't realize it was such an imposition. I think it might be best if I leave right now. Again, I'm sorry."

"Kabir, you don't leave till I say you can leave. Now besides being an incredible scholar, I am also a most beneficent one. Therefore, I tell you what I'll do, I'll let you have twenty minutes of my valuable time to state your case about this thesis proposal of yours. Again, I repeat, you will have twenty minutes, no more, no less." Warly reached down into a lower drawer and removed an egg timer. "I'll set it to ring after the allotted time. In this way I'll be sure you don't get more than I promised."

Vladimir began walking out of the office. "Where are you going Vladimir?" I asked.

"I will leave you alone with Dr. Warly. It will be better that way." Vladimir exited and I was alone with Dr. Donald Warly.

"Mr. Kabir, I noticed you were talking to yourself again. I don't like people who do that. Now back to this thesis proposal, what it the topic?"

I explained it to him as clearly and succinctly as I could. A certain gleam appeared in Warly's eyes and he smirked at me and bobbed his head spasmodically up and down. Then he rose furiously from behind his desk. Straight at me he came, forcing me to retreat a few steps. Next he circled, scrutinizing me attentively before singing in my ear, "Kabir, you're a new student here, that's all you are. I believe you have forgotten that very fact, but let us see, let us determine if you are a fool or not. Now, answer quickly, now, answer, have you read Henderson's Egypt Since 1691, or, Cramer's The Economic History of Arabia?"

"Well I. . . ."

"Have you, or have you not?"

"No."

"Hm, thought so." Warly strolled over to bookcase, purveyed the books and then like a dive bomber, raced up to me again and shot, "Have you read Pulsen's The Political Elite in Tunisia, or, Ani's astounding book, An Ode to Central Asia?"

"No, Dr., but I've. . . ."

"Sa-sa-sa-sa," sneered Warly as he circled. "You certainly must have read Paterson's Turkish Civilization in the Nineteenth Century, Harper's Medieval Yemen, and Paperdorf's Syria during the Time of the Second Crusade?"

"No, no, oh no, no, but, oh."

I was totally beaten, had it, was finished, caput.

"Tell me Mr. Kabir, have you ever opened a book?"

"Tha-that's all I do is open books and read, believe me. I've read many, many. . . ."

"Mm-Hm, Mm-Hm, Mm-Hm," hummed Warly with a mocking grin. "I want to be fair to you, quite fair, fair and practical.

Mr. Kabir now, right now, I want to know what were the factors inhibiting the growth of Turkish nationalism at the start of the twentieth century? Answer, answer, quickly, answer new student, quickly."

My being was stricken with immense terror. I couldn't think properly.

"I can't answer that right now. Give me a few moments. This is very. . . ."

"Fair enough. Another chance. Tell me in an organized and detailed manner all the problems Iran faced in the nineteenth century."

"I, ah, Iran, nineteenth century, ah, Iran." After those words, I stood before Warly dumbfounded and searching for words without success.

"You fool Mr. Kabir," growled Warly still grinning. "You come into this office, impose upon my time, irritate me with that stupid raspy voice of yours packed with emotion, and then, to top it off, I find you are a worthless human being. Why don't you act like a graduate student. Now listen here, never again will I allow you to set foot in this office until you have learned the value of facts and generalizations."

"Nobody every gives me a chance around here, nobody."

"I am not nobody, Mr. Kabir, I'm somebody, something, never ever call me a nobody again. Do you realize, are you aware that you are right this minute listening to the speech of the most important man in this Department. I, and not the gimpy, old Jefferson run this Department. That dope is only a figure-head whose only usefulness lies in his many contacts with dignitaries from various Middle Eastern countries which brings in the needed revenue each year. I am the leader, and the leader has pronounced judgment on you and that judgment is that you are lacking in almost every way and have the greatest of gall coming to me today. If I wasn't so nice I would have you thrown out of the Department entirely, but I am too generous a man for that. And as for this thesis proposal of yours, if you really want to get it passed one day then you will go home and learn to view the world in the widest possible terms and that if you want to be a true scholar than you will have to make yourself an instrument of knowledge. Until you reach that point Kabir, I can professionally assure you that your little thesis proposal will ultimately finds its way into the fires of Hell along with you."

Beaten, smeared, smashed, finished, I remained riveted to the spot. Dr. Warly, meanwhile, had turned his nose up to the ceiling, shimmied back to his desk, and sat there with fists clenched. Then he stared at me, stared for so long than he was soon staring through me.

"Dr. Warly, Dr. Warly," I cried, attempting to get his attention as well as trying to keep myself from completely being covered over with soil. "Please Dr. Warly would you say something to me, anything. Please don't turn me off like this."

Warly responded to my pleas in a way. "Part One A, B, C," he mumbled incomprehensibly. "The thirteenth century, the Mongol invasions of the Middle East. Mongol invasions, horrendous acts of violence committed. Genghis Khan their leader, bad. They burn, loot. Baghdad sacked. Skip. Fourteenth century. Not my specialty. Fifteenth century, the Byzantine Empire falls after one thousand years. The Turks take Constantinople, interesting, interesting. Good facts surrounding conquest of the city. The sixteenth century, the Turks conquer Hungary, amazing, unbelievable. New dynasty comes to power in Iran and India, great dynasties. The seventeenth century, Turks conquer to the gates of Vienna and then are pushed back until Hungary is lost to them."

Just then, the egg timer went off with an explosion of sound, signaling my time with Warly was over. Warly was woken from his trance. "Well times up Mr. Kabir. Out you must go. You must stop bothering me, stop it, so I can get on to other more important matters. I have so much research to do, tons and tons of it, tons and tons." Warly picked up the book he had been reading when I arrived and plunged his head into it.

"Dr. Warly, Dr. Warly, Dr. Warly," I whined. "A few more minutes, give me a few more minutes."

There was no use. Slowly, mournfully I made my way out of his office without Warly being conscious of me anymore.

*   *   *

Vladimir, Cyrus and Riza all waited for me outside Warly's office. Nobody said a word. I walked with all three men I didn't know where, but I walked. In the middle of the hall, we stopped while Riza pulled aside a small throw rug that revealed a trap door, opened it and descended down. We followed down many flights of stairs and in total darkness. Slowly, carefully we descended so as not to make a misstep. In a pitch dark cellar we arrived, a cellar that smelled of stale dampness. Riza left us for a minute to light a small red candle found somewhere in the corner of the cellar, turning the darkness into a red dimness. I could make out the outlines of a rocking chair which I was taken to and placed upon. Vladimir stood on one side of me, Cyrus on the other both pushing and pulling the chair which rocked me back and forth. Riza stood directly in front of me, but all I could make out of him was the shiny buttons on his shirt.

"So Kabir," began Vladimir. "You think you're no good, am I correct?"

"Yeah, I know it. Everyone is better than me."

"Do you think that could be corrected or not?" asked Vladimir.

"Yes, if I change. I want to change, become better by becoming a scholar, a historian, but, I don't know anymore. They won't let me make something of myself here."

"They won't let you, Mm, think Kabir, think, they won't let you or is it that you won't let yourself become something? Have you thought about that possibility? Maybe your spirit is too great for them, maybe it is rebelling against their attempts to mold you."

"My spirit! I won't let myself become something, I don't really understand."

"Think, realize, and get in touch with your vitals, Joseph. Understand their quest, to make you into something, that is, to make something of you. Maybe their attacks on you have come because you have resisted their designs. Now have you thought about that, Joseph?"

"No, but it makes sense."

"What are they Joseph Kabir? Who are they? Why are they?"

I did not understand the questions.

"Who are all those you want to become?" Vladimir clarified. "Why do you want to become like them?"

"Because they are very smart people who are accepted and respected by everyone."

Vladimir rocked me so violently in my rocking chair that I became dizzy. "Joseph, Joseph, Joseph," he honked. "Joseph, your vision is still cloudy. You do not realize yet the true reality. Those in the Department who are accepted are the dead ones, those without living souls, barbarians we may call them. Barbarians fit in there; nobody else fits in there. Which brings us back to you, Joseph. Do you know what you are, do you know?"

"I don't know anything anymore."

"Joseph, you are good, you are great, you are the best. You must realize that, you must face up to yourself and your own glory."

In the distance Riza belched, "Joseph you are good, you are good, you are good. We know it, they know it, we know it, they know it."

"I'm good, really. I'm not stupid like they say? I'm not a fool?"

"Ha-ha-ha," Vladimir chuckled. "Of course you're not. You are a genius, Joseph Kabir, a genius possessing an intelligence of the greatest magnitude."

"But they all call me stupid!"

"You still doubt," Vladimir wailed. "How can I convince you of your beauty. Anyone looking at your or who has talked to you for a second knows that you are not stupid. They call you names, slander your intelligence only to beat you down. That's the way they operate."

"But why should they want to attack me? I've done nothing to them."

"That's right Joseph, you've done nothing, you are nothing and right there is your crime. All you have is your personality and you carry it around with you everywhere and let it shine. But then to the barbarians your personality is so bright that it blinds, burns, hurts. They seek only to stifle the light, stifle the light which is them. You see, at one time all the barbarians were like you, but they trampled their glowing spirits until they became living vacuums."

"But why, why?"

"Because to live in the brightness, to live out of the personality is the hardest thing in the world to do. It means feeling pain, hurt, and depression. To merge with the world, into things, into words on paper, into concepts and conglomerates, into masses and democratic movements is easier, comforting, tranquilizing. Yes, that's true. But, it is also true that once you merge you become an empty vicious dog seeking only to make others, the pure ones, empty. From the time the pure soul emerges from the crib, the barbarians start their attack. The growing child, who initially radiates only the spirit, is ravaged from the start with ideas that his natural state of nothingness and oblivion is terrible. The barbarians yell at him: 'Stop acting crazy, weird, infantile, stupid. Act like an adult. Follow the rules. Obey your elders, sanctify tradition by becoming tradition. Make something of yourself. Be something, educate yourself into someone, medicate yourself into someone. No, no, no, stop being the child and acting out of instinct. Instinct is for animals. You are a thing above animals which is sanctified by God who is the God of all monotheists. No, no, stop the impulsive behavior. You can't act that way anymore, child. That's not rational behavior. Reality is our reality not your reality. Remember that.'"

"But still I..." began I before I was cut off by Vladimir.

"Another approach used by the barbarians in their attack on the true man like you, Joseph is to use lollipops as a major weapon. 'Come on little boy,' they say, 'come on, here is a nice lollipop for you. All I want you to do in return is to be a good little man. And, there will be more lollipops for you if you continue to behave, continue not to act like an inferior jack ass.' That's what goes on, Joseph. When the pure spirit grows up, the words of the barbarians begin to have their effect. The young individual grows up saying to himself, 'I'm no good, I must control myself, control it, suppress it. It's inferior. I must make something of myself in this world, become something. This is what was happening to you, Joseph, but, you managed somehow to hang on to what is important. And those who don't become, they are labeled as bums, vagabonds, baggage, bank robbers, murderers, rapists, hijackers, butchers, and are denounced. But Joseph these individuals are the best. They are not the scum of our world; they are the cream of our world, the messiahs seeking only salvation for each and every living creature. You must remember this during the relentless attacks of the barbarians."

"But these barbarians you speak of, they are people too who must have souls. If you believe that we were all good in the beginning, it must follow that these barbarians were once good. Can they become good again?"

"Of course they can Joseph. But, before proceeding further, I wish you to follow me upstairs. There is something there I wish you to see."

Cyrus grabbed me and virtually lifted me up from the rocking chair. With Cyrus on my left and Vladimir on my right and Riza up ahead, we went up to the surface through the trap door. I was escorted through the door opposite Warly's office, a door behind which a strange banging noise was coming.

Inside the door, I was immediately encircled by huge machines smelling of oil, long thin drills, power presses, saws, along with saw dust, rags, oil drums. In the middle of it, all was this one giant machine which stamped out dart boards out of pure white foam. Upon entry into this factory, we were all startled by the appearance of a man dressed in a light orange jump suit which had the map of the world on it.

"Hello there you all, glad, glad, delighted, happy, glad, fascinated, cheered, warmed, glad you could come, so happy," welcomed the map man in the orange jump suit. "Welcome to the Department of Middle Eastern Studies dart factory. Blue darts are made here, the best blue darts in the world, my world. We have been making blue darts for sixty years. All are custom made with the purchaser's name nicely engraved on each dart. Lately, lately, only lately we have taken to making dart boards. Our dart boards are made from the finest foam, the very finest. Would you boys care to see our assembly line where the needles, the very sharpest, the most sterile, the brightest and shiniest, are inserted into the dart's base. Come boys, come."

"No thank you," answered Vladimir. "We are quite capable of showing ourselves around."

"Fine, my fellow citizen, fine," the map man responded. "Show yourself around the world, around existence, show and tell, tell and show. But you shouldn't ignore me. I'm the world you know. How do you like my pants suit?"

"Nice, nice, we all think it's nice," said Vladimir.

"Aren't my latitude and longitude lines gorgeous? Dark and sensuous, aren't they? Ah, and how do you like my seas and rivers?

So blue, and calm and extensive. Most of my body is water, you know. I am composed of three fourths water and one fourth land."

We tried to pass the map man but he blocked our way. "The world was created I'd say, about a billion years ago or maybe more," he explained. "Of all the planets of the solar system, Earth is closest to Venus in composition. The Earth is layered. First, there's the crust, that's my favorite, then, there's the mantle, that's all right. I like the mantle, my mantle. Then, I have an outer core. I have no real liking for my outer core, arrogant it is. And finally, there is the detested inner core, which is all hot liquids, boiling hot metals, everything is boiling. I hate my inner core, just hate it. Don't you?" Once more, we attempted to pass but were blocked by the map man's outstretched arms or should we say peninsulas. "Look at my countries, look, look. So well proportioned." As he talked he pointed to the countries on his jump suit. "Spain is my favorite. Breathtaking. How she exists so lovingly above Africa. What a shape she has. There's no other country like her. I'd love to get a piece of her. But, lately she's begun to brake my heart by being a bit of a naughty girl. I thought she loved me the way I loved her, but alas, she dropped me to engage in an illicit relationship with her neighbor France. But still I love her, I can't help it. At least I can find solace with my South American sweetheart, Brazil. Unlike my Spain, she is always obedient to me and will do whatever I ask. Oh Brazil, Brazil, Brazil, a wonderful young lady. She never fights with anyone and is always the lady. If I wasn't so in love with Spain, I think I could have a long term relationship with her. But alas, it is not so. And soon, very soon, Brazil will marry Argentina and I will give her my blessings. After all, I cannot ask her to wait for me. That wouldn't be fair. And to tell you the truth, Brazil and Argentina make a lovely couple; they are so well matched in natural resources and other forms of wealthy."

We tried to pass the map man again, but again he stopped us. Vladimir was seething at the mouth; you could see the smoke coming out of his nose.

"I love the world, the continents, the nations, the alliances, the governments, I love them," map man continued. "My favorite shape, though, and here I'm talking continents, is Africa? Does everyone agree?"

Vladimir charged. The map man blocked. Vladimir swung and landed a punch to the little guy's pudgy nose. The map man went down, and Vladimir falling on him, ruthlessly began to soundly thrash him, ruthlessly pounding his head into the floor until there was blood. I stayed back while Riza and Cyrus went in to view the scene up close. Soon the body of the map man was limp.

"Come on Joseph, come on," Cyrus called to me. "We can pass now, the guy's dead, gone, kaput and in his rightful place, oblivion where he can roam unencumbered by the human body and the human concept of the body."

I inched closer to the body, close enough to view the blood and the gore.

"Look at it Joseph, don't turn from it, " cried Riza.

Just then, a man looking exactly like Zeno Beneen approached. He was wearing a black tuxedo and white gloves, and carrying a silver tray with little sandwiches. "Hello," the tuxedo man addressed us in a deep voice. "I am the butler and here to serve and make your stay in the factory comfortable. It would please me if you would take a sandwich." He pushed the sandwiches under our noses. Vladimir warned us not to touch a bite. Looking down at the corpse on the floor the butler exclaimed, "Oh, a dead body I see. Hm, I'll have to get the janitor to come and clean up the mess, yes, I must. Gentlemen, are you sure, you don't wish to partake in a sandwich? No, okay then, let me escort you through our factory. It contains some fascinating features which will astound."

The butler escorted us through the factory. All throughout the complex, there were tools thrown about loosely, a million tools, knives, scissors, chisels, back saws, files, soldering irons, all over, on work benches,, on floors, everywhere. The few workers we saw were old, gray-haired men in plaid aprons manning the machines with concerned looks on their faces. The dartboard stamping machine was operated by a worker in a silver hat who fed it large sheets of white foam which the machine grabbed, chewed, shook, digested, and then spit out into perfect dart boards. From there the worker in silver hat carried the dart board to the dying machine where it was colored a perfect sky blue to match the color of the darts.

"Now you must come and see our shiny silver conveyor belt," the butler advised, escorting us to the belt where the darts were assembled and its shiny needles were inserted into the base of the darts. Here we were commanded to wait for a moment, while the butler disappeared further into the factory complex. Then, from nowhere, music began playing and was all around us, shrill, high-pitched music which gradually increased in volume and was followed by the appearance of clowns from everywhere, clowns with a lot of makeup and funny red rubber noses who now encircled us. The clowns crept up to us pulling out and juggling little white balls; but, then, suddenly, violently, they threw the little balls away and some picked up sharp scissors, metal files, and other tools instead and juggled them. Vladimir tried to break this imposing blockade but was stopped when one of the happier looking clowns pulled a knife from under his costume. Vladimir rallied us then. Lining up behind him, we fled in single file past the clowns with their weapons. "To the exit," Vladimir commanded.

The clowns followed in pursuit intend on catching and probably destroying us. And they were gaining. Yet, the EXIT was just up ahead, just a few yards. But then, just before the EXIT, our path was suddenly blocked. Women appeared, hundreds of middle-aged females carrying large clubs and yelling, "We are women, we are women." We were trapped. Behind us, the clowns were closing in. We raced to our right hoping to escape, but our right was now also blocked. Men dressed as waiters brandishing empty champagne bottles had appeared and were closing in on us slowly. To the left we raced, to the left. Our path, our last opening, was also blocked, blocked by baseball players swinging large brown baseball bats violently through the air. There was no place to go, no place to hide. Everyone was closing in on us. I thought we were goners but then Vladimir calmly, like he had it all planned, ordered us to duck behind two nearby storage bins.

"Joseph, I want you to watch what is going to happen carefully," Vladimir instructed me. "Watch very carefully."

All our attackers converged. They looked for us and looked and looked all through the factory but didn't find us even though we were only a few feet away and were in plain sight behind the bins. After looking everywhere, they dropped the pursuit. The group of females were all making ugly faces, while the clowns still jumped from box to machine to box, up and back, up and back. The waiters clanked their champagne bottles against the palm of their hands, and the ballplayers still swung their bats swiftly through the air. The ballplayers didn't like the clowns, they jeered at them. Finally, one of the ballplayers in an outburst of rage at the clown who was making a condescending gesture at him, swung his bat mightily and landed the fat part of it squarely on the big red hose of the clown as he was jumping up and down. The clown went down with blood spurting from his face. The attacking ballplayer quickly went and hid behind his fellow ballplayers for protection against retaliation.

One of the group of females immediately raced to the side of the fallen clown, bent down over him, straightened up again and yelled, "You animal, you hurt this poor defenseless clown, you hurt him, you brute, all you brutes, all you ballplayers. The clown, you hurt him." The rest if the females took up a position behind her with clubs in hand. The waiters began new buzzing about something and making funny faces at the females. One of the waiters, in the middle of his fellows, took his bottle and smashed it over the head female. Down she went on top of the clown. The pool of blood grew. The females went into a frenzy over their fallen leader. They pulled their hair and then marched in force against the waiters. The waiters held their ground and raised their bottles. The baseball players , trying to keep both parties apart, got between them but just then the clowns swooped down upon the ballplayers. Pow, that was it. All hell broke loose thereafter while Cyrus, Riza and Vladimir and I hid only a few feet away to watch as the females took to clubbing the waiters, the waiters to breaking their bottles over the heads of the females, and the clowns - using great agility to weave in and out between the ballplayers - slashing them with scissors or any other sharp tool they could find. The ballplayers totally wild swung their bats, mangling one clown, one waiter, one female after another. The pool of blood was becoming a lake, overflowing its banks and spreading over to us. Vladimir dipped his hand into a little puddle of it and brought the hand to his nose. "The smell of warm blood is divine. It is what true humanity is sprung from. Take a whiff of the marvelous aroma, Joseph." I passed on experiencing that pleasure.

The battle grew in scope until every inch of the factory was embroiled in combat. The ballplayers were the wildest of the lot, swinging at everything, including at the machines which were left in pieces. After only a few minutes of fighting, things looked like a city after a nuclear attack. The blood, the crushed, dead bodies were everywhere. Despite the carnage, Vladimir, Cyrus and Riza were smiling and mumbling, "More, more is needed, come on, come on, more." This was followed by the patter of many tiny little feet scurrying in rows and the appearance of men carrying giant wooden crosses and dressed in purple woolen cloth garments with hoods who marched into the melee crying, "This is the first crusade recreated. You all here are in mortal danger of becoming heathen barbarian Turks, infidels, Saracens, Muslims that we slashed to death on the cross in the twelfth century. Stand aside all of you who would be Turks or our wrath shall know no limits."

The surviving clowns, women, ballplayers and waiters formed one solid line, blocking the line of the holy marchers with their crosses. At this defiant act, the leader of the crusaders reddened, spat down at the floor and yelped, "Heathens, Turks, I see here Turkish heathens in thy midst. Clowns I address thee first. Take off thy makeup and put on the holy vestments."

The clowns did not budge. The crusader leader spat again, looked down and examined his spittle. Then, with cross firmly in hand, he twirled about and landed the religious object squarely on the jaw of the clown. Reacting, the rest of the clowns pounced upon the crusaders and dodged their swinging crosses by climbing acrobatically on top of the machines, under the machines, revolving behind the machines and then sneaking up behind their adversaries and jumping, kicking, choking, killing. The baseball players, the females, the waiters, suspended for a few minutes like stones figures, now came to life and they too attacked the holy men, attacked and attacked and attacked. The factory suddenly caught fire and burned; there were flames everywhere. Still, clowns continued to beat crusaders, sometimes picking them up in their arms and throwing them into the rising flames; the crusaders did the same to the clowns. All were being thrown into the flames. Soon all was a jumble to the eyes, all smeared all against the walls. More intruders; men in blue, policemen came rushing through the door. "What's going on here? What the hell is this?" came a voice from amongst the men in blue. "Stop, halt, stop, halt, stop." The police charged into what was left of the crowd, wallowing through the blood and flames while fire sirens were be heard outside. The policemen blasted their way through the crowd with clubs while barking more orders. Fighting stopped. The clowns fixed their makeup and noses, the waiters dusted off their messy waiters' outfits, the women fixed their hair and arched their backs, the ballplayers put the bats at their sides and smiled and the crusaders held their crosses high. Firemen arrived with hoses and put out the fires.

Vladimir shook and cried. "I must do something," he wailed. "If I don't, all of this will have been for nothing." He burst forth from our hiding place and made his way past the police undetected. He was out of sight. A few seconds later, the lights went out. Screaming erupted, followed by banging, breaking, thumping, cracking. New fires broke out, worse then the previous ones. Cries of pain rang out, shots rang out. The sound of bodies falling rang out. They fought worse then before. The smoke was intense as it circulated through the factory, a choking smoke, a burning smoke, a killing smoke. I don't think I could have taken much more if the lights hadn't come on again. To my surprise, there was Vladimir standing over me, pointing to the place where the major part of the battle had been waged. The police were gone. The firemen were gone. Dead bodies were sprawled all over. Only a few clowns, a few women, a few waiters, a few baseball players, a few crusaders were left alive. They stood there shame-faced amidst the smoldering rubble. The fires were no more, nothing burned as nothing was left to burn. The building was no longer anything but a shell. It's my guess that the building later collapsed due to lack of support. The survivors of the holocaust stood looking at one another. It was odd to me because they had jubilant faces. Then, one clown began to strip, then another, then a female, then another, then a baseball player, then another, then a crusader until they were all naked and glaring at one another's bodies. Then, converging on one spot, they touched one another, hugged, kissed, and finally just milled together for a few minutes before one former clown took off effortlessly out of the factory. Then, the others followed. Never did two leave together.

Finally, all were gone except Vladimir, Riza, Cyrus and I. We walked through the burnt factory with its smashed machines.

"Now do you understand, Joseph?" asked Vladimir, stepping over a roasted body. "Has the nature of man's wickedness grown clear to you?"

"Yes, finally I understand. Man is wicked because of the things he becomes, those outward things which eat them alive."

"Yes, yes, yes, yes, yes, Joseph," applauded Vladimir. "Things do eat the individual alive, but the individual wants to be eaten, he longs for it. Man creates the things which destroy him, the things that make him evil, the things that make him trample another individual's emotions. Saying that Joseph, do you have any solutions?"

"All things must be removed within man's grasp," I answered.

"Only partially correct, Joseph. Things must be removed but the barbarians must also be operated upon by a butcher. Barbarians, who were once individuals, are also things, who must be made into human beings again like you and I."

"Now you have it, Joseph," Riza jumped in enthusiastically. "You know what must be done, you know that the Earth must be blown into a million pieces, forcing each individual who lived on that Earth to thereafter float in space alone. Finally, you know, you understand." Riza now turned his attention to Vladimir. "Is it time now?" he asked him. "Can I?" Vladimir shook his head affirmatively and Riza took off for all parts unknown accompanied by Cyrus.

Both men gone, Vladimir dragged the dead bodies to one side and piled one on top of the other; I assisted him. "These things are no good," Vladimir declared while working with the bodies. "Why must we have these things. We must go back to being cavemen. All the walls that now exist must be torn down, every structure, everything must be torn down, bodies must be torn down. Each one must be able to see the next one at all times, each one must be able to see the vapor and nothing else."

Riza returned with Cyrus a few steps behind. Riza was carrying a small, green, tin box. Cyrus joined Vladimir and myself in piling up the bodies while a mysterious Riza watched. When we finished our piling, Vladimir spat on the bodies and took the tin box from Riza. "Joseph, you are completely pure now," Vladimir announced to me. "You have the knowledge. You are aware you are not inferior and never have been. Along with this knowledge has come your new responsibility to bring life to the individual, and you realize that this can come only through violence. While you carry out your mission to free the individual, your spirit will glisten. Remember this Joseph, and remember to always be vigilante, to never put down your sword. Do that and there is danger you will become as they are."

"Remember, remember, remember, remember, remember!" seconded Riza and Cyrus in the background. "Always remember."

"Your fight must begin now, Joseph" Vladimir continued. "Your job, to push the barbarians to the ground, degrade them, encourage their natural brutalities, their unending wars until oblivion descends. Once everything is gone then the sun will shine forever and ever and ever and you will be free with the universal spirit." Vladimir gave the tin box to the laconic Cyrus who in turn presented it to me while making a little speech.

"In honor of truly finding yourself and the courage you have shown in keeping your purity despite the fierce attacks waged against you, we award you this gift which contains nothing but precious jewels. May you use it wisely and in good health."

Quickly, anxiously, I opened the tin box and found sticks of dynamite, a clock and all sorts of different colored wires.

"You will plant this," explained Vladimir, "amongst the barbarians in the Department. In exploding, it will release the souls trapped there, free them to float through the air. The Department is giving a party next week to celebrate the birthday of the Prophet Muhammad, and everyone will be there. You will arrive early to plant the device in a concealed place. Wait until ten minutes before it's set to explode to leave. You must talk to all the barbarians, remember the filth, and forever after be reminded what you have destroyed. Now Joseph, I think that is all."

"I shall do my best, Vladimir. I know this must be done and I know I must be the one to do it. I have an obligation as an individual with a radiating soul." Vladimir headed for the door of the burned out factory, then, with the others when I called out, "Where are you going? Are you going to leave me to accomplish this task alone."

"We must go and we must vanish," answered Vladimir. "You see Joseph, we too have become barbarians. We have banded together to fight the forces of darkness but in doing so we have become like them. Thus, we must cleanse ourselves, separate from one another and roam free. That is the only way to become pure again. I hope you understand, Joseph?"

I nodded in understanding. All disappeared behind the rubble of charred existence never to be seen again. I didn't even try to see them, see where they had gone. I knew they were no more and that was good enough for me. They were gone, I must accept that now, they were gone for good and I was on my own to do, to accomplish something so worthwhile, so philanthropic, so extraordinary that it boggled the mind.

CHAPTER 11

I apologize to my dear readers who desire to learn the truth, the hard facts about this case. What could I do? I'm a reporter. I asked the questions and that's how the lunatic answered them. What could I do but put them down the way they were related to me!

Of course, Kabir's story is utterly ridiculous, agreed, but, please don't reject it all outright. I believe Kabir's tale does shed light on the man's distorted mind, a mind I don't think any of you have ever been exposed to, a mind so twisted and perverted that it would make an excellent study for all criminologists. So what I think you get, dear reader, is insight into the inner workings of the criminal mind with all its perversities and justifications for violence.

To be honest with you, I tried to get Kabir to change his story and talk to me about reality, about the real world and real events which led up to the bombing but I couldn't get him to budge. Kabir would only say that he'd told me the whole truth and nothing but the truth and he said it with such conviction that I believe the maniac actually believed the story himself. And maybe I even started to believe him. For a time there, I thought that there possibly could be a Vladimir and friends and that the bombing of the university was part of a conspiracy like Kabir said. Yeah, maybe he wasn't lying, maybe he had just exaggerated or distorted the facts to make them seem unbelievable, but the underlying story was true. That's why I conducted my own little investigation later. I found not trace of the existence of this Vladimir or Riza and Cyrus. Nor did a later police investigation find evidence to support the conspiracy idea; in fact, the report conclusively showed that the bombing of the university was initiated, planned, and executed by no one except Kabir. Kabir's claims then were false, made by a maniac who resides in his own demented world.

Again though, I am just a reporter doing my job, taking down the facts as I was doing my job the night of the bombing while interviewing Joseph Kabir in the Officers Lounge of the precinct. He'd told me one strange story after another, but what could I do. We were now coming to the end of it. There was nothing to do now but let Kabir finish the story of the bombing. And we had to hurry. Dawn would soon break and with it, Kabir would be whisked away by the federal government, and I would never get the opportunity of interviewing Kabir face to face again, nor, I knew, would anybody else get the opportunity. So I sat and waited for the conclusion as Decarrie waited for the conclusion. This would be his last moments as precinct head, he knew it, he knew that Detective Talon had reported him and that with his record, he'd be stripped of command. He knew. But he didn't care anymore. He cared only that his friend's story, Kabir that is, be told to its conclusion and that the public learn the truth. I have to admire Decarrie for that. There was another interesting character, Decarrie. Ah, maybe he can be the subject of my next book!

*   *   *

The days before the Department's party went very slowly for me. It was hard. I had to pretend to be unchanged, pretend to still be the victim of barbarian attack. No, it wasn't easy, but I went through all the motions, attended my classes, smiled a lot in those classes, took my criticism in those classes, listened to the barbarians in those classes, went to the library and dealt with the ever cunning Jamila. But finally the day came, my day, that wonderful day.

I arrived an hour and a half early. The party was called for eight-thirty and was being held in this banquet hall on the floor above the History and Sociology Departments. The hall was empty of people except a few waiters and waitresses tending to long white tables with plates of all sorts of oriental delicacies, kebabs, roasted lamb, unusual vegetables and fruits, pastries, cookies and nuts. I entered and surveyed, looking for a place to place my tin box and set its timer. Besides the food tables, the room was barren of furniture except scattered chairs. In the back, there was the coat rack and a long bench in front of it. Underneath the bench would be a perfect place and quickly I made for it.

Nervous, I was very nervous. I kept wondering if someone have seen me coming in with the box? Could they have guessed what was in it? I would be captured, destroyed. They would have won and would torture me until my soul was stripped from my body. No, never, I had to accomplish my task. There was no choice. I rushed to the coat rack bench, making sure not to be seen by any of the help up front. Under it, I scurried and began my work when I was stopped by the sound of breathing and the sight of a pair of legs in green work pants. I remained still. Had I been detected? No, the green pants man moved away taking his footsteps with him. Cautiously, I resumed my work. I set the timer and attached the tin box to the underside of the coat rack bench. It was almost too simple, everything was so simple, one two, three, a, b, c.

My job done and still time before the party, I walked on campus and let my mind go and let my emotions take over. Not being rational, allowing for anger, and the hatred, and the love without moral standards, without rules of any kind, without religion, without any cloak of respectability, it was liberating. It was better than sex, better than dope, better than getting gifts from strangers. To be part of nothing, to have nothing, to have no past and no future, wow, to live for the absolute moment, it was something I wouldn't trade for anything. To see nothing, to perceive only the real, the feeling, to see through the phony, the obsolete, wonderful. Yet it was scary. To see human society as a giant trap, a snare, to denounce it, was frightening. What's next then? Where would I go next. Those were the thoughts I thought as I wandered the campus until it was time, time for the party that the world of empty humans would never forget.

Arriving at the banquet hall a second time, all were there. I stood at the doorway for a moment watching. For whatever reason, Jamila was calling everyone to order. "Come all," said she perkily. "Professors line up to the right of me, students to the left." Obediently they formed the requested lines. Now Alice, the doctoral candidate and worker in the library, appeared at Jamila's command, carrying a ton of red and white pamphlets and stood at her boss's side.

"Attention, attention, attention, I want all your attention," Jamila addressed those in the two lines before her. "Now Professors, listen up, the red pamphlets pertain to you. They are the revised edition of 'Scholastic Yearly' magazine. I want each of you to take one. There is much new vocabulary and phrases in it for you to learn as well as articles which detail the professorial behavior patterns you are to follow for the upcoming academic year. You are really going to enjoy it, I am sure." Alice passed out the magazines. After eagerly taking their copy, the Professors dispersed into the banquet hall.

Next Jamila, waving a copy of the white pamphlet, addressed the second line. "Students, Jamila hasn't forgotten you. Each of you will now get a copy of the 'New Student Guide.' It contains valuable articles on how to develop the proper vocabulary, how to please everyone, how to dress, how to talk with the proper accent, and the do's and don'ts of academic discourse. Read it well and read it long. It will help lead you to the promised land of scholarly accomplishments. Alice, please give out the guides." Each student took one and then scampered away, intently gazing at their guides.

I remained in the doorway until Jamila - now over by one of the food tables and serving tea to students and staff alike from a giant samovar - noticed me. Her icy stare sent me in motion into the hall where I now milled about. Most everyone avoided me. "Hello, hello there, how are you, hello, hello," I greeted. They turned their backs on me, the supreme snub. Bodies, that's all they were, moving about in space and time without rhyme or reason. But I did see one familiar face. Over by the pastry table, I spotted Zeno Beneen, my old dear friend. From the moment the conspiracy against me was hatched, Zeno had avoided me like the plague. Now there he stood before me stuffing his big mouth with gooey, syrup-laden pastry while reading his New Student Guide. I strode up to him boldly. "Hi there fellow, you old son of a guy," I greeted loudly in Zeno's ear. He lowered his head further into his New Student Guide hoping I'd go away. I repeated my greeting even louder; forcing Zeno to accept the inevitable.

"La, ah, la, la, ugh, ah, la, la, ah, ah," garbled Zeno with mouth full of pastry and eyes focused squarely on me. Zeno took two big swallows and somehow got the whole pastry down his esophagus while turning a pretty violet in the face. Finally, everything down its proper tube, Zeno shot, "Joseph my good man, you are a good man, you know. I'm so delighted to see you, delighted and so, so happy you could make it to the party to celebrate the Muslim Prophet, so delighted indeed."

"Zeno my dearest comrade in arms, are you telling me the truth. Down deep in that little heart of yours, are you really happy to see me? Really?"

"Oh, oh, oh, what a question, my dear fellow, what a question to ask. I am always glad to see you. Of course, though I may have to pay a slight penalty for holding a conversation with you. Dr. Jefferson, my colleague, may chastise me a bit for it but I say so what. You should know that I am always quite happy to see my fellow student, Joseph Kabir."

"Well maybe you're happy to see me now, but you wouldn't be if you knew the secret."

"What secret? Tell me the secret Joseph, you simple must tell me!"

"Okay, you twisted my arm. Last week I wasn't feeling well so I went to see a doctor. After giving me a thorough examination, he told me I was suffering from a bad case of infectious intestinal flu. It's not really serious. Once it's contracted, it only takes about three weeks before it disappears from your system. It's not so bad. The only symptom you have is throwing up, but once you get used to that, it isn't so bad. I probably shouldn't have come tonight, my flu is still infectious, but I just couldn't miss this party. Hopefully nobody will catch what I've got."

Zeno turned a nice shade of green and jumped back two feet. "Joseph," he exclaimed, "don't think for one moment that I am afraid of catching that disease of your. To me friendship comes before disease, whether the disease is infectious or not."

"An admirable point of view my dearest comrade, highly admirable. But if you are speaking with honesty and integrity, why then, may I ask, do you perspire so? Why then do you hold that napkin over your mouth?"

"Oh, you misinterpret things, my good man. I always perspire like this; it has something to do with my body temperature, I believe. And as for the napkin over my mouth, let me assure you it is simple a habit of mine."

"Yes, of course. Please excuse me for doubting your sincerity."

"Quite all right, quite," replied Zeno through his napkin. "Joseph, I think I best be getting on to the other guests now."

"Oh Zeno, before you go I must tell you that I was joking about the flu business and all. I'm as healthy as a horse. I don't know why I always like to tease."

"Ho-ho-ha-ha, you're a good man, Joseph, the very best, the very best."

"What a kind, gracious gentleman you are Zeno. If I teased another man the way I tease you, I probably would get punched in the nose. But you Zeno, gracious is the only way to describe you."

"Thank you, Joseph. I can never get made at you, you who understand the basic concepts of jocularity and expound your theories in words." Zeno moved closer to me, changed back to a normal color, removed the napkin covering his mouth and exclaimed, "Joseph, I would like to confirm a rumor which lately has found its way to my ears. Is it true that you've been having great difficulty getting your latest thesis proposal passed by the Board?"

"Oh yes-sir, yes-sir-re-Bob, yes sir-re Bobby, it is the truth you been hearing, my dear lad, tis the honest to God truth, tis, tis, tis. And you know what else, I can't even find a Professor to be my thesis advisor, and do you know why? Everybody thinks I am dirt, filthy, garbage, sludge."

Zeno smiled slightly. "I think you exaggerate slightly, Joseph, and possibly being humorous again with me. Anyway, to more important matters, I knew you were having difficulties. The grapevine here is always reliable." Zeno put his arm around my shoulder and proclaimed solemnly, "You know Joseph, my thesis proposal passed the Board immediately. I might possibly be able to help you with yours. Advice from me, I'd say, is quite in order. I think your problem, Joseph, my dear man, stems from your taking an improper approach. You must learn to view everything in its proper perspective. If things are approached scientifically, and in the proper schemata of generalizations, you will be able to view the whole better than the half."

"Zeno, Zeno, Zeno," repeated I in false admiration. "You are so wise, you have such a mind, a sage, a scholar. It is amazing how one man can be so stupendously brainy."

"Wisdom comes with experience, the type of experience I've had."

"It's such a pleasure to hear you talk."

"Thank you, but getting back to more serious issues, I've been hearing another rumor about you. They tell me that your use of footnotes and efficiency with spelling and commas isn't up to par. Is that rumor also true?"

"Quite, quite."

"Shocking. That is most undoubtedly another reason why you're your thesis proposal has been continuously rejected. To be a scholar, my good man, to be any type of scholar you must be proficient in these areas. And especially spelling, it is the very core of writing and goes hand-in-hand with the proper use of commas and footnotes. Now I know it is difficult to improve, but Zeno shall tell Joseph what do to. It's all so simple really. One hour and a half before bedtime each night study the three categories I just touched upon, devoting a half hour to each. Then, go to sleep immediately after. Exactly three hours later get up and study for another one hour and a half, giving an hour to each of your weaknesses. Then go back to sleep again, and sleep till the sun comes up. As soon as you wake up in the morning, go directly from your bed to a piece of paper and write something, anything applying what you learned during the night. And, that's all there is to it, my good man. A year after you adopt this procedure, I can guarantee you that will be touted as a great writer, almost as great as I."

"Mm."

"Mm, is not good enough, my man Joseph. For your own good, you must follow meticulously the elevated program that I just laid out for you, you simple must. I am a fine scholar whose dictums should not be trifled with."

"Oh, I know that Zeno, of course."

"Yes, I am a fine scholar, and do you know why that is?" asked Zeno who would not wait for an answer. "I am such an adroit scholar because I am a specialist who knows more about Algeria than anyone in this Department. Oh, wait, that's right, you haven't heard.

Well about two months ago, Joseph, I decided to specialize in Algeria, giving special emphasis to the communist movement there. Specializing is the only means to advancement. I expect that very soon I will be swarmed with requests from institutions of higher learning throughout the Western hemisphere to give lectures on Algeria. Specializing is the only way. I simple can't stand the sight of an unspecialized man. A scholar who lacks a specialty is like a man without a country. Joseph, do you have a specialty?"

"Why of course. I specialize in the senses. Through carefully applying the scientific principle, I have developed my senses to the fullest. Now I am able to detect, to the nearest centimeter, if there is substance or if there isn't any substance within a radius of twenty feet."

"Good man, you are a good man, and a funny one too."

Just about then, Zeno shut his mouth and took on a startled look. To the doorway, he pointed. I turned. Dr. Jefferson had come strolling into the room and was immediately accosted by a large group of the Indonesian students who bowed before him, muttered a few incomprehensible things, and quickly disappeared towards the back of the room where my bomb was planted and ready to explode in less than an hour. I would stay for about forty-five minutes to enjoy the festivities before departing to safer pastures from where I could observe the catastrophe.

I had all of Zeno I could take in my lifetime now. I excused myself from his presence then and crept over to Dr. Jefferson who, after escaping the Indonesians, stood all by his lonesome in the middle of the room. I noticed that some in the room took a few steps toward him, made frightened faces, roll their heads back and forth, and then retreated. However, I, fearless, with a triumphant gait, approached this monument of a man, took his hand and shook it. Everyone in the banquet hall eyed me with an amazed, stupefied look. Maybe I was too aware of them and that's why I accidentally stepped on Jefferson's foot, then. He was a foot wearing a white shoe. "I'm terribly sorry," apologized I.

"Kabir, Joseph Kabir, why have you come over to me, I, I don't really understand?"

"I come to pay my respects to you, Dr. Jefferson, the scholar, the leader we all appreciate and respect," explained I calmly despite the fact that they all still eyed me and despite the fact that Jamila was making absurd faces behind my back. Jefferson didn't seem to hear me; he was glaring down at his foot. "I'm terribly sorry, Dr. Jefferson," I repeated. "It's just that I'm so nervous in your presence. I hope I haven't ruined your shoe."

"Don't feel bad Kabir, it's nothing. So what if these are new shoes that cost me a great deal of money, so what if they were personally made for me by an artisan in Italy, so what!" Jefferson, gritting his teeth, placed his foot with its dirtied shoe over his foot with its clean shoe and scuffed up the good one. "Now they'll match," he snarled. "Everything must match. I demand everything match!"

"I'm really sorry," I cranked out again.

"Haven't I told you not to drop the matter, drop it now! I demand that. I'm a rational intellectual. I don't let little insane bits of life annoy me."

"Thank you for being so forgiving, so kind."

"I'm not either. I'm not allowed to be such things. I told you, I'm a rational man with a superior mind who cares not to view the non-intellectual facets of human existence."

Tic, tock, tic, tock, tic, tock came a faint ticking from the back of the hall, a ticking which meshed with Jefferson's voice. Was this ticking a beautiful melody? What was the ticking? Where was it coming from exactly? Why didn't anybody else seem to notice? I listened and followed the sound waves as they traveled from place to place until I discovered that the ticking was emanating from under the wooden coat rack bench. It was the bomb, it had begun ticking. All I could think of was being detected, failing, having them castrate my spontaneity which hung proudly from my heart.

"Kabir," cracked Jefferson, 'you are not paying attention to me, Kabir, eyes front. Look at me when I talk to you. Now yes, that's better. So Kabir, you've now been with us month after month that adds up to many months in multiple calendar years, what have you learned during that time?"

"If I may ask who in the phrase 'You have been with us' does the us refer to?"

"I'm referring to the department. Who else would I refer to? There is nothing else."

"Oh, I didn't realize, but such a fact is always useful to know. Now what have I learned from being in this Department? Interesting question. Well, let's see, I've learned that the Department is stupendous, fabulous, sparkling even. I've also learned that everyone here are thinkers whose great minds entitle them to stand mounted in famous museums while the people visiting the museum just stand in awe."

"Excellent Mr. Kabir, excellent."

"In poetic terms, let me say that this Department is spellbinding, a pearl in the midst of ignorance, an oasis amidst a barren sandy desert, a pearl amidst rotted pears, a. . . ."

"Kabir, your attitude is becoming excellent. I see you are beginning to make progress."

"A haven for the intellectual elite, an enclosure of unrivaled importance, an. . . ."

"Kabir, that's quite enough. I am relieved that you now see things clearly and are becoming part of our big, happy family." At that moment, all the happy family members were sprawled throughout the hall, but not looking happy. Jamila was the only person in the room with a smile her face.

My mind had drifted from Dr. Jefferson and was now floating through the hemisphere where a man can not look back, or go back, because there is nothing to go back to. My floating was rudely interrupted by Jefferson, of course who was trying to bring me down to the ground.

"Kabir," he barked like a German shepherd. "I'm talking to you, talking to you, did you hear me, talking to you. How dare you not pay attention to me. Don't you understand the rules of polite society? Were you raised on a planet all your own? Sometimes we around here think so."

"I'm was paying attention to you, Dr. Jefferson. "I always pay attention when an esteemed, wise gentleman like you talks."

"Mm, bad reports that's all I've gotten about you but it seems to me that they are not all quite true. There seems to be some intelligence there, maybe not a lot, but some. Could everyone have been wrong about you? Possibly! There still may be a chance for you. I tell you what, I usually don't take on cases such as yours but you, I think, I can help. What that means is I, Dr. Jefferson is going to give his free time to help you. Now I want you to make an appointment with my secretary for next week. The meetings then will begin."

"The meeting, office, next week?" cranked I incredulously. "Well I won't be here next week."

"You will be here next week, Kabir! How many times does Dr. Jefferson give his free time to students."

"But you won't be here, nothing will be here."

"Kabir, what are you talking about? Of course, I'll be here. And you'll be here too meeting with me in my office where you will receive my gracious assistance in becoming something in this world, something that the world can understand and accept."

"What type of help did you have in mind?"

"Kabir, what time is it?" asked Jefferson.

"Nine-fifteen."

"I must leave soon. I have an eleven o'clock flight to catch to Cairo. I'll be attending a two day conference with the President of Egypt and his chief of staff. We shall be discussing many things which I am not at this time at the liberty to divulge. Every year the conference is held and all the illustrious Middle Eastern scholars from North America are invited. We all gather around a large conference table with the President leading us and try to put our heads together to better piece together the history of Egypt, a history which the President uses to instruct his people on what it means to be Egyptian. It seems that in Egypt a vast majority of people don't care about anything; they seek only to farm their land. The President, in his vast wisdom, has decreed that everyone must be an Egyptian, and is using us scholars, as we have been used throughout the world, to brainwash the people toward this end. Yes, you see, scholars are important. We are in the vanguard of spreading ideas to the masses. We develop the concepts that the masses feed off. Without us, there we be no them, without us there would be no sense of humanity, no ideas of patriotism and nationhood and religious nationalism. We scholars are like major Gods."

The thought of Jefferson leaving and missing the blast sent me into a frenzy. I fell to my knees and grabbed at the man's ankles while Jamila stared from the distance. "Please, Dr. Jefferson don't leave the party."

Jefferson glared down at me. "Get up fool. I detest erratic behavior that springs from emotion. Emotion is the cause of all mankind's problems. It is unpredictable, untamable and outright evil. Now, get up off the floor and off my new shoes."

I rose. "I'm sorry, Dr. Jefferson. I just don't want you to leave. What will it be do without you. The party will come crashing down."

Dr. Jefferson pondered this for a moment. "Well, that's understandable. My presence does add to the pristine nature of this affair. I do have an obligation as the head of the Department. Yes, you're right, Kabir. I will take a latter flight and stay to the end. I am a man who takes his responsibilities seriously. Now, will you excuse me, Kabir. I have to make a few calls to rearrange my schedule. I will be back shortly."

As Jefferson exited, I had a vision: The bum would be walking down a dark street, when I'd jump him, punch him continually in the face, watch his blood flow, and then pull out a knife and carefully skin the bastard alive, slice out his heart and intestines and raise them to the sky in triumph with his blood dripping down my face and neck. My vision was interrupted, then, by a booming, familiar, unreal voice. I spun around in its direction. There, in the back by the hall, before the coat rack bench, stood Majnoon Jazzar - Professor of Arabic and lover of all things Arab. He was holding a long hollowed bamboo flute while students and Professors gathered close. I noticed that Professor Majnoon Jazzar was talking to himself and had pulled out a white handkerchief which he began to twirl while singing, "I am Arab from an Arab land, a land with sand. We tend sheep, raise ourselves for keep, and then put ourselves to sleep. I am an Arab from an Arab land, a land of sand. . . ." As a finale, Jazzar threw his handkerchief down, jumped up and down on it, and then picked up his flute, blew, and produced a series of notes forming an off- key oriental tune offensive to the ear drums. By the time Professor Majnoon Jazzar finished his performance, Dr. Jefferson had returned and stood once more by my side, "Bravo, bravisimo, excellent, magnificent," he applauded. "Come on everyone let's give our talented Professor a nice round of applause." From throughout the hall, clapping erupted while the ticking continued, sounding more like the heart beat of a lover in heat.

"Professor Jazzar is such an extraordinary man," Jefferson whispered in my ear then. "Do you know that this extraordinary man has singlehandedly helped raise hundreds of thousands for our Department. His contacts with the Saudi Arabians have built a lucrative pipeline for us. That is why we must clap for him. Without the funds he brings, we might have to eliminate some of our overhead." I noticed that Jefferson's breathing became heavy and he was pulling on his ear lob and looking over his shoulder.

"Dr. Jefferson, is there something the matter?" I inquired.

"Ah, Kabir this is no slight upon your integrity by any means, you have made superb progress, but I must leave you. I see Zeno Beneen waving at me. He probably desires to enter into an intellectual discussion. That always pleases me. Now as for you, I'll get in touch with you concerning my helping reconstruct you. There are still concerns, however. I do not truly know if it is possible or not, but we can try. Capturing and taming the human soul, putting it within a straight-jacket is an obligation that we all have as human beings."

As Jefferson walked away I crooned, "I hope your trip to Egypt is a safe and prosperous one. I hope your plane doesn't have to make a crash landing in some warm deserted place." He didn't hear me as he was already at Zeno Beneen's side and in heated intellectual discussion. I was on my own again amidst them all with thirty-five minutes to go. The eternal ticking reached a crescendo in my mind. I could swear that its ticks were notes that added up to 'London Bridge is Falling Down,' but maybe I was wrong. Anyway, there were other things to think about, Jamila was staring at me again and wasn't even bothering to conceal it anymore. Could it possible be that she knew everything? It seemed like it. But that was impossible, wasn't it? But it didn't make a different anyway. To hell with Jamila. Ignoring her, around and around the room I pranced like a seagull circling over a garbage dump. A coldness settled over my body which numbed my brain which ticked along with the bomb. The earth would explode and there was nothing to do about it but wait for the museum pieces to be destroyed.

Soon, almost magically I found myself in the back of the room by the glorious coat rack bench. Professor Majnoon Jazzar sat stooped upon it with one eye shut and the other closing fast, not seemingly bothered by the bench's vibrations. Then I heard voices. They were coming from behind some coats. I listened carefully and discovered the identity of the voices. They belonged to my good friends Mutt and Jeff who, it seems, finally made it out of the Students Lounge.

"What do you think of the phosphate situation in Morocco?" I heard Mutt ask Jeff.

"Atrocious," answered Jeff, "simply atrocious. I do believe government intervention is called for. This is a matter not only of domestic importance but one that has international implications and may well lead to African nuclear proliferation."

"Quite, agree, quite, agree," returned Jeff. "We know from past experience that a problem of this nature always has international ramifications. You'll notice that the CCN and the NDG are both using the phosphate issue to rouse fanatical elements. It is inevitable, especially so since many of the economies of the non-aligned nations have vested interests in the phosphate equation. In my way of thinking, unless the issue is immediately addressed, the global economy will be effected an a inevitable global conflict will ensue."

"Disagree entirely," thrust Jeff. "The matter is one of. . ."

I took my leave at that point to wander against amongst the white food tables in the hall. Slowly but surely, I made my way towards the entrance where I stood for a time watching, observing, seeing only human jelly fish. Twenty-five minutes to go, twenty-five. How many seconds was that? Then, I noticed, students and Professors all of a sudden began a slow migration to the back of the hall to the coat rack bench, slowly, slowly where the bomb was planted, circling it, circling while Professor Majnoon Jazzar still rested upon it. And there, Dr. Jefferson and Zeno Beneen moved to and, like father and son, comfortably plunged into talk of communist movements in Algeria. As I stood staring at the scene, a finger drilled me in the middle of my back.

"Well hi-yah Joseph," came a voice. I turned and there was Stan Lord, his finger, and his little wife Bertha. "Gee whiz, isn't it interesting us colliding into you like this," Stan further beamed.

"Hel-lo Joseph Kabir, hel-lo," grinded Bertha.

"Hal-e-shoma-chetori," squeaked Stan. "That's a Persian saying which means how are you?"

"Quilvahs I vahmasla-kitbam ast zandala boonah vat," mouthed I in gibberish. "That's Swahili meaning the telephone is ringing in China so don't answer it in Japan."

"Hooooo-hooooo-hoooo," crooned Stan in laughter while Bertha gave me a cutting look, understanding I had just made a booby out of her Stanley.

"That was Persian what you spoke, wasn't it Joseph?" inquired Stan earnestly. "You can't fool me, Joseph, that was Persian, a Persian dialect which they speak in the southern part of Iran. Now, finally I've got you. You are Persian, Joseph. There's no longer any doubt."

"Well who knows Stan, maybe you are right, maybe you are wrong, maybe you are in between," dueled I enjoyably.

"You are a Persian!" persisted Stan.

"I don't know what to answer you, Stan. The bit of information you so desire slips my mind at present." How I could dance! What marvelous precision of motion I was.

"Oh, oh, oh, oh, for months you won't tell me. Why won't you admit that you're Iranian. Don't be ashamed of your noble heritage, don't be scared to admit your glorious race which makes you better than most. If you'll just admit you're Iranian, you know what I'll do?"

"No, don't know."

"I'll bend down and kiss your feet."

"Stan," cried I in an alarmed tone, "you can't do that, no. If you value your health and the health of your loved one, you can't do that. The last one who did wound up in the hospital suffering from an acute bacterial infection."

"Heeeeeeeeeeeeeeeeeeeee, that's a joke Joseph, right, that's a joke isn't it now," mooed Stan.

Bertha gave me another one of her wicked looks.

"I tell you what Stan, you want to know my race, well I'm a Swedish man, born in Sweden on a farm where me and father raised cows. Can't you hear my accent and tell I am Swedish or Svedish as we say in the old country"

"You must be Iranian," hammered Stan. "You're funny like an Iranian. Iranians are the funniest people in the world. Read any of the great Iranian writers both past and present and you'll soon discover that they all use comedy as a major vehicle to introduce their themes."

"Wow, isn't that a coincidence, them and me, me and them, I, and the collective idea, I and the man as the masses."

Bertha's attention had turned towards the white food tables. "Stanley," she meowed. "Why are you talking to your friend and ignoring me. Stanley, I'm your wife and never forget that." Bertha jabbed Stan in the stomach with her finger. As Stan, rubbing his belly, turned an interesting shade of green, Bertha continued to yap, "Now Stanley, you have this terrible tendency to forget I'm your wife. You must not forget in the future. I hate being treated as just another person. You must perceive me in the proper way or you'll get yours and you know what I mean. Okay, now tell me Stanley, what are we going to do?"

Stan, perplexed, pulled on his beard, jerked at his groin area, raised and lowered his eyebrows repeatedly. "Do-do, do-do, do-do about what-what?"

"Oh God, Stanley," moaned Bertha. "Will you look around the room." Stan looked but still didn't understand. "So what are we going to do?" she repeated.

"About what, Bertha, gee whiz, golly, about what? I don't know what your talking about and that's the honest to God truth."

"Stanley, Stanley, my fool of a husband, Stanley don't you see they aren't serving any freshly cut vegetables here. What are we going to eat? I wanted to eat before we came but no, you always have to have your way. Now we're in a terrible mess. What are we going to eat, Stanley? I want an answer, and I want one right now. Do you think I want to starve. I'm hungry."

Stan looked at me for a second for moral support. "Perhaps it would be wise for us to partake in some coffee now and then once the party's over we can go out to eat somewhere."

"Coffee! Stanley, what are you talking about, we never drink coffee, never. That is definitely a taboo food for us. Coffee is bad for the heart and kidneys. We don't want our endocrine system perverted, do we? I thought we agreed on that point years ago when we got married. Have you forgotten that we've agreed to drink only carrot, tomato, and prune juice. So what are we going to do?"

"Perhaps later we can go out to that nice vegetarian restaurant downtown, the one next to the pet shop. We can have some of their nice sun-dried asparagus, cream corn and carrots. You know how you love their cream corn."

"Yes, yes, their cream corn, so exquisitely prepared, so voluptuous, so impregnated with the wonders of the palate. I could just smear it all over myself. I could fill my insides with it, pad my outsides with it. I dream of the smell and the taste. If I had a choice to be anything it would be a plate of their cream corn and their unbelievable boiled baby carrots."

"Excuse Bertha," apologized Stan to me. "She gets like that sometimes. I can never tell when she'll snap out of it."

"I understand Stan, snapping is a difficult process. Snapping in takes effort, snapping out takes inhuman effort. Snaps, they are important to society. Without them, a woman's dress would fall, bags and purses would open in mid-stream and plastic sandwich bags would not be able to hold the moisture out."

"Perhaps, gee whiz, maybe," said Stan like he knew what I was talking about. He then changed the subject. "You haven't heard the good news Joseph, have you?"

I shook once for no.

"Well Bertha here has been awarded a year's scholarship to do paleontological research in the Sahara Desert. She'll be joining one hundred other eminent paleontologists."

"You don't say."

"Yes, and you know what, Bertha, God bless her, is going to take me along. Oh what an opportunity this will be. I'm going to bring all my books on Iran with me and in the peace and quiet of the desert will be able to study almost non-stop. Perhaps I'll even be able to memorize the English-Persian dictionary. Gee whiz, this is going to be so, so great."

Bertha who had been chewing on her finger for some time, now stopped. "Fossils, I love fossils," she exclaimed. "I see fossils everywhere. Stanley, you are a fossil. Civilization is a fossil, but strangely, you, Joseph Kabir are not a fossil. What are you? You are something modern, something definitely not buried. That's why I am not interested in you, Joseph Kabir. I am interested in fossils. All I see are fossils. I am a paleontologist. I see fossils. I am a fossil." Finished with her oratory, Bertha went off into her hypnotic stupor once more.

Stan looked embarrassed by the outburst. "Joseph, I'm sorry. I don't know why Bertha goes off like that sometimes. She's done it ever since I've know her."

"Stan, forget about Bertha, Stan," said I. "I like you, I really do, and that's why I want to give you a chance before it is too late for you. I want to spare you and to do that you will have to tell me who I am?"

"I don't understand, " Stan answered. "You're beginning to sound like Bertha?"

"I never go off, Stanley, I am always off and Bertha over there is always on but just changes into different wardrobes from time to time. I'm giving you a chance to be spared, Stan. Don't you understand. If you don't want to tell me who I am, tell me who Bertha is? Who is this woman you call your wife? Do you really know her? Have you ever known her or do you know the label? Are you the label, are you?"

Bertha had begun tugging at Stan's arm, "Stanley, we must go," she whined. "This man, this friend is attacking us, we must go. You must not associate with him. We must go to meet other people here. Stanley, now."

Stan stood his ground, not knowing what to do.

"Can you answer my questions, Stan?" I pounded on despite Bertha's attempt to stifle me by making many crude faces. "Can you tell me who I really am, who she really is?"

Stan gawked at me and said nothing.

"Can you feel my glow? Do you see it? Can you bask in it? Can you unite with it? What do you see in Bertha? Can you merge with what you see? Can you harvest the crop?"

"Gee whiz, I really don't understand."

I was in a panic to penetrate Stan Lord's thick head. "You must know me Stan."

He still had a perplexed look on his face while his wife continued to pull at him.

"If you don't know me, that's all right. But you must want to get to know me, please you must, are you willing?"

"I'm sorry, but I have no idea what you are talking about," Stan answered.

I reacted by violently pulling out some of my hair, throwing it in his face and yelling, "You must get beyond this, you must Stan, please look, please look deep into me."

Bertha tugged at Stan a lot harder, but Stan remained glued to the spot.

"I think you're joking again, Joseph," chirped Stan like a dodo bird. "You are joking, yes, of course, that's what you are doing."

"Do you know me, Stan?" asked I.

"Of course, you are a student in the Department and an Iranian who is ashamed to admit it. Yes, you are an Iranian, yes."

"I'm afraid Stanley that you are lost, a hollow tree trunk that's been dead for over one hundred years. But I will help you." I grabbed Stan's arm while Bertha took hold of the other. I kissed the arm I captured, gradually working my kisses up to Stan's neck. Stan tried to wiggle away but was unable to fight me or Bertha off and kept yelling, "Perhaps, perhaps," as the tug of war continued. Any minute I expected Stan's arms to snap off. Surprisingly this incident did not capture the attention of the others; they went on with their party, not even glancing our way. In the end, I found it impossible to hold my own against Bertha who was whining "I told you he was wicked, Stanley," she yelped. "I knew it, knew you should never have associated with him. He's our enemy, don't you understand Stanley, our enemy."

I lost my hold. Bertha now held Stan, her prize, tightly around the mid-section and then scowled at me triumphantly. As Stan was dragged away, he managed to exclaim, "Ah, ah, ah, Joseph, I don't know what to say, ah, ah, ah, I'll see you I guess, I don't know, I'll see you." Yes, I had lost and Stan was lost. The only thing left for him was the removal of his body to release his spirit. There was no choice. Yes, I watched him sadly, as Bertha dragged him away, to the magical coat rack bench in the back where Jefferson now stood with Zeno while most of the others milled about them. The exception to this was Dr. Warly and Professor Lunwi. Both were standing in the middle of the hall, holding coffee cups. I didn't have much time but I couldn't somehow resist going over having a little talk. Approaching, I could hear Warly fiercely explaining something or other to Lunwi, something that sounded like dignified gibberish. As Warly talked, he blinked his right eye feverishly. Neither Warly nor Lunwi noticed my approach so I snapped my fingers and stamped my feet to get their attention.

"Hi there," I greeted them. "How are you two on this glorious evening celebrating the glorious birth of the glorious Prophet of Islam, none other than the glorious Prophet Muhammad, member of the glorious house of Hisham?"

Both took on sinister looks while trying to ignore me. But I would have none of that. I snapped my fingers some more, stamped my feet and danced around them in a circle like a talented flamenco danger. "Nice party we're having, don't you think?" I sang while I danced. "Why don't you folks answer me. I said, don't you think we're having a nice party?"

"What do you want, Kabir?" queried Warly, red-faced as he and Lunwi retreated backwards toward the coat rack bench. "Why do you always bother me?"

"I don't know, maybe it's the luck of the draft. Now what I want, yes, you asked that. Dr. Warly, dear Dr. Warly, I want nothing but oblivion. I just stopped over to give you both a hearty hello and a solemn farewell. I want to remember your existence as it now stands, solid, frozen, incapable of movement. That's what I want to remember."

"Insolence," cried Professor Lunwi in a touching tone of voice while continuing the retreat. "Why do you approach us in such a rough manner, Mr. Kabir?" Lunwi demanded to know.

Before I answered, I looked at my watch and told both my adversaries that it was only a few moments until there bath time and bed time and resurrection in a glorious morning. They looked at one another as if I was cracked to which I do agree. "Professor Lunwi, you said I approached you in a rough manner, correct, correct," I finally answered. "Let me declare for the record that I wasn't aware of that. But, if you tell me where the rough manner is, the exact spot, I'll let you smooth it out for me. Isn't that fair. But, why do you keep retreating? Are you afraid of my essence? Can you visualize the furnace within me? Can you see flames?"

"Aren't you aware, the least bit aware. . . ." she began to answer.

"I'm not aware of anything really, that's why I'm wonderful," I interrupted.

"Aren't you aware," Lunwi tried again, "that there exists a proper way to act at social gatherings?"

Warly, in the meantime, was staring at me while sipping his coffee.

"But I don't care about social gatherings, Professor Lunwi. As a matter of fact, I want to be rid of social and gatherings."

"Mr. Kabir, you are a sick young man," blasted Lunwi. "You seem unaware of all the social graces. Are you a complete animal then?"

"Excuse me, your Lady-ship, let me offer my humblest apologies." I attempted to kiss her hand which she pulled away. Her face became pale while the coffee cup, she held, shook. Warly continued sipping.

"Mr. Kabir," exclaimed Warly stepped in, "your tone is abominable. Scholars should never be sarcastic. But what am I saying, you are no scholar. God knows what you are. You're not worth much to us. You are the equivalent of an insect that spreads disease and a fool let out of an insane asylum."

"You're right, Professor Warly," bitched Lunwi. "Everyone knows he's stupid. He can't even spell properly or use commas in the correct fashion. This doesn't surprise me. From the first day he came to my office, from that first minute I laid eyes upon him, I classified him as one of them and I was right. I have a sixth sense about things. I am like a God the way I know, the way I can discern and the way I pass judgment."

"I concur with Professor Lunwi's appraisal," said Warly, politely. "I too noticed your deficiencies as soon as you opened your mouth. Your speech, ha, ha, isn't speech, is filled with guttural slangs like a dog in the field. Ghastly, and the way you walk, ha, who walks like that! You're a common hooligan. But there is still hope. The canvas can still be wiped clean and a nice Picasso put in its place."

"Yes, Dr. Warly," pumped Lunwi, "there may still be some salvation. The first thing that must be done is to develop that brain of his. Get it connected up to that tongue and heart. We must gain control over that brain and direct it towards the desired goal."

"Yes," answered Warly between coffee sips. "We must then make him take on a particular way of talking and acting."

"That shouldn't be too difficult, but we must get him alone and get him reading the proper materials. The first thing he should be made to read is Weinbrook's, <u>A Handbook On the Proper Way To Write Scholastically</u>. Mr. Kabir, you haven't read this book, have you?"

"No, but I've been planning to read it. It's just that I've been so busy reading Burdette's, <u>Egypt Faces The West</u>, Oddwell's, <u>The Taxation System In Modern Tunisia</u>, Kilvenny's. <u>The Nationalization Of The Wheat Industry In Syria</u>, and Brolnavitche's, <u>Political Disenfranchisement In The Modern State of Afghanistan</u>."

"Mm, admirable, but funny," clucked Warly. "I've never heard of any of those books. Now how could that be? I've read everything."

"Mm, it is strange," tongued Lunwi.

Warly handed his coffee cup to Lunwi and then produced a piece of paper and pencil from his back pocket. "Please Mr. Kabir, repeat the names of those books to me slowly again. I shall take them down. I must read them immediately. I don't know how in the world I could have overlooked them."

"Proceed with what?" I cranked in blaring tones. "You dirty, no good, son-of-a-bitch, dirty-fucking-bastard. Drop dead both of you, drop dead. Stick every book you own up your fucking asses. Steel beings, iron that attaches itself to any magnet no matter what color or size." I caught the attention of everyone in the room. They all circled, hissed and jeered. I was surrounded and I was forced to retreat to the back of the hall and the coat rack bench. They crowded around the bench before me and hissed and hissed while I riddled them with words: "Where have you hidden yourselves? I know as I know everything. True knowledge comes from me. I am a genius like Jesus, Muhammad, Moses. But they, these Prophets of yours lost their genius and became barbarians by catering to your needs. You are the guilty ones, you who have hidden yourselves in the past, in religion, hidden yourselves in the walls, in the lights, in your thoughts. But why? I will not answer that. I will only say that you're dirty now, filthy, each and every one of you here in this hall. What's worse, you want to stay dirty, you delight in it. There's your real crime. But I won't stand for it. I will not allow criminality to go unpunished. I've made myself the judge and I have been elected to pass judgment on you barbarians, and my judgment is that you must go through a process of purification. The stink will be washed from you. That is the ruling of this court and the process is almost here and so I must take my leave. There's almost no time left, ha, ha. Here take my watch." I ripped it off and threw it into the crowd. All stood around the bench stiffly erect as if posing for some picture.

Then, I ran, ran, ran. Five minutes. No time. Would I make it out? Would I die too? Maybe it was supposed to be this way? No, my will to exist as an individual and breath the air of the divine spirit was to great. So I ran like I've never run before, but I should have blown up. The time had passed, but the bomb hadn't blown. There was no explosion. Out of the building I ran. I looked up, up, up towards the floor where they were. Lights blinked on and off through the windows of the banquet hall. What? Lights blinking, why? Then, it came, the expected sight and sounds. Bang, boooooooooooom, biiiiiiiiiiiiiiiiiiiiiiiiiing, booooooooooooooom, baaaaaaaaaaaaaaang. Bricks, cement, glass, chair, tables, arms, legs, guts, flew out of the windows and fell to earth like giant snowflakes. Explosion followed explosion. It's like everyone at the party was being blown up individually. Sparks and bright lights ascended to the sky while I watched until the top floors of the building disintegrated in flame. Fire blazed, burning the remains of the rubble. I stood in awe thinking only of them and their ripped and torn bodies. When the smoke cleared somewhat, fire trucks came, police cars, ambulances came, miserable crowds came, everyone came but could be nothing.

For a long time I stood watching them all behind the barricades as they stared at the bombed out floors. I couldn't bear it anymore, I couldn't just stand there. I raced to the barricades amidst all the men in blue and the crowds of short-sleeved humanity and yelled, "I've cured them, I've cured their cancer, yeah, I've done it and all it took was a little bomb, I've done it. I've saved all their lives. I have freed them. I'm a hero, a saint. Disperse, all of you disperse I say. I command all of you to disperse and burn down your homes and then roam through the countryside naked. Disperse."

All made noises, looked at one another strangely and then charged me. Everyone wanted a piece of my carcass, but the men in blue intervened, thankfully to disperse the mob with clubs and guns. The mob ran in all directions, ran cussing and spitting, and then came together again some distance away looking for an opening to attack again. But the men in blue were too efficient for them. They quickly shackled me, put me into one of their blue trucks and drove me away with the mob raced behind, throwing stones and sticks. We barely made it here to the precinct, but thank the spirit of the universe, the divine perfection, the soul of all that we did and that I live to tell the tale of my existence.

Well, that's it. I wish that was it for everything, but at least that's it for the story. Bombser, I hope you got everything down. I want it all told, I want everyone to know, everyone to feel for me, be for me, be good for me, be kind for me, care for me. That's why they must all know and once they know if they still remain barbarians then each must be sliced into little pieces as if they were all sides of beef.

*   *   *

Stillness pervaded the room. Kabir had a peaceful look on his face that signified accomplishment, the doing of a great deed. The night had passed now. It was almost six o'clock in the morning. A strange aura of doom now pervaded the room as it hadn't pervaded it before. This remarkable interview-interrogation, question period-story period, or whatever you would like to call it had drawn to a conclusion but strangely, it left me wanting more, left me thinking there was more, that there had to be.

Detective Decarrie went over to Kabir and patted him on the back and whispered something or other in his ear which made Kabir smile. Both jumped up and looked at me with a ghastly vicious look. "You think Joseph is a criminal who committed an atrocious act," barked Decarrie, forming his hands into claws. "You think Joseph is insane, a lunatic, a pervert, you think. . . ."

Kabir ran toward me, hands outstretched as if he was going to try to choke me. Closer he came to me and my neck. I thought I was a goner. But no, Kabir stopped and stood like stone before me. "Fool, you empty fool," he yapped at me. "You need to be destroyed with all the rest. I'm a hero, but you don't understand that. I stemmed the tide of a great epidemic, but you don't understand that. If you did, you too could be a hero. But no, you want to be a son-of-a-bitch reporter, which is nothing but a beast that accepts the world of illusion and treats it as the ultimate reality. You are nothing but a perverse bastard, Bombser."

Kabir turned from me and ran throughout the Officers Lounge. He was screaming at the top of his lungs: "Filth spores, Novocain beings, trash, die you bastards. Go visit Dr. Warly, he is waiting. Go visit Dr. Jefferson, go visit Jamila, go visit my friend, Zeno Beneen, go visit them all. Don't hide from me. I see you. You are the couch and chairs and the pool table and the windows. I see you. I understand. There's no use in hiding from me anymore filth spores. Go visit my friends. I'll be glad to show you the way."

Ten Federal agents with guns raced into the Officers Lounge now. Kabir went running towards them screaming a long scream. He dived and fell right into their waiting arms. They punched and kicked him to the ground and then carried him out the door as he were to be cooked and served for dinner. Detective Decarrie made no attempt to save his friend. Instead, his eyes never left mine throughout the outburst. A little wrapped piece of paper lay on the floor between where Decarrie stood and I sat. Decarrie suddenly took his eyes off me, bent down, picked up the paper, tore it up into a million pieces, threw it into my face, turned away, and defiantly marched off with tears in his eyes, off to somewhere, someplace from which I was to never see him again.

Everything was quite in the Officers Lounge once more. Peaceful, yes, peaceful, but was it really? Was it just contentment? Was it just a break until hatred flared once more as it always had in the past? Was it just a break that would end with us all back in the ice age?

                    *   *   *

An after note, Joseph Kabir was never seen or heard from again once he left the Officers Lounge that morning. I tried to locate his whereabouts but nobody seemed to know. Nobody knew anything or wouldn't say. Subsequently, I have heard from a very confidential source that two days after Kabir committed his crime, he was taken to some out of the way place by a huge reservoir of water in a bullet proof black limousine. Once in this out of the way place, Kabir was made to enter a dirty wooden shack where an old judge and twelve respectable citizens waited to put him on trial. For a half hour, witness after witness was brought in and testified against Kabir. Kabir kept interrupting, wanting to speak and give his side of the story, but guards came, punched Kabir, tied him to his chair and stuffed a large blue kerchief in his mouth. Kabir now sat quietly watching and waiting.

The Judge walked over to the squatting jury in their jury box. "I don't need you," the Judge is supposed to have said. "I have passed sentence on this monster. He is guilty, there is no doubt, he is the one, the guilty monster." He then returned to his pedestal and sat.

The guards untied Kabir and he was brought him before the Judge who gave him a choice of sentence, either death by pouring white hot ashes down his throat done right there on the spot, or, life in a top secrete scientific laboratory where he would be used as a human guinea pig to help discover cures for diseases that plagued humanity. Kabir chose to become a guinea pig. That is all I've heard. Kabir is in a laboratory somewhere, or maybe dead in a laboratory somewhere. Either way, he's finally doing good for the first time in his perverted life. That's all.

I also tried to publish the facts of Kabir's case in my newspaper, including parts of the interview I did, but my editor wouldn't let Kabir's story go to print. He gave me no reason, just an order. The public was simply told that there had been a fire at the university and 300 hundred people were killed as a consequence. But, I wouldn't let the story fade away. I couldn't let the fascinating, deranged mind of Kabir escape public attention. I believe the public has a right to know. So I wrote this book and am very proud that I did. Hopefully it will be a lesson for us all of the evil that lurks within the body politic, of the madness that is amongst us. Our democracy, human society hangs in the balance as such people as Joseph Kabir are allowed to exist. That is all I will say for now.

But we all must be careful out there and always watchful.

-THE END-

Made in the USA
Charleston, SC
19 January 2011